PICKING CHRYSANTHEMUM

PICKING CHRYSANTHEMUM

P L Hampton

iUniverse, Inc.

New York Lincoln Shanghai

Picking Chrysanthemum

iUniverse, Inc.

For information address:
iUniverse, Inc.
2021 Pine Lake Road, Suite 100
Lincoln, NE 68512
www.iuniverse.com

ISBN: 0-595-27450-1

Printed in the United States of America

To my biggest fan and my harshest critic. You believed in me, when I did not believe in myself. Without you this would not be a reality.

I love you Tonya.

"Of all our studies, history is best qualified to reward our research."
                                                        —Malcolm X

CHAPTER I

▼

Georgia, Post Civil War—1868

Nettie had felt the warm gentle breeze spring to life from out of the west long before Timmy or Massa Jackson came to where her and Celia stood in the cotton field. The wind had run up and over the fields in swift leaps and bounds like a gazelle in flight, sneaking up on them ever so quietly. Nettie found it strange, she had not heard of its arrival in the clap of thunder in the distance nor in the shape of a rain cloud upon the horizon. It was like the breeze had been conjured up by black magic or voodoo. Despite its unexpected arrival, Nettie did not complain for it was a much welcome guest in a field where the sun beat down on her like an overseer's whip. Nettie stood up, in hopes of resting her weary back. The feel of the fresh air filling her lungs was refreshing. The way the wind cooled her skin was comforting. On a hot summer day, a nice cool breeze was much more soothing than an ice-cold glass of water.

Nettie peered down at her daughter, Celia, who had also stopped picking cotton in order to give her cramped fingers and weary back a rest as well. It did not matter if you were young or old, the stress associated with picking cotton wreak havoc on anyone's joints and back. Cotton tied many of people's fingers, both young and old into knots. If someone were to walk by the field that day and see Nettie and Celia standing there with their heads tilted towards the heavens, one might think they were awaiting some celestial being to descend down from the sky and save them from such exhaustive labor. Instead, they simply enjoyed Mother Nature's gentle caress and sweet embrace as it enveloped them.

Nettie could feel the wind weave its fingers through her tattered garments, drying the rivulets of sweat beading down her back. She remembered seeing Timmy pass by earlier as he hurried to The Big House, but she had paid him no mind. However, now that he returned with Massa Jackson trailing close behind, she paid him closer attention. Judging by the haste in their step, it was obvious to Nettie something was amiss. They were trotting through the field pretty fast even by her standards.

When Massa Jackson was within shouting distance, he called out to her. "Nettie! It's Cletus 'gain!" As soon as she heard him yell the boy's name, Nettie knew who conjured up the mysterious breeze.

"Where he at?" she hollered.

"He's on top of y'alls quarters! Timmy, sazs he's tryin' ta fly!" Nettie took off running towards the cabin, upon hearing of her son's latest stunt.

"Lawd, dat boy isn't goin' ta learn til dere's a rope aroun' his neck," she proclaimed, running to save her son.

The closer Nettie got to the cabin, the stronger the wind became. Just getting there in the midst of such a gale was a task within itself, but she knew she had to get there before Cletus did something they all would regret. When Nettie got into the clearing in front of her quarters, she found Cletus standing on top of the roof with his arms extended into the wind. His fiery red mane blew violently in the wind. He looked like a strange bird trying to take flight. Nettie found it strange, how everyone else found it hard to stay upright, while Cletus balanced himself effortlessly in the wind.

"Cletus! Cletus!!" screamed Nettie, trying to get the boy's attention over the din. "Cletus!" she shouted, this time shouting loud enough to break his concentration. "Cletus! Git ya tail down heah boy, befo' I takes a switch ta ya," she demanded.

"But Ma—" stammered the boy.

"Did ya heah wats I says? I says git down heah now!"

"But Ma dey—"

"Boy don't makes me cum up an git ya!" yelled Nettie, her tone conveying her anger. There was no way she was going to climb up there and bring him down. However, she knew that if she could strike the fear of God into him with the prospect of possibly being at the receiving end of a switch, it would be enough to convince him to come down.

"Yes'um," he conceded.

As Cletus descended the small cabin, the trees began to lose their sway and the wind slowly died. With the show over, Massa Jackson begun shooing the children whom had gathered around the cabin away. As soon as Cletus' feet touched the ground, Nettie commenced to scold the young boy for his latest exploit, which instantly brought tears to his eyes. As soon as all of the children had dispersed, Massa Jackson let Nettie know he was not pleased.

"I told ya Nettie, ya gat ta keep a handle on dat boy! He aint goin ta bring nuttin' but trouble aroun' heah, an' I can only protect y'all for so long!"

"I hav' done all I can! It's hard tryin' ta raise a bull headed boy by yo' sef! He needs da strong hand of a man aroun'! Ya his pappy, Clayton, why don't ya do sumthin'! I mean, he may be a lil' slow, but he's no fool! Ya spends more time in my bed, than ya do in Da Big House! Heck, he and his sista are almost jus' as white as ya!"

"Now looks Nettie we hav' been over dis a million times! I tells ya once, I tell ya 'gain. Ya should be glad that I still provide for ya! Slavery's been over, and I still lets ya work my land ta keep shelter and food on y'alls table!"

"And yas should! Dese heah are yo' chirrens!"

Clayton grimaced. "Lissen Nettie, jus' handle Cletus!" he snapped, grabbing Timmy by the hand and dragging him off towards the mansion.

Nettie didn't care how mad Clayton got. In her opinion, he had it coming to him. Besides, she felt she was doing nothing more than telling the truth. As soon as Clayton was out of sight, Nettie walked into the cabin to find Cletus still in tears.

"I saw-saw-sorry Mama. I didn't mean ta-ta cause ya no trouble. I didn't mean ta do no wrong. P-P-Please don't whup me," he pleaded. "It was jus' dat dey-dey kept a teasing me, callin' me slow. Ah aint slow Mama!"

Nettie listened as her son stumbled over his words. At times even pausing to make sure what he said came out right. Nettie could empathize with her son. She could feel his pain. "Look Cletus, I knows ya not slow. But ya mus' understan' boy dat ya are blessed an' not everyone is goin' ta understand God's gift he's dun givin' ya like I do. Ya heah?"

Nettie loved Cletus with all her heart, and the last thing she wanted was to see him hurt. So, she attempted to express to him how special he was. He was after all, her first born. The fact he was different than all the other children made him that much more special to her. She never looked upon Cletus as being slow or retarded. She saw Cletus as being gifted. In Nettie's eyes, God had seen it fit to bestow a blessing upon her, so he gave her Cletus.

"But Ma-Ma-Mama dere-dere names hurt my feelins." Nettie could see the tears swelling in her son's eyes. She tried her best to protect him from the cruelties of the world, but she found it to be a daunting task she often failed at. It was often at times like these, when Nettie could not protect her son that the weight of the world came crashing down on top of him.

"Don't ya fret none boy. Ya mama aint goin' a let anythin' happen ta ya. Ya heah? Nobody, an I means nobody is goin' ta hurt mah babies," Nettie assured him, wiping away his tears.

If there was one promise Nettie intended to keep it was that one.

CHAPTER 2

▼

"I'm tellin' ya Clayton, ya got ta do somethin' 'bout dat dere nigger," insisted Tom. The six of them, all of them either friends or business associates of Clayton's in some sort of fashion had crammed themselves into his parlor to discuss Cletus' latest stunt and the racial tension he was creating amongst the town's folk. News of Cletus' latest feat had traveled fast. It had already reached a friend of Clayton's in a neighboring county. Every little thing Cletus did only made the myth surrounding him grow larger.

"Yeah, ya got ta do somethin' 'bout that dere nigger. He dun gat da good niggers in town thinkin' he's Christ Almighty, himself, for God's sake. Ya should hear how dey yap 'bout him. Sayin' he can talk ta da animals an' bring plants an' animals back ta life and all wit only a touch. Hell, preddy soon dey'll have him raisin' da dead...If dey haven't gat him doin' dat already," said Orville, adding his two cents.

Clayton glanced around the room at the other gentlemen in his parlor; all of them nodded their heads in agreement. These were all tales Clayton had heard before; in fact he had personally witnessed a few of Cletus' miracles himself. Although these tales had been embellished upon, the stories were not too far from the truth.

"I tell ya Clayton, if ya or dat niggra bitch can't control dat lil' mutt we will," Tom demanded, turning complaints into threats.

"Are ya threatenin' me Tom?" questioned Clayton with a hint of anger in his voice.

"Aw shucks Clayton, we've known each other fo' years! I know we aint goin' ta let no nigger come between us," proclaimed Tom. Tom was Clayton's closest friend as well as his closest neighbor. So, the news of Cletus' feats always reached his plantation first, which meant it had the most immediate effect on the Negroes sharecropping his land. So, out of all of Clayton's friends, Tom usually felt the financial implications of Cletus' exploits long before everybody else. Many of the Negroes sharecropping Tom's land had come to believe Jesus Christ himself had moved in next door. They truly believed that Cletus was going to deliver them to the Promised Land. So, many of them believed they did not need to harvest the land, since they would soon be on their way to Heaven.

"Not only are dey callin' da nigger God. He dun' made 'em think dat dey can jus' sass off at da mouf ta decent white folk…Why, I had ta rake a young niggra across da mouf da otha day, cuz she refused ta walk in da street wit da rest of da animals. Ya know wat she told me, 'I iz a free Negro an I can walk where I pleases.' She's lucky I didn't tie her up and whip her right dere on da spot. If dat would have been a nigger I would have strung him up right then an dere," exclaimed Orville.

"I tell ya dis nigger gats all da colored believin' dey's God's chosen people, instead of God fearin' white folk as it states in da good book," Joseph chimed in.

"An' we cants be hav'in dat," Orville chafed.

"Dat's right. Befo' ya know it, dey'll be sneakin' in da dark from house ta house an' from bed ta bed cuttin' our throats like dat devil Nat Turner," added Joseph.

"Dat's right! We have ta do sumthin' 'bout dis once an' for all ta stop dis nonsense," exclaimed Harvey. Harvey was a friend of Tom's, still to hear his displeasure in Cletus gave him a good reason for being there.

"So, wat do ya plan ta do 'bout it?" asked Tom.

Clayton sat in silence. He could sense the gravity of the situation weighing heavy on him as all of them sat there awaiting his response. Every one of them in his house that day had told him how Cletus was affecting their livelihoods and stirring up relations with the town's Negroes. These men in his house were not individuals he considered strangers. They were people whom he called his friends, his neighbors, and fellow businessmen. They helped him rebuild their town from the ashes that remained after the Union Army's departure, back into a town of bustling commerce. Each one of those men was a respectable, upstanding, citizen of the community. Yet, they sat there in the comfort of his living room, working them selves into a frenzy. Why? Because they feared a little boy who had never harmed a soul. They had come to his home to hear what he intended to do about Cletus, but in all honesty they truly only wanted his blessings to commit murder. They had already made up their minds how they intended to deal with Cletus, long before they had set foot into his home.

Clayton wanted so desperately to side with them, but in doing so he knew he risked forsaking everything he believed in. Still, he could not rightfully stand by and bless the murder of a ten-year old boy. Clayton could not help but wonder if Cletus truly were a blessing sent by God, an honest to God angel. He had seen for himself the wonders Cletus possessed with his very own eyes. He questioned how he could sleep peacefully at night knowing he may have sided against God. However, he knew if he sided against those sitting in his parlor that evening he would be damned. Yet, if he sided with them he could be courting eternal damnation. In either case, he knew it was a no win situation. He could not rightfully stand up and protect a colored woman and her child, even if that child was his own. It would be sacrilegious.

"Gentlemen, I hav' informed Nettie on several occasions 'bout how she mus' control dat boy. But it seems, I hav' dun all I can do," Clayton sighed. His displeasure at having to make such a decision was obvious. A silence filled the room as everyone in attendance realized what exactly Clayton's reply meant.

"Well, I'm sorry ta hear dat Clayton…Real sorry," answered Tom. Clayton's answer was not the response Tom wanted to hear, but he understood it was the best Clayton could do. Everyone in town knew Clayton was sweet on Nettie. Tom had hoped to save his friend the shame of the rumors that were sure to go around if he decided to protect her. His decision to do nothing at all saved him some face. Nonetheless, Tom could not help but sympathize with his friend's predicament. Because of this reason and this reason alone, Tom did not demand Clayton to give him a better answer than the one he had provided.

As they filed out of his home, Clayton knew they would waste no time. Cletus had riled up the town's colored folk into believing he was the second coming of Jesus Christ. For that reason alone, they would not want to waste no time in putting a stop to this blasphemy in an attempt to make a statement. Clayton wished he had the nerve to stop them, but he had to think about his own two kids, Jane and Timmy, and his wife, Emma. He could not risk his life or theirs, protecting Nettie. Clayton was certain they would act that evening. Although he was unable to protect Nettie, he felt it was his obligation to warn her.

*   *   *   *

When Nettie spotted Massa Jackson walking up the trail in the haze of twilight; she figured he was coming for his regular nightly visit. Despite the dim sunlight caused by the setting sun, Nettie could see Clayton walking up the trail in a deliberate fashion. She had seen him walk that same path many of times before in the waning hours of daylight. She had figured this evening would not be any different than any other night. Her and the kids had finished supper and she had settled down to sit a spell in her rocking chair to read them a book. A skill she insisted Clayton teach her in exchange for his nightly visits. However, Nettie could sense that something was amiss by the way he grudgingly walked up the path that particular evening. She had seen the men go in and out of The Big House around suppertime, and she was certain their visit was not a social one. She knew those men were there to talk about her beloved son, Cletus, and whatever verdict they rendered, Massa Jackson was there to deliver their sentence.

Clayton came and sat on the porch. At first he said nothing, simply pretending to listen to the chorus of crickets singing in the brush. When he had managed to gather his thoughts, he told Nettie, "Can I hav' a word wit ya Nettie?"

"Massa wonts ta talk ta me? Lil' ole me?" she teased. Clayton knew Nettie would still be sore at him for the way he treated her earlier. However, Clayton believed if Nettie had any idea of the pain, the torment, he was going through, she would understand and be lenient on him.

"Please Nettie?…Alone," begged Clayton.

Nettie stared at him for a moment before sending Cletus and Celia inside to bed. "Wat ya wont?" she snapped, when she was sure the children were out of earshot.

Clayton took a deep breath. "I jus' met wit sum of da town's folk 'bout an hour ago, upstandin', respectable folk Nettie."

"So wat dat gat ta do wit me?"

"Dey came ta see me 'bout Cletus, Nettie."

"Mah boy iz none of dere biz'ness!"

"It doesn't matta. Dey've made 'im dere biz'ness…Dere goin' ta be comin' for 'im tuhnight."

"Wat ya mean dey goin' ta be comin' for 'im? He aint dun nuttin' an' ya know it! He aint nuttin' but a boy! Grown men afraid of a lil' ole boy! Y'all ought ta be ashamed of yo' selves! Anyways, ya his pappy why don't ya say sumthin' ta stop 'em!"

"Nettie it's not dat easy…Dere is nuttin' I can do…I cares fo' ya an' all, but I hav' a wife an' two kids ta think of. I can't be goin' aroun' protectin' a niggra…I mean how would dat look?"

"Dese heah are yar chirren too!"

"They from me, but dey not mine."

"Youse goin' ta tell me, youse not lay down wit me an' gives me dem dere babies!" yelled Nettie, pointing into the cabin.

"Nettie ya got ta understand."

"I understands a'ight! I ask God ta bring me a man, and he brings me ya! No other man will even look at me now, cuz dey say I da massa's whore! So, I live heah alone! No man, jus' two chirrens! But he dun' heard my prayers cause he broughts me Cletus ta dry my eyes, an' I tells ya nobody is gonna take my boy away from me…Ya heah me Clayton Jackson…nobody!"

"Nettie, I jus' came ta warn ya."

"Well, ya dun' did wat ya was told ta do! Now git!" Clayton hesitated for a moment, wishing he could say something that could change everything, but he knew he couldn't. The words were there, but he had lost his voice. Even if he had said something, Nettie would have surely ripped his tongue out of his mouth before he could speak a word.

"Git, I say! Go on an' go! We don't need ya comin' aroun' heah no mo'!"

Clayton knew as he started back up the trail, it would be the last time he would ever make that twilight walk again. Although he wasn't supposed to, he felt sad. He felt he had lost something special, something he had lost for no apparent reason. Nettie, on the other hand felt betrayed. She watched Clayton walk back up that trail like a hawk until he was out of sight. Clayton could no longer be trusted. He was right when he said, 'he was one of them.' So as soon as he was out of sight, Nettie hurried inside the cabin to wake up Cletus and Celia.

"Git up now! Cum on git! Da both of ya!"

Fortunately for her, she had planned ahead just in case for such an occasion. Nettie knew someday, Cletus' luck would run out, and they would have to leave in haste. She knew she had to hurry up because nightfall was already beginning to seep across the sky. Nettie had to get Cletus out of there, and come back for their belongings later.

"Wats wrong Mama?" asked Celia, wiping the sleep from her eyes.

"Nuttin's wrong jus' git dressed." Nettie glanced outside, in search of anything unusual. For the time being everything was the way it was suppose to be. Nettie didn't have much time, and she knew it.

"Cum on we gat ta go!" yelled Nettie.

When they were ready, Nettie led them out back into the dense woods where despite the advancement of night, she was still able to find her way. She had come this way many times before, so, it was hard for her to forget especially at a time like this. The children bickered amongst themselves as kids often do. They were scared and uncertain of what was happening, but Nettie paid them no mind. She had to focus her energy on making sure they did not get lost. It was the first time she had ever tried to find her way amongst the trees at night. Even though she was apt at navigating through the densely packed thicket, the possibility of her taking a wrong turn somewhere along the way was possible. Just when Nettie thought she had done just that, she managed to wander into the small clearing she was in search of. She could not help but thank God for showing her the way on such a night. Now, realizing she didn't have much time, Nettie quickly started a small fire and told Cletus to stay put, while she went back to the cabin to gather up the rest of their belongings.

"Cletus, now, ya stay put till mama cums back for ya, ya heah?" The boy simply nodded his head, not sure what to make of this late night excursion.

Nettie could sense her son's fear. She wanted so desperately to explain to him why she was leaving him there all alone. Yet, due to her lack of time, she could not afford to give Cletus the explanation he so desperately sought. She had to get back to the cabin as soon as possible and get their things before it was too late. Nettie figured she would have plenty of time to explain it to him later. Until then, she could do nothing more than hope he minded her and stayed put as she had asked. Now, when she was sure Cletus was comfortable, Nettie stole away back into the night towards the cabin with Celia by her side.

*   *   *   *

Nettie had just finished stuffing her carpetbag full of what little belongings she had and ready to make her way back to Cletus, when she heard the thunder of hooves in the distance.

"Go inside!" she screamed to Celia, who rushed back into the cabin.

Nettie had nothing to defend herself with other than her ornery ole temper. Although, she was smaller than the ordinary woman, she felt her temper more than made up for her lack of size and in some instances gave her the upper hand when it came to fisticuffs. Of course, that was when it was a fair fight. Yet, she knew, no matter how venomous her temper, she could not beat a man. Still, she had sworn to herself that she would never cower to men who hid behind sheets. Above all else, Nettie intended to make good on that promise. The thunder of horse's hooves grew loud as they drew nearer. When masked men finally brought their horses to a halt in front of her cabin, Nettie's fists were clenched so tight that her knuckles had turned a ghostly white.

"Where's da boy at bitch?" asked one of the masked marauders.

"Aint no boy heah!" proclaimed Nettie.

"Don't lie ta me niggra, we know ya gat 'im aroun' heah sumwhere!" he shouted. Nettie quickly deduced he was the leader.

"I tells ya dere aint no boy heah!" she screamed.

The sheet doing all the talking looked back at the other six Klansmen, who had joined him on this late night ride of terror, and instructed them to, "Go aroun' back an' see if he's hidin' sum were back dere." Two Klansmen quickly galloped off on their horses around to the back of the cabin.

"Ya think ya a smart lil' niggra, don't ya bitch?" yelled their leader. As he dismounted his horse and made his way towards Nettie, Celia came tearing out of the cabin screaming.

"Didn't I tell ya ta stay inside chile?" Nettie hollered.

"But Mama dere haunts out back!" Celia screamed. Just at that moment Celia noticed the same ghostly white sheets she had seen out back were also in the front. "Mama wats goin' on?" asked Celia, grabbing on to her mother's tattered skirt.

"Hush chile!" Nettie warned.

One of the Klansmen whom had rode around back came riding back, "Aint nuttin' back dere. Joseph heard sumthin' in da bushes, so he's checkin' it out. Probably nuttin' but a possum."

Upon hearing this, the head Klansman walked up to Nettie and seethed, "Ya think yar a smart niggra, don't ya? Well, let me tell ya sumthin bitch we aint leavin' here tuhnight empty handed!" snatching Celia away from her. "Sumone is goin' ta hang tuhnight! If ya don't tell us were da boy is at, it's goin' ta be ya lil' girl heah!"

"No, not my baby!" screamed Nettie, attempting to pull Celia back. Her attempts were in vain for the other night riders had quickly restrained her. Celia kicked and swung her arms wildly, but it was no use.

"Didn't I tell ya, dere is goin' ta be a hangin' tuhnight? Whether it be dis one or da boy it doesn't matter! We need ta send a message ta ya niggers!"

Nettie had not intended for this to happen. The Klan was supposed to leave once they realized Cletus was not there. They were not supposed to take her baby. Inadvertently, in her attempts to save the life of her son, she had jeopardized the life of her daughter.

As Nettie struggled to reach Celia, there came a cry from out back. "Tom back heah!"

*   *   *   *

Now, Cletus was never one to disobey his mother, but in this particular instance, he was frightened to death by the thought of sitting alone in the woods where the shadows shifted and moved. On top of that, he couldn't understand why his mother would want to leave him behind as she stole away back into the night. So as soon as Nettie and Celia had disappeared amongst the thicket of shrubs, Cletus decided to follow. A couple of times he had gotten lost, but the sound of Nettie and Celia's voices in the distance guided him back home.

When he had made it to the cabin, he was shocked to find haunts roaming about. Cletus watched in amazement as the ghosts moved here and there as if they were searching for something or someone. His mama had told him once about haunts and their wicked ways, but he had never seen one with his very own eyes. His fear of them had gotten the best of him for it had frozen him in his tracks. Cletus thought he could feel his heart skip a beat when one of the ghosts had gotten so close to where he hid, that he could hear him breathing. He didn't know whether to run or be still. Regardless of his intentions, the snap of a stray twig giving way beneath his feet betrayed him. It was then when Cletus heard the demon call out to another, that they had found him. Before he knew it they were everywhere. It was then that Cletus heard his mother scream.

*   *   *   *

"Run Cletus!" screamed Nettie, before being struck across the mouth. She could taste her own blood wash over her tongue as she attempted to pick herself up off the ground. Nettie slowly rose to her feet, refusing to remain on the ground. She figured if she were going to die, she would die standing up. It sickened her to her stomach to hear the Klan rejoice in the capture of her boy. They had her precious son, Cletus, and she could do nothing about it other than call out to him.

"Ya stupid bitch did ya think we wouldn't fin' 'im! Harvey and Orville, ya two go out back and help Joseph string that damn nigger up! It shouldn't be that difficult stringing up a retard! John, hold dis heah lil' girl! Butch and Elmer, ya hold dis wench down." Tom handed Celia over to John while Butch and Elmer, wrestled Nettie to the ground.

"Da rest of ya torch da place...As fo' you niggra bitch, I heah ya like white folks...especially da men folk. How 'bout I give ya a lil' sumthin' ta remember dis special night by?" quipped the Klansman they called Tom.

Nettie tried to fight to get back on her feet, but before she knew it there were hands everywhere, groping, tainting her skin. They ripped her clothing, so they could fondle her breast and ultimately pry her legs apart wide enough to force themselves inside of her. As one after another took their turn mounting her, Nettie withdrew into a world of madness. It was only there that she did not feel their hands upon her skin or their pants and hurried breathing upon her neck. However, even there, even in the farthest reaches of her mind, she clung to the thought of Cletus.

*   *   *   *

Nettie had no idea how many men had their way with her that night. Nor, how long she had lain there with her back against the earth, before they had rode off. She had lost track of time the second they had forced themselves inside of her. If not for Celia's constant cries for her to get up, Nettie might have remained there on the ground until God, so, mercifully decided to take her.

Nettie gathered together the rags that remained of her clothes and attempted to use them as best as she could to cover herself. The home she had known was no longer. A mound of smoldering wood and ashes was all that remained. As Nettie stood there, gazing into the fire one lone thought entered her mind...Cletus. It was Cletus that sparked some sign of life inside of her. Despite, being badly beaten Nettie refused to let herself die without first knowing the fate of her son. Not until then, not until she knew what became of her precious Cletus, would she invite death to finish the job it had already begun that evening.

Celia helped Nettie around the charred remains of what was once their home and into the clearing where they both were greeted by the sight of Cletus hanging lifeless amongst the trees, his body dangling listless in the amber moonlight. At that moment, at that very second, Nettie's will to live took flight. All her hopes and desire, drained from every limb of her body, only to pool at her feet as she wailed in grief

It was at that very instance, sheer madness wrapped its cold arms around her in a frigid embrace and vowed to never let her go.

CHAPTER 3

▼

The Present

The sunlight broke through the balcony doors, landing on the dull hardwood floors like the so many disparaging puddles of rain, left behind on a rainy day. Chris lied in bed awake, watching the reflection of the sun dance on the ceiling as it shimmered off the pool outside. She was so glad that she had once again awakened in her bed.

It was Monday morning, the beginning of the workweek for Frank, but just another day for Chris. At times, her days simply blended together and she could only tell the difference from a weekday and the weekend was by whether or not Frank got out of the bed by six o'clock in the morning. Unfortunately, every morning started out the same, her invariable waking up in a panic, with her heart racing at a feverish pace. Followed by, the horror of envisioning herself standing in a field somewhere, next to the smoldering ruins of what was once a home with the sound of someone's piercing screams playing in her ears. Once she had assured herself it was only a dream, her anxiety would eventually ease. However, it was generally around this time the pain began. It usually started at the small of her back, before wrenching its way up her spine, tightening each muscle and sinew along the way like a vice grip, until the pain came to rest comfortably in between her shoulder blades and the nape of her neck. There it would stay for the remainder of the day. This routine played out day in and day out for Chris without fail, and this particular morning was no different. She tried massaging the muscles at the base of her neck, in hopes of untangling them. She knew it was nothing more than a symbolic gesture. However, she figured trying to do something was far better than doing nothing at all.

Chris pulled herself up out of the bed, to the sound of Frank singing his rendition of Eric Clapton's, *Tears In Heaven*, while he showered. He did both the song and her ears a disservice. Yet, who was she to tell him he could not sing. He would later bounce down stairs for breakfast as he did every morning and proclaim how he should have gone into the music industry, instead of marketing. She would agree with him and smile as she did every morning. She did not have the heart to tell him he stunk. Besides, she believed everybody had the right to dream.

Chris threw on her housecoat and slippers, before heading downstairs to make Frank's breakfast. She made sure to walk gingerly, to ensure she did not set off a host of alarms along her spine. As she walked into the kitchen, she could smell the morning blend of coffee brewing. For Chris, there was nothing like the smell of freshly brewed coffee in the morning to wake the senses. She poured herself a cup. She preferred it black in the morning. She stood there and stared out the kitchen window onto a brand new day. While she sipped her coffee, she noticed a group of birds gathered at the bird feeder in the backyard. A few of the birds acted as if they noticed her standing there in the window. It was something she had noticed from time to time over the past few months. As usual, a couple of birds flew over to the window and perched themselves on the windowsill. At first Chris had found it odd, how they gathered at the window's ledge every morning to greet her. However over time, it had become nothing more than a morning ritual, she had grown accustomed to.

She could hear Frank's footsteps, slide across the floor upstairs as he made his way from the bathroom to the bedroom. That usually was her cue to get breakfast started. If she timed it right, Frank would be coming down the stairs right around the time she would be placing his plate on the table. So, Chris turned her attention away from the birds, and towards preparing Frank's breakfast.

By the time Frank had made it downstairs into the kitchen, Chris had just finished scrambling his eggs, and was in the process of taking the toast out of the oven. Frank preferred his bread to be toasted in the oven, instead of in a toaster. He liked the butter to be toasted right into the bread, rather than spread on afterwards. He also liked his eggs runny, not wet just runny. After several years of marriage these were just a few of the many idiosyncrasies of his, Chris had managed to perfect.

Frank sat down at the table in silence. There was never a "Good morning" nor "hi," just the clank of his fork against the plate as he ate. Over time, it had become the way he greeted her in the morning. It was another annoying habit of his; Chris had learned to live with. Frank grabbed the morning paper as he did every morning and threw it up like a makeshift barrier, separating the two of them. He always read while he ate. Chris, saw it as an easy excuse for him to avoid talking to her. Upon completion of his meal, he finished off his coffee and gave her a quick peck on the cheek on his way out the door. It was his customary morning goodbye. He was so predictable Chris could set her watch to his routine. In the beginning Frank's chronic rigidity drove her crazy, but like everything else she grew use to it.

When she heard the car pull out of the driveway, Chris went upstairs and put on her sports bra and shorts. Although, she knew a brisk morning run would do nothing but aggravate her back further, Chris was determined to get out of the house. She had already had her fill of it. From time to time she viewed her home more like a prison, rather than a sanctuary. There were days she could not wait to escape its confines. Unfortunately, days such as those were becoming numerous, especially of late. However, there were days she could not wait to cuddle up on the couch with a good book and relax either. She never really knew what mood she was in until she had progressed along into her day.

This particular morning, Chris had pretty much decided to get out and leave the house behind. An early morning jog usually provided her with the necessary excuse to escape. Other than gossiping with Beverly, keeping tabs on her favorite soaps, or the occasional charity work to keep her mind occupied; jogging made her feel alive. Of course, she received gratification from being in shape. Still, jogging seemed to give her a sense of purpose. Of course, the charitable work her family provided for the community gave her satisfaction as well. Nonetheless, it did not allow for her to have time to herself like a nice long jog did.

Chris had tried her hand at working, but she found the level of stress it gave her unbearable. Besides, she really did not see the need to work, especially since she did not have to. Frank made more than enough money to support the two of them, and if that wasn't enough she had her inheritance to fall back on. Her inheritance was more than enough money to take care of them for the rest of their lives. So, there really was no real need for her to work. If Chris wanted to work, she figured picking and choosing, which charity rightfully deserved her family foundation's money was taxing enough. So, other than splitting her time between jogging and charity work, Chris usually spent her days gossiping with her best friend, Beverly, whom she had a luncheon date with that afternoon. Although, the early morning jogs and afternoon lunches with Beverly had become routine, they provided her otherwise mundane life with some type of structure.

Chris stepped out onto the front yard and was immediately greeted by the unbearable heat and humidity of a typical Atlanta summer. Although the day was new, the heat coupled with the humidity had already made being outdoors unpleasant. She contemplated returning to the comfort of an air conditioned home, but Chris knew if she did not force herself to go through with her morning jog, she would see its effects of neglect on her hips later in the week. As she stretched out in the front yard, Hector, the neighbor's cat came by and wished her a good morning. Something he did every morning with a gentle nudge of his head against her calf. It was a morning ritual similar to the one with the birds.

"Good morning Hector, how are you doing this morning?" asked Chris, stroking him along his spine. Hector arched his back and purred with satisfaction. He was sufficient company until Chris was limber and she sent him on his way.

Since many neighborhoods in Atlanta, including hers, lacked sidewalks, Chris was forced to jog along the outer edge of the road. The omitting of sidewalks in certain neighborhoods were a constant reminder to possible interlopers that strangers were not wanted, especially in swank Buckhead. Despite having to run with the traffic, Chris learned running into oncoming traffic made it easier for drivers to see her and her them. Otherwise, if she ran with traffic, she risked not being able to see the drivers who strayed dangerously too close.

Each fall of her feet upon the firm and unyielding concrete, sent shockwaves of pain up and down her spine. The thought of turning back, crossed her mind several times, however, she was resolved to push on. She occasionally waved at a few neighbors she happened to encounter in passing. Many of them were the housewives of successful husbands such as her. Their lives were predominately spent shopping at the mall, or at some country club gossiping over Bloody Marys with other women just like themselves. Some of the women passed the time by sleeping with the golf instructor or the cabana boy, who was most likely some college student working to pay his tuition; boredom manifested itself in many different ways. Chris was not the country club type. Although, Frank often attempted to force it upon her, she never really felt a connection to the women who frequented them.

Chris jogged passed the governor's mansion, which were only a few houses down the street from hers. For years, Chris had begged Frank to move. Despite the fact she was born and breed in Atlanta's high society, a product of old money, Chris did not care for the status and air of affluence living in Buckhead brought with it. Frank, however, loved living in close proximity to the city's power brokers, not to mention he enjoyed the prestige that came along with living in Buckhead on West Paces Ferry Road. Chris on the other hand, could have cared less for the exalted status he so dearly coveted.

Since the day was heating up faster than she had expected, Chris decided it was best she cut her jog short and head back home. Not only was it hot, but also her back was beginning to scream out in pain. She usually could focus beyond the pain while she ran, however, this particular morning she was having a difficult time doing so.

Chris was glad she arrived at home when she did. She seriously doubted she could have taken another step. She stood there in her yard for a moment waiting for the pain to subside, so she could walk. It took a while, but it eventually eased. When she was certain she could walk without wincing in pain, Chris hurried inside to get cleaned up. She needed to run a few errands before meeting Beverly for lunch.

CHAPTER 4

▼

"How's your back?" asked Beverly, popping an escargot into her mouth.

"Terrible. You know, I think it's getting worse. I hardly get a good night's sleep anymore," complained Chris. Of course, Chris did not dare tell Beverly another reason why she was having trouble sleeping was because she was having nightmares. Chris felt telling Beverly about her back pain was about as personal as she wanted to get.

"How long has it been now…six months?" asked Beverly.

"Let's try more like nine," stated Chris, correcting her.

"Chris, I'm telling you, you need to go see my chiropractor, Samir Deshpande. I'm telling you, he is a lot better than those quacks you've been spending your money on. In my opinion, he's the best chiropractor in Atlanta, and a hell of a lot cheaper than the guy you're seeing now. Besides, he is about the cutest little East Indian man I've ever seen in my entire life." Chris rolled her eyes. Beverly always based everything thing she did on whether or not she would find her next lover from it. It seemed hard for her to simply base her advice or opinion on simply a man's merits, such as in this case her chiropractor's ability to fix her back.

"I keep telling you, Beverly, I'm not going to see your witch doctor. So, will you stop with the sales pitch already."

"Okay, but I'm telling you he is the best. Especially, when he lays those soft hands of his on your back and massages those healing ointments of his into your skin."

"Don't tell me, he makes you get undressed?"

"He doesn't make you get undressed. It's your choice," responded Beverly.

"He sounds more like a pervert to me," stated Chris.

"Come on Chris, lighten up. You sound more like you're forty-two going on eighty-three," chided Beverly.

"I've never gotten undressed for no man other than Frank and my gynnie."

"Maybe that's your problem," quipped Beverly. Chris shot her a cold glare. "Don't look at me like that it's probably the truth…As I was saying, maybe you need to go to Dr. Deshpande and get one of those massages. Your back might feel a whole hell of a lot better. I'm telling you, every once and a while I let him massage the front too." Beverly giggled.

Chris couldn't believe her ears. "You expose yourself to a complete stranger? How do you know he's not videotaping you or something?"

"I just do it to give him something to look at. You know, let him know I still got it. Oh, he tries to keep his cool, but I know he gets a rise out of it. Besides, his ointment is good for the skin. Firms it up…You and I both know, neither one of us is getting any younger. I especially have to look my best since I'm single," stated Beverly. It was not like the tummy tucks, breast implants and Chris couldn't imagine whatever else cosmetic surgery Beverly had done did not enhance her appearance already.

"And if he's taping it, oh well. At least somebody is getting their rocks off. I sure in the hell am not. I need to start going to the gym," said Beverly, nonchalantly sipping her Chardonnay.

"I can't believe you. If you have to go through all that hassle to get a man to look at you, then why bother."

"I'll tell you why, because men are pricks. Whatever way their little weenies are pointing when the wind blows is exactly where you'll find them, married or not. So, in order to compete you have to look your best. That's why," snapped Beverly, popping another snail into her mouth.

Ever since Beverly had caught her now ex-husband, Harry, with their nanny, she harbored a deep resentment towards the opposite sex. Simply put, she did not trust men. It was also the reason she never stayed with one guy for too long. It was understandable, after going through such a bitter divorce and enduring a nervous breakdown in the process. So, Chris did not bother to debate with Beverly, when it came to men. Frank was far from a saint.

"Speaking of pricks," Beverly said, washing the escargot down with another sip of wine. "How's yours?" Chris gave her another icy glare. "Okay I'm sorry…Anyway, how are things going?" she apologized.

"You know, Frank is Frank."

"So, basically nothing has changed. He's back to his old self again. Frank could probably careless if you were dead or alive. I swear Chrysanthemum, you need to leave the jerk. It isn't like you need him." Only Beverly and her mother called her by her full name. "If it was me, who caught him having an affair with a client, I would have relieved him of it. Just like I almost did Harry. I would have just grabbed those scissors in one hand, and his dick in another and snipped it right off. Harry would have been dick less for the rest of his life, if he hadn't of woke up. Can you believe, I was this close to relieving Harry of his little pecker?" exclaimed Beverly, holding her index finger and thumb about half an inch apart. "As you can imagine he was scared shitless," she said, laughing.

"Yeah, I can bet. He probably had visions of John Wayne Bobbit flashing through his head," Chris commented, trying not to laugh.

"Do you think," Beverly said, cracking up. "But really," she rambled, once the laughter had subsided. "I mean, what do you expect. You let him back in the house only after two months." Chris had quickly grown tired of her mouth, and had begun to tune her out. "You didn't even make him grovel. Frank, probably thinks he can get away with murder now."

"Okay, that is enough," Chris admonished. She hated being reminded of Frank's infidelity. "I don't want to talk about it no more," she said, sternly.

"Fine. We won't talk about it," snapped Beverly, finishing off her glass of wine. "I'm just worried about you. I don't want to see you hurt again. That's all," she said, motioning for the waiter to refill her glass. It was close to one o' clock in the afternoon and Beverly was already working on her fourth glass of Chardonnay.

"Can we just drop it Beverly. Besides, he gave me his word."

"Yeah, and the wolf told the sheep he wasn't going to eat them either."

Chris had had enough of her snide remarks. "I've had just about enough from you for one day!"

"All right already. It's dropped," professed Beverly.

Beverly was Chris' best friend, but at times she did not act like it. She would often do and say the exact opposite of what Chris thought was appropriate. It was often this nagging characteristic of Beverly's to be her polar opposite that absolutely drove Chris crazy. There were times when she wondered if they had anything in common. Despite this annoying fact, Chris loved Beverly like a sister. Beverly often had an ugly habit of crossing the line, but Chris knew that if it were not for Beverly's blunt honesty, she would be lost. If there was one quality about Beverly, Chris found endearing, it was her honesty. Beverly always gave it to her straight. Sometimes her frankness was a little too harsh for Chris' taste, but it was nonetheless what she needed to hear.

Lunch ended on a sour note. The two of them promised to call each other later that evening. However, it would not have mattered if they had ended lunch on pleasant terms, they still would have called each other. They spoke to each other at least twice a day. Since Beverly left in a hurry to show some rock star a condo in Buckhead, Chris was left with the bill.

*   *   *   *

Chris went home, her excitement for the day was now over. She went home to an empty house, where there was nothing for her to do except check her voice-mail and watch television. Upon checking her messages Chris discovered there was only one. It was from Jessica Rhimes, the director of the College Park Youth Center in southwest Atlanta, reminding her about the youth meeting Tuesday. Since Chris' family donated heavily to an organization ran by Ms. Rhimes called Save Our Kids, Chris felt it was only right she knew how her family's dollars were being spent. She also realized, she had forgotten all about the meeting, so she made a point to input the date into her palm pilot. After placing it in her palm pilot Chris noticed, she had made it home just in time to catch the tail end of *General Hospital*. She figured since she had time to watch *General Hospital*, she might as well watch *Oprah* too. However, somewhere in between *General Hospital* and *Oprah*, she unknowingly dozed off.

Chris awoke to the sound of the telephone ringing in her ears. She instantly awoke in a panic. Once again, she was glad to wake up at home and not in a field. Why she continued to have the same dream over and over again was a mystery to her. However, the reason for the dream did not matter once she noticed the time. At that point, a different kind of panic consumed her. Frank would be home any minute expecting dinner to be ready.

However, her rush to prepare dinner turned out to be premature. It was none other than Frank on the phone, informing her he had to work late and would grab a bite out to eat. Chris could not help but immediately think about what Beverly had preached to her earlier that afternoon. She tried to block Beverly's comments out of her mind, but simply couldn't. Of course, Chris had her reservations about Frank, however, she knew if she did not place some trust in him things between them would never work out.

'After all he did give me his word,' she told herself.

Since Frank was eating out and she was still somewhat weighed down by lunch, Chris felt there was no need to cook. So, instead of cooking she decided to take a nice hot bubble bath to help her relax.

By the time Chris had gotten out of the tub and climbed into bed, Frank still had not made it home. She tried to beat the thought of Frank with another woman out of her mind, but the idea persisted. She tried watching television to preoccupy herself with thoughts of something else. Yet, visions of Frank and another woman continued. Chris attempted to wait up for him just to ease her fears, but the comfort achieved from a relaxing stint in the tub coupled with the feel of the warm blankets wrapped around her, eased her off to sleep long before Frank arrived home. Still, thoughts of Frank and another woman bled their way into her dreams.

CHAPTER 5

▼

Tuesday morning started off the same way as Monday. Beginning with the daunting task of overcoming a vicious panic attack. Once Chris was certain, she had awakened in her bedroom; she was able to calm down. The only difference between Tuesday morning and Monday morning was that the excruciating pain that typically worked its way up her back to her neck was more severe. Sometimes there were days like Monday, when the pain started out bad then subsided as the day wore on. Then there were days like Tuesday, when the day started out painful and built up to a crescendo of agony, that only went away after Chris had taken an excess of pain killers.

Chris looked over at the illuminating red digits of the alarm clock on the nightstand, to see it read five ten. She checked on Frank to see if he was still asleep. By the sounds of his loud snoring, he was sound asleep. Chris knew it would be impossible for her to go back to sleep while in so much pain, not to mention Frank's obnoxious snoring. The best thing for her to do was to go downstairs where it was nice and quiet and hope she could fall back to sleep down there.

As she placed her feet on the floor, Chris could not help but coil from the bite of the early morning cold upon the soles of her feet. The sun had yet to break through the dusty gray curtain of dawn and warm the bedroom floors. She searched frantically for her slippers but could not find them. She was quite sure they had been drawn into the proverbial black hole underneath the bed, where all slippers went when they did not want to be found. It was always the unobtainable, always just out of her reach spot, beneath the bed. It sort of reminded her of the dryer, when it came to socks. They went in, but they never came out. Even if she wanted to find them, Chris knew she would have to get on her hands and knees and crawl under the bed to get them. However, in her condition, she did not have the strength to go on such an expedition.

Frank stirred as she stumbled into the bathroom. He voiced his displeasure when she turned on the bathroom light, which shined the brightest on his side of the bed. He grumbled something under his breath before rolling over to avoid the light's glare. She went about getting the prescription bottle of Tylenol with codeine out of the medicine cabinet, totally ignoring Frank.

Chris popped open the jar and downed two tablets. "I need to really find someone who can do something about this, before I become addicted to pain-killers," she said to herself in the mirror. As she stared at her reflection, Chris noticed the crow's feet at the corners of her eyes becoming more pronounced. The laugh lines that had only been barely visible a year ago were now etched into her cheeks.

Chris glanced over at Frank for she heard him moan something in his sleep; this time she listened intently. She silently hoped he would repeat himself. Frank had a bad habit of talking in his sleep. So, bad at times he kept her awake at night. As with everything else Chris learned to live with it, especially after he called out his lover's name one night in bed. If it had not been for his hapless rambling, Chris may have never found out about Rita Thorin. After hearing the name, Chris did a little investigating and was able to put a face to go along with the name.

Rita Thorin was a client, Frank's company was aggressively wooing at the time of the affair. She was a successful Atlanta luminary. She had managed to take her grandfather's fortune; he made in the citrus business and turned it into a media empire. Rita was relatively young, thirty-two. However, she was also very attractive and above all else ambitious. She exemplified, everything Chris was not. Of course, Frank denied ever having slept with her to the bitter end. Yet, when he had ran out of lies, he confessed to his infidelity. In the end his excuse was that his affair with Rita was to ensure the firm received her business. His story of taking one for the team was one Chris found hard to believe. Still, Chris did not press him. In her mind, Frank simply did not have the courage to tell her, he did not love her anymore. And in all honesty, Chris doubted if she could handle hearing him say such a thing, even if she felt the same. Although the spark in their marriage was lost, their lives had seemed to develop into a co-existence Chris had grown familiar with.

When it appeared Franks' mindless chatter had ended, Chris returned to her visage in the mirror. She glanced at the tangled crop of auburn hair that crowned her head and quickly ran her fingers through it trying to work out the kinks. She noticed a few wisps of gray lining her bangs. Her eyes had begun to rest a little further back in their sockets as often dictated by the advancement of time. From somewhere deep inside her body, Chris could hear her biological clock mocking her.

Depressed by her reflection in the mirror, Chris made her way downstairs where the first signs of daylight weaved its elongated fingers of red and orange through the fading dawn. As she stood there watching the day as it laid claim to the heavens, Chris could not help but think about the time when her life was pain free—both physically and emotionally. It was hard but she could remember a time, when she did not wake up in pain. When she did not have to struggle every morning to get out of bed. For Chris, it now seemed like a distant memory.

The coffee would not begin to brew its magical concoction of high-octane caffeine for another hour. Chris, on the other hand could not wait that long for a cup. She needed her caffeine fix right away. Now, Chris was well aware of the dangers of mixing medication with caffeine. Still, she was willing to take her chances. Once she had gotten the coffeepot brewing, Chris walked outside down to the mailbox to retrieve the morning paper. She felt it would help her pass the time until Frank woke up expecting breakfast. So once back in the house, armed only with the morning paper in hand, Chris sat down at the kitchen table with her cup of coffee reading the newspaper as she waited for Frank to wake up. She made sure to keep the paper neat and in order, so, Frank would not be able to tell she had read the paper before he did. He was a stickler when it came to someone else reading the newspaper before him.

The combination of Tylenol mixed with caffeine worked like a charm in deadening the pain. She experienced a brief episode of the jitters, but they passed. If she had her choice between the jitters and chronic back pain, Chris would choose the jitters any day. She had just about finished reading the local section of the paper, when she heard Frank slam the bathroom door shut upstairs. By all accounts, that meant he had awakened on the wrong side of the bed. By the scowl on his face as he descended the staircase after showering and dressing, Chris was certain that was the case.

When Frank arrived at the breakfast table his newspaper was in a neat, tidy, stack next to his plate of eggs and bacon. Still, it was evident to Chris, judging by the grimace on his face as he glanced over his morning meal and beloved paper that was not enough.

After looking over the paper, he glared over at her and growled, "Up early this morning." That was it. He said nothing else. Instead, he went to eating his breakfast and reading his newspaper. He did not bother to inquiry as to why she was up early; instead, there was just his snide remark.

It was at times like these when Chris did not understand, why she even tolerated his insensitive behavior. Especially, since she did everything in her power to please him. She often found herself wondering what happened to the campus geek, she had fallen in love with at Ole' Miss. The guy whom all her friends had claimed to be nothing more than a weirdo, but to Chris was nothing more than an extremely shy guy. It took him two and a half years to finally ask her out on a date. Up until that time, Frank was simply content with being her friend and occasional tutor when she seemed perplexed by a particular subject. Their first date was a one-dollar movie in the student union hall, *Taxi Driver*. Frank was a big Robert De Niro fan. That night he walked her to her dorm and they clumsily made love. It was apparent they both were inexperienced in the art of love.

Frank was her first, not to mention the only man she had given herself to. Chris disdained her college roommates, who hopped in the sack with every dumb jock or frat boy that tickled their fancy. Instead, Chris had saved herself for Frank, the man she knew she would one day marry. However, after all these years of hoarding herself for one man, her reward was a geek who had turned into an asshole. Although Chris knew she loved Frank, she also knew she was not in love with Frank. She questioned if staying with him threatened to turn what little love that remained into hatred. Life simply had not worked out the way she had planned it to.

There was a time when Frank adorned her with love and affection. Now, Chris was lucky if he gave her a second glance. In the past Frank seemed to genuinely care about her. Now, it often appeared as if he could have cared less. She often wished she could turn back the clock, to a time when there was no corporate ladder to climb and power lunches did not exist. For it was when he got the job at Simpson & Simpson, the marketing firm that employed him, that everything began to unravel for them. It was then when power lunches and dinner parties became more important than her. With each step up the corporate ladder, time spent together became a rarity. Often, it was business trips. Other times it was corporate meetings. The only time she saw her husband was when he threw himself into bed at night, exhausted. As can be expected, they drifted apart. Ultimately, Frank and Chris became nothing more than roommates.

In the beginning Chris was supportive. She did her best to play the role of corporate wife. She hosted dinner parties and fraternized with Frank's colleagues' wives at the country clubs. Regardless of how much she despised the corporate wife charade, she forced herself into playing it. Believing, that she was doing what was best for Frank's career, while keeping her true feelings and goals a secret. For Frank, Chris suppressed her own dreams out of fear that it might interfere with Frank's success. That was until he ran into the arms of Rita Thorin.

After that tearful night when Frank admitted to sleeping with Rita, Chris had tried several times to leave him but found it hard to do. She had even gone so far as to pack her bags, only to have them sit by the front door staring back at her. It was almost like she felt some type of loyalty to him that barred her from leaving. Yet she knew, the reason she refused to walk out that door was due to her innate fear of being alone. Just the thought of being by herself at the age of forty-two conjured up images of Beverly, and her constant bed hopping in search of love. Chris did not want that for herself. She wanted stability and security, instead of uncertainty. She could remember the days leading up to their marriage, the advice from numerous married women. "Things change when you get married," they warned. Now, at this juncture in her life, Chris hated to admit how right they were. She only wished they had been a little more specific on how drastic things would change.

"What time did you get home last night?" asked Chris, trying to make small talk.

"Ten," Frank said, through the business section. He knew the question was not one to initiate conversation, but instead one devised to probe the legitimacy of his answer.

"Excuse me, I didn't hear you?" Chris had heard him. She simply wanted Frank to put the paper down, so, she could see his eyes.

"I said ten o' clock," repeated Frank as he laid the paper down. Although Frank, kept eye contact with her, Chris could sense he was fishing for possible excuses just in case his answer did not satisfy her curiosity. The last thing he wanted to do was arouse her suspicion.

"Things must be getting busy at the office?" Chris said, pretending to be satisfied by his response.

"Yeah, we're in the midst of trying to land this new account," replied Frank, once again pulling the paper up in front of his face.

Over the years Chris had gotten good at being able to detect when Frank was lying to her; he always avoided eye contact. His eyes would dance around, avoiding her gaze. However, it appeared he had learned how to mask his dishonesty. Although, he had managed to look Chris in the eyes and answer her question without flinching, Chris still found his story hard to believe. The reason being the time at which he told her he came home. Chris remembered, glancing over at the clock around a quarter to ten just before dozing off. She found it hard to believe, Frank had came home only fifteen minutes after she had fallen asleep and did not wake her from her slumber. So many other nights, she had awakened when Frank climbed into bed. Chris found it hard to believe she did not wake up when he climbed into bed the night before. The only way Frank would have been able to get in bed without Chris noticing it would be if he came home extremely late. Chris contemplated challenging him, to see if he got flustered or attempted to change his story. However, she decided to let it go for fear of hearing the truth.

'Why did you even come back, if nothing was going to change?' she thought, watching him shove a slice of bacon into his mouth. 'Why did I even take you back for that matter after what you've done to me?' she scolded herself. It made no sense to her why they even continued on with this farce day in and day out. Even though they slept in the same bed, Chris could not remember the last time Frank had even touched her.

As it was everyday, Frank cleaned his plate after reading the morning paper and headed out the door. However, this morning he conveniently forgot Chris' routine peck on the cheek. Chris knew that was on purpose. It was his way of letting her know, he did not appreciate the cross-examination she gave him at the breakfast table. After Frank had left for work, Chris fixed herself something to eat and finished reading the rest of the paper, she had to abandon in haste. She was elated that Frank was gone. In fact, his absence put her at ease. She did not care if he was angry. Besides, Chris felt she had a good reason to question him about his whereabouts. She was after all his wife. In all honesty, Chris felt, she was the one who should have been upset. Regardless, Chris did not want Frank's callous behavior to ruin the rest of her day, so she did her best to forget about him.

After finishing the paper, Chris contemplated taking a jog but decided against it due to her back and a serious lack of motivation. She also considered canceling her engagement at the youth center, but decided it was an appointment she should keep. If there was one thing Chris enjoyed more than anything, it was working with the children at the center. Since her doctor had informed her some years ago that she could not bear children, spending time at the youth center was the closest Chris came to being a mother. Of course, an affluent white woman, being the mother to forty black kids in one of Atlanta's roughest neighborhoods was a bit far fetched. It was, nonetheless, a comforting thought.

With Frank gone, Chris ascended the staircase to her room. She tried to push aside thoughts of Frank. Instead, she tried to fill her head with thoughts of the kids at the center and how happy going there for these meetings made her feel. No matter, what mood she was in those kids always seemed to brighten her day. In her room, Chris set her clothes out on the bed and began to run her bath water in the bathroom. Just the thought of children always seemed to lift her spirits. After bathing, she put her clothes on before rushing out the door to College Park.

*   *   *   *

The one problem that always seemed to bother Chris, whenever she returned home from such meetings was that she suffered from an acute case of depression. Just discussing the plight of those children living in horrendous conditions, always seemed to bring her down. The deplorable conditions some of those children lived in sickened her to her stomach. Yet, Chris knew, no matter how much money she donated to any organization dedicated to assisting children such as the ones in College Park, there would never be enough money to change the lives of every single one of those kids. It was a hideous fact Chris had a hard time grappling with, but one she had to live with. Chris often wondered, why she was cursed to never bear children while there were so many women out there who had children but chose to neglect them.

As hard as it was, Chris tried to place the thought of the kids out of her mind. She was home and whether she liked it our not, she needed to shift her focus more towards getting dinner started for Frank, rather than thinking about the children at the center. As usual, Chris listened to the messages on her voice-mail-box. Many days, the pre-recorded messages left behind by family and friends was about as close as she came to human contact. Fortunately for her, a day spent in College Park did not allow voices on voicemail to be her only form of human interaction.

Chris only had one message. She hated to admit it, but she was sort of disappointed by the fact there was only one. She often enjoyed hearing from so many different people during the day. It made her feel important. Yet, this particular day only Beverly called. In many regards, Beverly did not count for she spoke to her on a daily basis. Chris pressed erase, cutting Beverly off in mid-sentence, when Chris realized she was not saying anything of importance. Chris walked into the kitchen and poured herself a glass of milk. It was while she stood there when she noticed a note taped to the refrigerator door.

Chris—

Gone golfing with Russell. Don't bother with dinner. I'll grab a bite out.

Frank

Russell Crandall was Frank's best friend. Frank was always, going somewhere or doing something with Russell. "He might as well fucking marry him," said Chris out loud.

Frank always ended his notes with just Frank. That was another thing about him that bothered her. His notes never ended with the customary, "Love Frank," or "Sincerely Frank." It was always just plain old Frank. Just the sight of his letter made her think about that morning. Chris could remember, when just the sound of Frank's name gave her goose bumps. Now, it only invoked a sense of disgust.

'He must have came home to get his clubs,' she deducted. The thought of Frank in another woman's arms briefly crept into her mind. After all, he was spending plenty of time away from home. Chris tried to let go of such thoughts as she drunk her milk.

While she sipped from her glass, she watched a flock of sparrows gather at the bird feeder outside. There was one sparrow in particular that caught her attention. There was nothing unusual about the bird. There was just something about it that drew her to it. Chris watched in amazement, as the bird seemed to sense her watching. It was uncanny on how it appeared to gaze back at her.

Just as Chris said, "It acts like it knows I'm watching him," the bird flew over to the windowsill.

"If I wasn't mistaken, I would think you knew I was watching you," she uttered, to the sparrow perched outside on the ledge.

Chris watched the bird for a moment, before finishing off her glass of milk and contemplating what to do next. Once again, there was no need to cook dinner, since Frank would not be home anytime soon. Also, by how clean the house was it was obvious the maid had stopped by. So, that ruled out cleaning up. Chris contemplated taking a jog, but once again she lacked the motivation. Besides, it was too late in the day and she didn't want to aggravate her back anymore than she needed to. It would have made it quite difficult for her to get a good night's rest. The pain was just beginning to subside and she wanted to keep it that way. Still, Chris felt if she did not do something, she would go crazy simply staying at home alone.

Chris called Beverly, but she was not home. She left her a message, in regards to lunch the next day, before hanging up. She pondered going to see her mother, but she quickly remembered she had not returned home from her cruise in the Mediterranean. Chris did not expect her home until the following morning. So, her efforts to conjure up company or something to occupy her time had resulted in nothing and basically put her right back where she had started...alone. There was only one thing Chris knew she could do that did not require the company of another. Plus, on top of that it was something she enjoyed doing—shopping.

*   *   *   *

When Chris had finished her little jaunt to Lenox Mall and Phipps Plaza, it was late and it was safe to say she had spent a small fortune. It did not matter how much she had spent because money was never an issue between her and Frank. Besides, Frank never really cared what she did anyway. As she pulled the car into the garage, she noticed Frank's Mercedes. For some unknown reason she was glad to see he was home. She did not know why nor could she explain why she felt that way especially after that morning. She just did. Maybe it was because if he spent another long evening out, Chris could not help but suspect he was seeing another woman. She knew deep down her sudden longing for him came from the need to feel loved and most importantly wanting to be apart of his life in some shape or form. In a way, it made her feel good that he had came home to her instead of staying out late with Russell.

Once inside the house, Chris put the shopping bags away and hurried upstairs to see her husband. The bedroom lights were out, which was not a good sign. Usually, such a sign meant that Frank was exhausted and did not want to be disturbed. Yet this evening, Chris did not care. She yearned to feel his touch upon her skin, to feel as if she indeed did fill some vital part in his life. The distaste that had once consumed her had dissipated and now all she felt was a burning arousal gathering in her loins. She no longer wanted to fuss and fight, instead she wanted to be loved. She wanted to feel needed. She wanted to feel him caress her in a way that made her feel that despite it all, they were meant to be. She wanted so desperately to hear Frank whisper in her ear, 'I love you.'

Chris quietly slipped off her clothes and slid into bed next to him, trying her best not to arouse him from his slumber. She indeed wanted to wake him, but she wanted to wake him her way. She gently began to kiss him upon the nape of his neck, working her supple lips down his back. It was a technique she knew would provoke from him the desired response. It did not take long for Frank to reply to her gentle kisses with a soft moan. When it became too much for him to bear, he turned towards her and embraced her in a deep, passionate, kiss. For a fleeting moment, Chris believed Frank had not evolved into the self-centered boor she had lived with the past few years. For a brief moment, she sensed Frank needed her just as much as she needed him. However, all that faded in an instant. Whatever initial feelings of closeness and tenderness Chris may have felt were quickly erased when he climbed on top of her and forced his way inside of her, only to began pumping furiously like a piston in a supped up hot rod. His maniacal pumping and gyrating was intended for no one's pleasure but his own. He had failed to give Chris' body ample time to naturally lubricate itself. Thus, each, cold, emotionless thrust was raw and painful.

There was no intimacy. No words of love were spoken in the heat of passion. Instead, there were only the guttural grunts and groans from a man, who rode her to his satisfaction. It did not matter that Chris had asked him to take his time. Neither did it matter to him when Chris pleaded for him to stop. Frank did not hear her. Frank did not want to hear her. It did not matter to Frank if he was hurting her. Chris' pain was secondary to him in reaching his own gratification. And when that goal was obtained, he rolled off of her similar to if he had gone to the bathroom, instead of just having had sex with his wife. He did not utter one word, because he did not care. He simply rolled over and went back to sleep.

Chris laid there in shock.

The smell of sex that filled the room repulsed her. The entire affair had traumatized her so much that she had became numb. She simply lay there frozen. He had not made love to her. There was no emotion of love exchanged between them. He had simply fucked her like she was nothing more than a body there for his pleasure, plain and simple. He treated her no different than a prostitute he may have picked up off the street.

The first thought that crossed Chris' mind once Frank had gotten off of her, was to leave. Simply, pack her stuff and run as fast and as far away as she could. She did not care where she went just along as she got away. Then the thought of going downstairs into the kitchen and finding the biggest butcher knife she could find and burying it into his back crossed her mind. That thought scared her. She had never thought about physically harming anyone in such a manner, especially Frank.

When Chris gotten up enough strength to get out of bed, she made her way to the bathroom. She wanted to scrub his smell off of her body. Once in the bathroom, Chris ran herself bath water. In her mind a bath was the only way she could rid herself of Frank's touch and smell after he had defiled her in such fashion. The feel of the steamy hot water surround her as she sank into the tub until water crept up just below her chin. As she sat in the hot water a sea of emotions washed over her. She was consumed by anger, but also grief. She could not believe she had truly contemplated doing Frank harm. Yet as she lay there another thought crept into her mind.

Chris looked at her wrist and envisioned them slit with blood spewing out onto the slick ceramic tile floor. She could imagine Frank walking in the bathroom in the morning and falling to the floor because he had slipped on her blood that had pooled and started to congeal on the floor from the night before. She could not help but see him falling and cracking his skull as some sick form of poetic justice for the way he had treated her.

However, she viewed slitting her wrist to be too painful a procedure to perform on her own. She doubted if she had the nerve to inflict such mortal pain on herself. If she planned to go, she wanted to go peacefully. Chris wondered if Frank would even notice if she simply stayed in the bathtub and drifted off to sleep.

CHAPTER 6

▼

The next morning Chris awoke in bed. She had purposely set her alarm clock to go off earlier than Frank's, so she could be up and out of the house long before he even woke up. After what took place the night before, Chris did not want to speak to him, let alone look at him. So as soon as Chris got out of bed, she put on her jogging suit and headed out the door. Regardless, of whether it tormented her back or not, she was going to get as far away from that house as possible and jogging provided her with an excuse.

At first Chris tried running, but the pain was too much to bear. So, she settled for a brisk walk. As she walked through the neighborhood, Chris could not believe she had contemplated suicide the night before. The thought of suicide had not crossed her mind, since Frank admitted to having an affair. That evening she needed her stomach pumped because she had tried to overdose on sleeping pills. After a brief stay in a psychiatric ward and time spent with a psychiatrist, Chris felt she had gotten beyond blaming herself for their marital problems. Yet, she had still considered drowning in her own bathtub. All this time, she had thought she had grown beyond self-pity only to discover that she had made no progress at all. She could not help but feel ashamed.

'It's his fault,' she said, to herself. 'That jackass is probably in a tizzy because his precious breakfast is not waiting for him,' she thought, enraged.

As she made her way back home, Chris could picture Frank coming downstairs to find no breakfast or morning paper on the table waiting for him. She was quite sure he would fly off the handle just before storming out the door in a rush to get to work.

When Chris returned home, she found the morning paper still outside in the mailbox. Inside the house, not one single dirty dish cluttered the kitchen sink. The only visible sign, Chris had seen of Frank having ever been there was a sole dirty glass that sat on the kitchen counter. She went upstairs and peeled herself out of her sweaty clothes, so she could take a shower. As she bathed, she could not help but think of him raping her the night before. Just the thought of it made her sick.

After taking a shower, Chris started getting dressed for her nine thirty appointment with her chiropractor, Dr. Loewn, followed by brunch with Beverly at ten o' clock. Chris wondered why she even continued to see Dr. Loewn, when he did nothing when it came to remedying her back. She had at first sought the help of a medical doctor when her back began to flare up, fearing she possibly had a slipped or herniated a disk. However, the doctor found nothing. In fact, the doctor had told her, her back was in excellent shape. Despite, his proclamation of good health, the pain persisted. After listening to advice from Beverly, Chris began seeing a chiropractor. Eventually, her quest to find one who worked led her to Dr. Loewn.

Although Dr. Loewn was one of the best chiropractors in Atlanta and Chris paid him handsomely for his time, Chris had yet to see any results. Her back felt the same way it did the first day she stepped into his office. Chris figured she went to see him, more out of habit than anything else. Just like her luncheon dates with Beverly, Dr. Loewn's weekly visits gave her life some type of structure.

The doctor's office was located in Midtown, so, Chris left the house early hoping to avoid traffic into downtown along Peachtree Avenue. Fortunately for her traffic was light. She was able to get to Dr. Loewn's office, fifteen minutes before her scheduled appointment. However, despite her early arrival, Chris was still forced to wait half an hour before being seen. When he did see her, the doctor rushed her in and out so quickly; Chris did not have enough time to ask him if he noticed any progress in her condition.

So, after spending half an hour in the waiting room and ten minutes in Dr. Loewn's office not to mention one hundred and ninety-five dollars, Chris left his office feeling no better than when she arrived. Unfortunately, it was how she felt every time she left his office. It also did not help matters none that she was also late for brunch with Beverly, due to the doctor's inability to adhere to his schedule. Fortunately for Chris the restaurant was in Midtown, so she did not have to drive far.

When Chris arrived, Beverly had already ordered. "Sorry…My chiropractor decided to take his own sweet time this morning," she apologized, taking her seat.

"I thought you were going to stand me up, like the jerk I had a date with last night," snipped Beverly. "I hope you don't mind, but I took the liberty of ordering without you."

"No problem," said Chris, motioning the waiter over to the table. "So, tell me about this guy who dumped you last night?" asked Chris. She knew the only reason Beverly brought it up was so she could complain.

"Ah, he was a real jerk. And for your information, he did not dump me; he stood me up. There is a difference you know…He was some sport's agent, I met while showing homes in Alpharetta. It kind of perturbs me, because he was the one who asked me out. I should of known it was too good to be true. He left me sitting at the bar all night long waiting on him."

"Sorry to hear that," Chris said, handing her menu to the waiter upon ordering.

"Oh, don't be. The whole night was not a total loss. The bartender was a blast, not to mention extremely cute."

Chris knew what that meant. "So, when are the two of you getting together?" she said rather uninspired.

"Oh, try to contain your enthusiasm," said Beverly mocking her.

"Sorry," Chris apologized. She would have gotten more excited about the guys Beverly met, if she was not always meeting a new one every week.

"His name is Jeff, and we're getting together tomorrow night," replied Beverly, flatly.

"I tell you Beverly," Chris intoned, in disbelief.

"Enough talk about me already. What's been going on in your life? Let me guess…oh, nothing." Chris couldn't help but think of how Beverly could be such a bitch at times.

"Oh, shut up," said Chris, while the waiter placed her salad in front of her.

"I tell you Chris, you need to get out of the house more often. Instead of sitting at home waiting on Frank's every beckon call."

"Not today Beverly," warned Chris. "Besides, I do not wait on Frank's every beckon call."

"Like hell you don't. You know, I'm just looking out for you. You need to leave that bum, I'm telling you. He doesn't give a damn about you."

"And do what? Jump in the sack with every guy I meet," said Chris.

"Oh, that was a low blow Chris," seethed Beverly.

"Sorry."

"Besides, I never said my life was perfect but it is at least mine."

"Beverly please, I don't really care to get into this today. I really am not in the mood." After last night the last thing Chris wanted to do was spend her afternoon talking about Frank.

"Fine. It's your life, not mine. Enough with that subject…What did your chiropractor have to say about your back?"

"What do you mean what did he say? He did not have time to say much of anything. He just laid me down on the table and cracked my back just before asking me for one hundred and ninety-five dollars and sending me out the door."

"And how's your back?" inquired Beverly.

"Terrible. I couldn't even jog this morning. I had to settle for a brisk walk."

"I keep telling you, you need to see Dr. Deshpande," stated Beverly.

"Oh God Beverly, I'm sorry I even entertained the subject. Are you pitching for this guy or something? Every time we get together you're touting how great this guy is," insisted Chris.

"I'm telling you, the man works miracles," professed Beverly.

"If I tell you I'll go see him, will you stop pestering me about this man?"

"Only if you go see him."

"Here, write Mister Magic Fingers' number down, so you can get off my back," said Chris, handing her a napkin.

"I'm telling you Chris, he's the best," said Beverly, searching for his number on her palm pilot. "He gave me a mud bath yesterday, that absolutely invigorated me," she stated, while scribbling his name and number on the napkin.

"Oh Lord, Beverly. The next thing you're going to tell me is that this guy has a long tongue and can move it a hundred miles per hour."

"Hmm," said Beverly, grinning. "I don't know about that, but it might be worth looking into."

"Dear God, give me the number," exclaimed Chris, snatching the napkin away from her. "Thank you. Now that I got the number, and I've promised to call him, can we please eat?"

"Sure thing," proclaimed Beverly. She was obviously pleased that she had finally gotten Chris to cave in to her persistent nagging.

From that point on, Chris spent the rest of afternoon listening to Beverly complain about men and how picky homebuyers were driving her crazy. If she was not griping about men and finicky homebuyers, then she was worried about finding the right shade of eye shadow to compliment her tan. Chris loved Beverly, and there was not anything she would not do for her. Nonetheless, there were times she could not help but realize how shallow she could be.

Following brunch, Chris returned home to unwind. It was a typical hot and humid August day. Out of all the seasons of the year summer was the worst in Atlanta. The only salvation from the heat was a well air-conditioned home. This particular afternoon, the weatherman had warned of a thunderstorm or two but from what Chris could see there was not a cloud in the sky. It struck her as a good day to sunbath by the pool. So, when she got home she slipped into her bathing suit, grabbed her radio, and headed out to the pool. She plopped herself onto one of the deck chairs next to the pool and soaked up the rays. The sounds of Gloria Estefan, emanating from the radio made it easy for her to relax as the sun transformed her uneven tan into a solid golden bronze. All thoughts of Frank and her nagging back faded into oblivion. In one of those rare occasions, Chris was at peace. She simply let her mind drift and let nothing interrupt the serenity. For her such calm was a rare thing. So, when Chris was able to achieve it, she let nothing get in her way of enjoying it. The only thing Chris allowed to enter her inner sanctum was the pounding of the bongos, and Gloria Estefan demanding everybody do the Conga.

*   *   *   *

The clap of thunder in the distance and the feel of rain upon her face woke Chris from her nap. It was good that it did, she had barely made it inside before the downpour. It took no time for the few droplets of rain that had danced upon her face to turn into translucent sheets of water. Such was the way of a southern storm.

Chris headed to the bathroom for she feared; she might have burnt herself by laying on one side for too long. She was not pleased to see as she glanced in the mirror that she indeed did. The golden bronze tan she had envisioned was more like a beet red.

"Great. Just great," she whined. "I look like a lobster." Chris sighed in disgust as she opened the medicine cabinet and pulled out the sunburn ointment.

"Wonderful," she murmured as she looked at herself in the mirror.

Chris opened the jar of ointment and applied it sparingly to her burns. When she was done, Chris thought about going to the Jackson family foundation headquarters to check on things. She still had plenty of time to kill before Frank got home. She had not been to the office in a week and although there was someone there to run the foundation's day-to-day operations, Chris liked to check in every once and awhile and see how things were going. Since her mother retired from running the foundation, Chris saw it as her responsibility to make sure her family's affairs were being handled properly. She glanced over at the clock; shocked to see she had slept for over an hour.

"No wonder I'm beet red," she said, aloud.

When Chris was done putting ointment to her burns, she meandered up the stairs to her bedroom in search of clothes to wear that were definitely loose fitting. As she combed through her closet for just the right dress, she noticed the napkin Beverly had given her during brunch with her chiropractor's phone number written on it sitting on the nightstand. Chris glanced at it for second, contemplating on whether she should make the call or not. She knew if she did not call Beverly's quack while it was fresh on her mind, she might never call him at all. So, she strolled over to the nightstand and picked up the napkin, noticing his name and phone number scrawled on the napkin in eyeliner pencil. Chris really did not have any desire to see the man. Although, Dr. Loewn lacked a decent bedside manner, she did at least feel comfortable with him. What Beverly had told her about Dr. Deshpande made her leery. Regardless of her skepticism, Chris had promised Beverly she would at least call the guy and schedule an appointment. Chris knew if she did not at least do that, Beverly would continuously nag her about it until she did. So, Chris figured it was best to go ahead and get it out of the way sooner rather than later.

She picked up the phone and dialed the number. The phone rung for sometime before someone picked up, which disappointed Chris for she was on the verge of hanging up by that time. She could have easily told Beverly that she had called, but did not get an answer. That would have been the end of it.

"Doctor Deshpande's office. How may I 'elp you?" someone said into the receiver. The person had a thick accent that made it almost impossible for Chris to comprehend what they were saying. The accent was so thick; Chris could not help but wonder if someone was joking around.

'Great, they don't speak a lick of English,' Chris thought. "I would like to make an appointment to see Dr. Deshpande."

"Iz tis your fist visit see Doctor Deshpande?"

"Excuse me?" asked Chris.

"Iz tis goin' to be your fist time to see Doctor Deshpande?" came the response, this time a little bit louder. Whoever it was believed Chris was deaf, instead of realizing she was having a difficult time understanding their English.

"Yes, it will be my first time."

"Kay. When would you come in?"

"What? I'm sorry, but I'm having a hard time understanding you," Chris confessed.

"I say when would you make an appointment?" Chris was beginning to decipher that the individual she was speaking with was a woman. "How is two o'clock Friday?"

"Hold on please." Chris held the phone away from her ear, just in case the doctor's receptionist felt the urge to yell again. Chris grabbed her palm pilot and checked Friday. She was booked; she had a lunch date with Beverly.

"Can't make it," said Chris, automatically checking the following Monday. "What about Monday?"

"Um…" there was a pause, "How bout Monday at nine?"

"Perfect."

"Kay, we'll see you Monday."

As Chris hung up the phone, she thought about suggesting to the doctor when she met him that he hired someone who spoke proper English. Regardless of his receptionist's poor English, it was done. Chris no longer had to worry about Beverly nagging her about her chiropractor Dr. Deshpande. She had set up an appointment to see him and once she did, she would return to Dr. Loewn without having to hear a peep out of Beverly ever again.

As Chris placed the receiver back in its cradle, her thoughts went suddenly to her mother. Chris was quite certain she had arrived home from her cruise in the Mediterranean. She debated on whether to call her, to hear how her vacation went or simply drop by to hear it first hand. Chris realized dropping by might be inappropriate, especially since she had gotten into town early that morning. She was certain her mother had yet to recuperate from the change in time zones. Thus, making it highly unlikely that she would be in the mood to entertain guest. In such a case, Chris decided it was best to simply give her a call so she at least knew she made it home all right.

"Hello?" said her mother, answering the phone on the first ring.

"Hi Mom it's me."

"Chrysanthemum, how are you doing?" sighed her mother, sounding exhausted.

"Fine…How was the Mediterranean?"

"It was great, beautiful people and beautiful country," replied her mother. Just the mentioning of the word, Mediterranean, seemed to perk her up a bit.

"I was planning on going up to the Financial Center and check on things at the foundation. I thought, maybe since I will be in the neighborhood that I stop by and see how you are doing. However, I'm not certain that is a good idea judging by how tired you sound."

"Oh, that is nothing…I'll get over it. It just takes an old body like mine, a little longer to bounce back from jet lag. You know, you're always welcomed here. This is your home too."

"Are you sure?" asked Chris, unsure if she should disturb her.

"Chris please, I'll be expecting you," her mother insisted.

"Okay," replied Chris. "I'll call you when I am leaving the Financial Center."

"I'll see you then," her mother replied.

"Bye, mom."

"Good-bye honey."

*   *   *   *

Chris' mother, Agatha Jackson-Moore, lived in an elegant estate not far from the Financial Center. Her parents had purchased their home when Buckhead was stodgy and a place of old money, long before it became a chic place to live by the nouveau rich. Although Chris had a home of her own, her home never made her feel the way her parents' house did in it. Whenever she walked through those doors she always felt as if she belonged, despite, the ever-lingering spirit of her father that permeated throughout the estate.

Following the passing of her father, it appeared that only one room in her parent's house sustained life—the kitchen. It had become the only place in the house where her mother entertained guest, and spent the majority of her time. The rest of the estate had sort of become frozen in time. It was almost like her mother had made the remainder of the house into a shrine in honor of her late father. From his favorite chair that still reeked of cigar smoke, to the water stain on the end table where he use to place his drinks. Her mother refused to erase any sign of her father's existence. In her mother's mind, it was all she had left of him to cling to. In some regards, it was how she coped with his death, a house full of constant reminders of him. On the surface Chris found it to be quite morbid, but deep down she understood her mother had loved her father dearly.

On several occasions Chris had suggested to her mother that she spiff the place up, maybe even move some of her father's belongings upstairs into the attic. Her mother would not hear of such a thing. For Chris to even mention it to her was profane. In her mother's mind, that cigar smoke infested chair and that water stained end table kept him alive. It allowed him to always be there with her. It did not matter to her that Chris' father had passed away five years ago. It would not have mattered if he had passed away ten years ago. Her mother was going to forever cling to his memory.

Of course, Chris did not think her mother's reluctance to give up the past healthy. Yet, whenever she suggested to her mother possibly selling the place and moving into something a little more economical, her mother totally disregarded her. Of course, the ghost of her father played a hand in that but another reason her mother refused to move was because she was bred into Atlanta's high society. For her to relinquish her home for a smaller one, gave the impression to those in her social circles that she had fallen upon hard times and that was the last thing her mother wanted.

Her canned remark, whenever Chris broached such an idea was always, "Your father would roll over in his grave if he ever knew I had even entertained the idea of moving out of this house." So, after a while Chris stopped even asking.

After checking on things at the foundation, Chris drove to her mother's house to find a hot cup of coffee waiting and a sympathetic ear ready to listen as soon as she arrived. Chris' mother was an avid coffee drinker. She roasted and grounded her own coffee beans. Her mother made a point to collect coffee beans from all over the world. It did not matter the vast majority of the beans she collected where the same Colombian coffee beans she had at home. Her vast assortment of coffee beans from different locales around the globe was a source of pride for her. And as Chris had suspected, her mother had bought coffee beans while in Europe and could not wait for her daughter to taste test them.

"I bought these beans while I was in Sicily. I thought you would like to try them out, since you have an affinity for coffee like I do. I think you'll like it," her mother said, taking a seat next to Chris at the kitchen table. Chris loved coffee just as much as her mother. It was an affliction borne out of her mother's addiction to the beverage.

"Sure why not?" Chris told her. "So, tell me about the Mediterranean?" asked Chris, trying to ignore the constant omnipresence of her father.

"Great, I had a wonderful time. I met the cutest little Italian man. He was simply adorable." Chris could not help but snicker upon hearing her mother speak fondly of a man other than her father. "I see you on the other hand, stayed in the sun a bit too long while I was gone."

"Yeah, I fell asleep while sunbathing this afternoon," admitted Chris.

"You better put some ointment on those burns," forewarned her mother.

"I did."

"Good…So, besides getting burnt, how is everything going at home?" Her mother was always curious to know how things were going between Chris and Frank.

"Fine, I guess."

Chris' mother was no different than any other concerned mother. She could sense by Chris' response to her question that all was not well between her daughter and her husband. "What is the matter now?" she quipped. Chris simply shrugged her shoulders, implying she did not want to talk about it.

"Let me take a wild guess…It has something to do with Frank?" exclaimed her mother. Not really wanting to discuss it but feeling she had no other choice, Chris reluctantly nodded her head in affirmation.

"What is it? Has he taken up with a mistress again?" questioned her mother, sounding concerned.

"No…not from what I can tell," Chris assured her.

"Then what is it sweetheart?"

"It's not the same anymore Mom. I feel like we're just going through the motions. There no longer is any love between us. We wake up in the morning and go to sleep at night like two total strangers sharing the same house instead of as husband and wife…I just don't know anymore?"

Her mother took a sip of coffee and gently patted her daughter on the knee before telling her, "Chris, I warned you that marriage wasn't going to be a romp in the park. It takes work. You're going to have your ups and your downs. You just have to ride them out, sweetheart. Remember, you do have some of that Jackson blood coursing through your veins…

"If your great-great grandfather could hear you now, he would be smitten with shame. If he could withstand the siege of the Union Army and the destruction of his very own town during the Civil War, not to mention your father and I can survive the 60's. I think you can definitely survive a few marital spats." Her mother, Agatha, always gave Chris the great Jackson family speech, whenever she dispensed advice. It was a pre-requisite with her.

"Mom, I have heard this a million and one times. Although I'm very proud to be a Jackson, this is different. This is my life…This isn't my great-great grandfather's life or you and Dad's life. It's mine."

A very serious look appeared on her mother's face, just before she told Chris, "Let me tell you something Chrysanthemum." She always called Chris by her full name when she was angry or intended to drive home a point. "I never told anybody this before. For years I kept this secret to myself because it is what an upstanding lady should do, but now I see it would do you some good if I let the cat out of the bag. Your father at one time had gotten himself a mistress too. It was during a rough patch in our marriage. He didn't lead me to believe there was anything wrong. In fact, I thought everything was wonderful. Yet, one day by accident, I found out he was keeping company with another woman.

"As you can guess, I was devastated. This woman had come into my life and turned it upside down. I don't need to tell you those were some rocky times for your father and I, but we managed to work it out. It's what marriage is all about, Chrysanthemum. It's what it means, when you say for better or for worse.

"Besides, you have to understand your father was a pillar of the community, similar to Frank. Your father played golf with the governor every Wednesday, and ate dinner or lunch with Richard Nixon, whenever he came to town for Christ's sake. For me to leave him would have shattered his public image. Besides, we had you to think about. If not for anything else, we needed to remain a family at least for your sake.

"Now, I know you can't bear children, and I know how much that hurts you. But even if you don't have the attachment of a child to keep the two of you together, you must realize there are other factors you must consider. Frank is not your father but he is a decent man who is going places. He is definitely a man you need to hold on to...Believe me when I say, things will work themselves out." Chris often wondered why she even bothered confiding in her mother. All she ever did, whenever she gave advice was make apparent the generation gap standing between them.

"Now Chris, I know you and I don't always see eye to eye on everything. I also know times have changed since me and your father was married, but I think you need to listen to me on this one. Give it time...Time heals all things. You're my only child and I love you, but what I'm telling you is the truth"

"Thanks Mom," sighed Chris.

"Anything for you snook'ums."

Although, she had visited with her mother for another hour following her mother's lecture on how to handle her predicament with Frank, Chris could not help but feel disheartened.

Chris left her mother's house in haste, she figured Frank would be upset when he got home and found out dinner was not ready. Yet, once again, he was not home. There were no messages on the voicemail nor was there any note on the refrigerator door. There was nothing. To not leave a message or a note was not like Frank. He usually let her know if he was not going to be home in time for dinner. Since there was nothing, Chris instinctively feared the worse.

'He hasn't came home for dinner the last two nights!' she reminded herself. Once again, her mind began to run wild with visions of Frank and another woman. Chris knew, there was only one way to ease her conscience and that was to simply pick up the phone and call him.

Not until Frank picked up the phone and greeted her with, "This is Frank Adams," did Chris' suspicions begin to die.

"Frank?" she said, surprised to find him still at work.

"Yeah, who else would be answering my phone?" he replied, sarcastically.

"I hadn't heard from you, so, I was beginning to get worried something might have happened to you," Chris lied.

"I'm sorry Chris. I've just been swamped. I should have called to let you know I was going to be home late, but there was an afternoon meeting that turned into an evening meeting. When I got back to my desk, there was a stack of papers I needed to sign off on before tomorrow morning. I apologize."

"No problem. I understand." Chris tried to sound understanding.

"I swear to you, I'll be home in an hour. What's for dinner?" Frank inquired.

"I don't know what do you want?"

"Why don't we go out tonight, I pick the place?" he replied, seductively.

"You got it," stated Chris, smiling.

"Oh, Chris?"

"Yeah."

"I love you."

"I love you too."

"See you in an hour," sighed Frank, sounding exhausted.

"Bye."

"Bye."

Frank's sudden shift in attitude caught Chris off guard. She wondered if his sudden change in heart was from some sense of guilt he may have felt from the way he treated her the night before. Regardless if that was the case, Chris decided she was not going to complain nor question the shift in his personality. She had learned long ago to take advantage of the few times Frank decided to act civilized.

As Chris searched her closet for something to wear, she could not help but wonder if her mother was right when she told her, "everything will work it self out."

CHAPTER 7

▼

For Chris that weekend was marital bliss. She felt as if she was married to a totally different man. She figured Frank's good behavior was probably due to guilt for the way he acted the other night. That weekend there were no dinners alone. In fact, Frank was home every night. He was also very receptive to Chris' needs. The two of them even spent part of the weekend at their cabin on Lake Lanier, something they had not done together as a couple in some time. Before that weekend going to the cabin had mainly become a solitary activity for Chris, whenever, she sought to escape the rigors of marriage. Chris did not know what to make of this sudden change in Frank, but instead of questioning it she decided to enjoy it. And judging by how Monday morning began that was a wise decision.

Chris felt the change coming on Sunday evening. She could sense the tension easing back into their lives, when they arrived home from the cabin. So, the return of the old callous Frank on Monday morning did not surprise her at all. Instead of getting upset, she decided to ignore Frank and cling to her memories of the weekend. It was memories of time spent at the lake that drowned out his Monday morning complaining about breakfast. As Frank left out the house that Monday morning for work, Chris nonchalantly prepared for her early morning jog before being reminded by the chirping of her palm pilot of her appointment with Beverly's chiropractor, Dr. Deshpande. It was an appointment she would have much rather have skipped. However, she knew if she did not go, she would never hear the end of it from Beverly.

It took Chris the better part of an hour to find Dr. Deshpande's office. It was tucked away in a Sandy Springs strip mall. Her inability to find the place had made her twenty minutes late. The first thing Chris noticed about Dr. Deshpnade's office when she walked in was that it was completely empty. The place was deserted. The only person there was his receptionist. This struck Chris as odd. She had grown accustomed to seeing a waiting room full of people at Dr. Loewn's practice.

The doctor's receptionist appeared to be of East Indian descent. Judging by her thick accent when she said, "May I 'elp you?" Chris quickly deduced she was the individual she had spoken to on the phone.

"Yes, I had a nine o'clock appointment with Dr. Deshpande," stated Chris.

"You are late," replied the receptionist, scolding her.

"Yes, I am," replied Chris. "I had a hard time finding the place." Chris wanted to tell her that Dr. Deshpande needed to do a better job in making his practice more accessible to his patients, but she bit her tongue.

"Kay, sit and I'll tell Dr. Deshpande you're waitin'." Chris glanced around the room then back at the receptionist to indicate to her that no one else was in the room.

Despite her being the doctor's only patient, the receptionist stared back at her and insisted she, "Sit." Chris replied with a sigh of disgust.

Chris did not want to prolong her stay any longer than she had too. She wanted to get in and get out as quick as possible. She contemplated leaving once Dr. Deshpande's receptionist left the room to retrieve the doctor. Chris figured at least, she would not be lying to Beverly when she told her she went to see him. Although, the thought of leaving crossed her mind, Chris figured since she had spent almost an hour trying to find the doctor's office, she might as well stay and hear what he had to say.

Chris took a seat in the waiting room as instructed. The first thing Chris noticed, when she sat down was the immaculate East Indian artwork that adorned the room.

"Dr. Deshpande will be with you soon," stated his receptionist, interrupting Chris' thoughts.

The doctor's receptionist returned five minutes later, to instruct Chris to follow her into an adjoining room. "Please, take seat. Doctor Deshpande, will be wit you soon."

"Thank you," said Chris. Chris took a seat in one of two chairs in the room.

She immediately noticed the absence of a tub for mud baths and a chiropractor's table. However, she did notice mats tucked away in a corner. 'How can he be a chiropractor without a chiropractor's table?' she thought. Just then an elderly gentleman entered the room. He appeared gaunt and frail, almost fragile. He moved like it pained him to walk. Chris could not help, but wonder if he was ill based on his appearance.

"Good morning, Mrs. Adams," he exclaimed, walking into the room. The doctor took a seat across from her. "My name is Samir Deshpande. I apologize for the wait, I was convening in my morning prayer." Unlike his receptionist, Dr. Deshpande spoke perfect English. "Did you have any trouble finding my office?" he asked.

"In fact I did," replied Chris.

"I have been trying to find a better location for my practice for some time, but with not much luck," he professed. "I see you've stayed out in the sun a bit too long," he said, examining Chris' sun baked skin.

"Yeah, I fell asleep while sun bathing" admitted Chris, somewhat embarrassed.

"If you don't mind me asking, but how did you come to hear of my practice?" questioned the doctor.

"Beverly Ostrum referred your practice to me."

"Ah yes, Ms. Ostrum, such a delightful woman. However, she suffers from so much inner pain, that she believes she can only dispel through her vagina." From the sounds of that comment, Chris was certain she was in for a very interesting visit with the good doctor.

"Before we begin," Dr. Deshpande continued, "Let me first tell you a little bit about what I do here...I am what you would call a healer, Mrs. Adams. I am a practicing Hindu of the Brahmin caste. In Hindu tradition, individuals of the Brahmin caste are priest or doctors...What I like to call spiritual healers. So as a practicing Hindu in that caste, I believe all pain originates or emanates from one's spirit or what you may call your soul. The deeds partaken in one's past lives may be the source of the pain or the remedy by which to cure the patient. As a healer, it is my job to determine which one it is, and fix the problem.

"The techniques I use may seem unconventional, or unorthodox in comparison to what you may be accustomed to with other chiropractors or medical practitioners. However, I assure you I know what I am doing. Now in my therapy, I use a form of yoga called Laya Yoga to help me seek out the source of the pain as well as heal it. I treat no two patients the same, because no two people are alike. I am not here to make money, but mend souls. It is my calling in life. So, without further ado, unless you have any questions let's begin?"

"If you say so," answered Chris. She was curious to find out how a practicing Hindu intended to cure her of her chronic back pain.

Dr. Deshpande began, by going around the room lighting fragranced candles. As he milled about from one candle to the next he asked her, "So, what seems to be your problem?"

"I've been experiencing severe back pain for the last nine months," she replied, catching a whiff of the vanilla fragranced candles lilting through the room.

"Well, let me see what I can do about that," said Dr. Deshpande, once again taking his seat.

"Do you need me to lay down or something?" asked Chris. She was unsure how it would work without a chiropractor's table.

"No, no…No need for that. If you could do me one favor and just merely close your eyes and try to relax. Now, I may touch you in places you may find uncomfortable and odd, but I assure you…it is necessary."

With that said Chris gave him a wayward glance, which caused the doctor to chuckle. "I assure you there is no need to worry. There is no need for me to touch you in those places." Chris glared at him once more, to make it clear that she was not going to tolerate any funny stuff, before reluctantly closing her eyes.

Chris was uncertain of what to expect from this man who claimed to be a natural healer. She could not be positively sure he was nothing more than a pervert especially after hearing the stories Beverly had told her about him. Although the doctor had stated he might touch her in some unusual places, Chris did not feel comfortable when he began to slowly massage her temples before moving slightly above the crest of her eyebrows to her forehead.

Dr. Deshpande could sense Chris becoming uneasy. "Please, keep your eyes closed and just relax," he instructed.

The one thing about Dr. Deshpande's request that troubled Chris the most was the fact that at the time he still had his eyes closed. Unless he peeked, Chris was baffled as to how he could have known she had opened her eyes. Despite the mystery, Chris did as she was told.

After rubbing the spot in the middle of her forehead for sometime, the doctor worked his way around to her neck where he began to gently massage. Although his hands appeared to be nothing more than bones with flesh stretched over them, the feel of Dr. Deshpande's hands upon her neck felt relaxing. His touch upon her skin was sensual. As he gently worked out the kinks in her neck, Chris drifted off into a semi-conscious, almost meditative, state filled with beautiful colors of sky blue punctuated by bright colors of red and orange. Chris could not help but agree with Beverly when she said the doctor had a gentle touch.

After massaging her neck, the doctor moved down Chris' spine in a slow rhythmic motion until he reached her tailbone. The pressure of his thumbs against the tip of her spine just at the point her butt started alarmed her. She could not help but come out of her trance. "Please, keep your eyes closed," ordered Dr. Deshpande. "Just close your eyes and think about easing the pain," he instructed.

Chris, somewhat apprehensive, did as she was told. By some miracle, the pain was indeed being lifted with each caress. It felt so good to be relived of the pain for the first time in such a long time. She became so entranced by the feeling of no pain and the relaxing massage that she did not realize Dr. Deshpande had finished.

"You can open your eyes now, Mrs. Adams," said Dr. Deshpande, with a smile. He was once again sitting in the seat in front of her.

"How do you feel?" he asked.

Chris turned her head, from side to side before exclaiming, "I feel great! I have not felt this way in a long time. I don't know what you did, but I haven't felt this good for some time! What did you do?"

"I helped you reach a realm of higher consciousness, a place were you can reach your inner self and rid yourself of the pain troubling you. This temporarily healed the wounds of your spirit by releasing the pain through the portal between your eyebrows called your third eye and your tailbone, these are two of the five centers of energy in Laya Yoga."

"What?" Chris asked, confused.

"See, your body has five energy centers that act sort of like portals to your soul from which a higher consciousness can be obtained. Right here," he said, touching a spot just above her eyebrows in the middle of her forehead. "The area of your spine at the base of your neck, your sacrum in the middle of your back behind your heart, the base of your spine behind your navel and at the very tip of your spine, or what we like to call the tailbone. As I said, all I did was open these portals in order for you to reach a higher level of consciousness, so, you could easily dismiss your pain. Whether you know it or not, every human being has the gift to heal themselves, however, most of us do not know it nor how to use it."

"I guess so," said a bewildered Chris. "All I know is I feel great."

"Good," Dr. Deshpande said, getting up to blow out the candles. "That means I have done my job. So, I take it I will be seeing you again?"

"If I can continue to get results like this, you bet your life you will see me again," exclaimed Chris.

"Good, your problem requires me to see you at least twice a week. How about, Thursday morning at the same time?" asked Dr. Deshpande.

"Sounds good to me," said Chris, gathering her belongings.

"Good, make an appointment with my receptionist, Sasha, on your way out. Don't worry about my fee I can bill you," he assured her.

Chris eagerly made an appointment with Sasha for the following Thursday as he had instructed. However, she did not do so without first checking to see how much he was charging her for her weekly visits. Chris was pleasantly surprised to see, he charged far less than Dr. Loewn. Two visits with Dr. Deshpande was far less than one visit with Dr. Loewn. So, not only did she feel great, she was also saving herself a great deal of money.

CHAPTER 8

▼

"My, you're still peeling," quipped Beverly. It had been over a week since Chris' ill-fated attempt at sunbathing and she still had some remnants left.

"I know," snapped Chris. She had grown tired of having to continuously answer to people's persistent questions about her sunburn.

"So, what do you think of him?" quizzed Beverly.

"Who?"

"Dr. Deshpande silly!" By this time, Chris had been seeing Dr. Deshpande for over a week. She had been anticipating, Beverly to sooner or later breakdown and ask her about him, but she had kept quiet up to that point. It now appeared Beverly was going to burst if Chris did not share with her, her opinion of him.

"I think he's great," exclaimed Chris. "A little on the eccentric side, but other than that he's great. The best chiropractor I have ever had, and you know I've had many. I haven't had an ache or pain in my back going on a week now. I've been able to go jogging and run errands without no problems."

"What did I tell you? The man is a god." Chris could understand now, why Beverly had been singing the man's praise for so long.

"I hate telling you this, but you were right," admitted Chris. It hurt for her to admit to Beverly, she was right.

"Did Dr. Deshpande say anything about me to you, when he asked who referred you?"

"Nothing," said Chris, smirking. "Enough talk about me," Chris stated, "Tell me about this new guy you're seeing."

Chris listened as Beverly ranted and raved about her new beau, who was ten years younger than her. Of course, Beverly made sure not to leave out any sordid

details about their sex life, details Chris could have done with out. Beverly probably would have sat there the entire afternoon talking about herself, if she did not
have to go home and get prepared for a night out on the town with her newest
boy toy.

After parting company with Beverly, Chris went home to an empty house.
This time around, however, her home was empty by choice, instead of by chance.
Frank had left that morning for New York on business, so, Chris was once again
home alone. Still, no matter if it were by accident or choice, Chris never truly felt
at home when she was there by herself. In such instances, she could never stop
imaging a house filled with the sound of a child's voice to give it character. It was
a harsh reality to face, but Chris knew whenever she came home, the only sound
she would hear would be silence.

Frank was gone and she had already fulfilled her daily lunch appointment with
Beverly. The only other pressing task for Chris was to check her voicemail and
even that was a bore, only Frank and her mother had called. Frank simply called
to assure her he had arrived in New York safely. Her mother on the other hand
called requesting a favor. She wondered if Chris could attend the Founding
Father's Day celebration in her place, the following week. The Founding Father's
Day celebration was an annual celebration held in a small rural town in Georgia
called Jacksonville, a town named after Chris' late great-great-grandfather, Clayton Jackson.

Now, Chris' mom routinely attended the yearly festival. However, this year
her mother had committed herself to another engagement, which she was finding
difficult to break. Since her and Chris were the last two remaining descendants of
Clayton Jackson, she felt that if neither one of them attended the annual celebration it would be a travesty, thus, the reason for her asking Chris to attend.

The idea of attending the annual festival in her mother's place did not bother
Chris; in fact she looked forward to it. Especially, since it allowed her to get out
of the house for more than just an hour. The thought of getting out into the
countryside where she would be more overcome by the sound of the crickets than
the blaring sound of car horns thrilled her. The last time she had visited Jacksonville, she was a little girl and had very little recollection of the place. Her mother
had only taken her there once. Chris never understood, why she never returned.

Chris returned her mother's call. Her mother was not home, so, she left her a
message letting her know she would be delighted to go in her place. After hanging
up the phone, she went into the kitchen to get herself a glass of milk. It was
unusually warm in the house, so, she decided to quench her thirst. Chris made a
mental note to check the thermostat to make sure the air conditioner was work-

ing properly. As she poured herself a glass of milk, she glanced out the window at the bird feeder. There was a beautiful array of birds at the feeder that afternoon. She often found herself amazed by the shear beauty as well as the mere number of birds that gathered at the feeder daily.

As she stood there drinking her milk, Chris could not take her eyes off the assortment of colors the birds came in. There were different shades of yellow, brown, red and blue. It appeared that at least one bird represented every color of the rainbow. As they did every morning when Chris entered the kitchen, a sole bird flew over to the windowsill. It was a fiery red cardinal. Yet, this afternoon a blue jay, then a sparrow and a robin joined the cardinal at her ledge. Before she knew it, her window ledge was suddenly crowded with an assortment of different birds, which was unusual for birds rarely intermingled. If she did not know any better, she would have thought that someone had sprinkled birdseed along the ledge to attract them.

As each bird perched itself upon the windowsill it began to sing. At first no two bird's song was alike, each one was unique in its own way. But eventually each bird's song began to meld with its neighbor's until they were singing the same song. It was one of the strangest things Chris, had ever seen or heard of before in her life. What was even stranger was that the birds sung in unison, like a church choir. It was by far, the most beautiful song she had ever heard. It was pure rapture to her ears. Although it seemed crazy, Chris imagined that she could hear the lyrics to their serenade playing like a song on the radio. Of course, she knew this was impossible. For one reason, birds could not talk. Yet, the more they sung the louder their voices became. To Chris it felt like someone had turned up the volume inside her head for there were suddenly a thousand voices calling out, demanding an audience. The longer the birds sung the more amplified their voices became, until it reached the point were the chatter reverberated throughout her mind.

Unable to withstand the sudden deluge of chatter, Chris threw her hands up over her ears, without thinking about the glass of milk she had just let drop to the floor and shatter into a thousand pieces.

"Be quiet!" she screamed.

And just as abruptly as their singing had commenced, it had stopped. The birds no longer sung, and the voices inside her head ceased. Instead, there was an eerie silence. In fact, it was too quiet. Chris glanced over towards the window to see the birds still there. She was not sure, but they appeared to wait for her to do something, to say something. Uncertain if it was indeed quite, Chris slowly eased her hands away from her ears. There was no singing, in fact there was nothing at

all. It was deafeningly quiet. She glanced down at the glass of milk that had top-
pled to the floor and shattered. She had regrettably smashed one of her favorite
glasses.

"I must be going crazy," she said, somewhat disturbed. "Why don't you guys
just shoo!" Chris yelled, flaying her hands in the air.

As if heeding her command they flew off. Chris could not believe her eyes. She
was speechless. Chris knew there was no way they could have understood her; yet,
they acted like they did. They had become silent on command and even flew
away when she had demanded them to.

She was shocked. "Dear God, I must be losing my mind."

For a while Chris simply stood there in amazement. It took a while for her to
shake the feeling long enough to clean up the spilled milk and broken glass off
the floor. She could not believe there was a chance the birds understood her. She
found herself, repeatedly trying to convince herself that birds do not understand
English. For Chris to even fathom such a thing was next to impossible. Nonetheless, she could not deny what she had seen with her very own eyes. Although the
birds were gone, the affect they had made on her was lasting. Their singing along
with the mysterious voices had given her a splitting headache. So she walked to
the bathroom, in search of aspirin to ease the endless pounding in her head.

Now, up to that point, Chris had no reason to believe she was not at home
alone. Frank was in New York on business. However, she would swear to the
police officers later that she had stumbled upon a little boy hiding in her bathroom.

Chris had a hard time recounting the incident when the police officers questioned her. However, she did recollect, walking into the bathroom and noticing
no one there. Yet, she remembered opening the medicine cabinet and grabbing
the bottle of aspirin and then closing it. It was at that point she saw the reflection
of a little boy in the mirror. From what she could tell, he was young, no older
than eleven or twelve. He appeared to be frightened or scared. Despite all of this,
he was still an intruder in her home and being as such, Chris' reaction was an
instinctive one. She fled in horror to her next-door neighbor's, where she stayed
until the police arrived.

When the police arrived, Chris did her best to describe the little boy to them.
The only problem was that she did not remember much about him, other than
the fact he was black with a light complexion and that he had red hair. His hair
was so red it was almost the color of fire. Chris could not forget his red hair.

CHAPTER 9

▼

Once the police had searched the home and found nothing, not even any signs of forced entry, they began to doubt Chris' story of an intruder. Instead, they began to handle it as a case of a lonely woman's imagination running wild.

"God damnit I know what I saw!" shouted Chris, to one of the officers who sounded cynical. "I'm not blind officer, I know what I saw!" she screamed. The police officers decided it was best to simply take her statement and leave, rather than argue with her on the fine points of breaking and entering.

Once the police had left, Chris found herself very uneasy about going back into her home alone. She thought about calling her mother over, but decided against it because she would simply worry her to death. So, since ruling out her mother and with Frank in New York, Chris' only choice was Beverly. She felt guilty calling Beverly, and basically asking her to come over and baby sit her, especially since it meant Beverly would most likely have to cancel her date with her new boyfriend. However, Chris had no one else to turn to. Besides, Chris knew asking Beverly to come over was far less a hassle and cheaper in comparison to staying in a hotel room for the night, which was her only alternative.

*   *   *   *

Beverly came over and ultimately wound up staying the night. By the time, Frank had finally decided to return Chris' calls the following morning; Beverly had already gotten dressed and left for work. Chris was somewhat irritated by Frank's lack of urgency in returning her pages. The fact that he had taken his own sweet time in calling her back, after Chris had continuously paged him and alerted him to the fact someone had broken into their home, only affirmed his lack of concern for her. When Chris questioned Frank as to why it had taken him so long to return her phone calls, he gave her his customary excuse of being tied up with work. Chris contemplated making a big deal out of his lack of compassion, but decided to wait until he returned home from New York. So instead of fussing with Frank long distance, Chris simply updated him on the prior day's events, omitting the incident with the birds. A topic she had intentionally excluded from telling Beverly as well for fear of being committed to a psychiatric ward. Once Frank felt he had heard enough, he hurried Chris off the phone by telling her he was late for a meeting. Enraged by his lack of concern, Chris hung up the phone without saying good-bye.

Not certain if she was being stalked, Chris cancelled her appointment with Dr. Deshpande for Tuesday. Although, she knew canceling her appointment bordered on paranoia, especially since it was only Monday. Still, Chris felt it was better to take the precaution and be safe rather than be sorry in the end. She tried to ease her own sense of guilt in missing her doctor's appointment. However, her nerves were way too frazzled for her to properly relax for Dr. Deshpande to work his magic.

Tuesday morning arrived to find Chris in pain. It was almost like her body knew she had cancelled her appointment and was torturing her for it. Of course, she could have partially blamed some of her pain on the couch she had slept on the night before. She was too afraid to sleep in her bed alone. She could not stop having visions of lying in bed asleep with a little boy jumping out from underneath the bed trying to suffocate her with her pillow. She knew it was crazy, but she could not get the image out of her head. Chris figured that at least by sleeping on the couch, she was close to the front door in case she had to make a quick getaway. Still, despite her body's protest, Chris refused to see Dr. Deshpande that morning for fear someone might be watching her. Instead of using Dr. Deshpande's services, she figured taking two Tylenol would be sufficient enough to relive the pain.

The Tylenol did very little. She had tried her best to bear with it, but by noon Chris could no longer stand it. Having to put paranoia aside, Chris made an emergency call to Dr, Deshpande. Fortunately for her, he had a slot open at one.

When Chris walked into Dr. Deshpande's office, she was in excruciating pain. His receptionist, Sasha, immediately showed her to his office. "So, how are you feeling this afternoon?" asked Dr. Deshpande as he glided into the room.

"Terrible," stated Chris, wincing in pain as she sat down.

"Well, let me see what I could do about that," he said, smiling. With that said Dr. Deshpande, went to work healing her ailing back.

Chris did not have a clue what it was he did, but whatever it was she loved the end result. "Do you have any idea, what is causing me such pain?" asked Chris; after the doctor informed her he was done.

Dr. Deshpande hesitated a moment before saying, "You would not believe me if I told you, Mrs. Adams."

"Try me," pressed Chris.

"Do you really want to know?" asked the doctor. He was uncertain if he should tell her. "It is a topic, most westerners find hard to understand."

"Yeah," replied Chris.

"Do you believe in reincarnation Mrs. Adams?" he said, timidly.

"Please, call me Chris. My full name is Chrysanthemum, only my mother and Beverly call me by my full name. I was named after my great grandmother's favorite flower."

"It is only appropriate for a beautiful lady to be named after such a beautiful flower. It is fitting," stated Dr. Deshpande.

"Well, thank you," said Chris, embarrassed.

"No need…But as I was saying, do you believe in reincarnation or unsettled souls?"

"Unsettled souls?" echoed Chris.

"You know ghosts," the doctor stated.

"No, not really."

"Well, reincarnation it is a basic tenet of my religion. Most Hindus believe in it. It is apart of the natural order of life. Our caste system is constructed around it. See, in our religion what you did in your prior life is reflected in your status in the present. How close you get to heaven in your succeeding lives depends on the deeds performed in your prior lives. Take me for example; I was a nun who tended to the wounded during The Crusades. Before that I was a witch doctor for a small Tutu tribe in what is now the Congo. All throughout my lives, I specialized in healing. It is my calling. It is the path I must take in order to reach heaven. The same can be said about you."

"And what is that?" replied Chris smirking. She could not help but believe this was all some kind of joke.

"Well, I have not been able to tell yet. What I can tell you, is that there is some unfulfilled deed from your past beckoning you to complete. Also, I can tell that either in your prior life or in the life of a spirit that haunts you, his life was taken from him abruptly. It is his inability to fulfill an important deed that is at the root of your emotional pain and the manner in which he passed away is the cause for your physical pain."

"He?" interrupted Chris.

"From the visions I have received from treating you in this brief time and the colors of the aura surrounding you, I would have to say the spirit or essence that embodies you is that of a young boy. An African American child, lynched to death sometime in the 1800's. His lynching is the reason for your unbearable neck and back pain. The deed he left undone, is what is at the center of your emotional distress."

At first, Chris sat there quietly. It was obvious the doctor was not joking. She suddenly became shaken by what she was hearing. She did not know whether to laugh out loud or be frightened to death by this man. Chris could not think of how to respond to his explanation for her back pain, other than by saying, "Well, thank you for sharing that with me doc," and gathering her belongings. "It's been a pleasure," she told him, on her way to the door.

"See you Thursday?" replied Dr. Deshpande.

"Yeah, sure thing," answered Chris, rushing out the door.

When Chris got out to her car, she could not believe how stupid she had been letting Beverly talk her into ever going to see such a lunatic. Dr. Deshpande may have been the best chiropractor she may have ever had, however she questioned his sanity after hearing such an improbable tale.

Nonetheless, once she had started up the car, Chris could not help but remember the little boy she had found in her bathroom.

CHAPTER 10

▼

Chris decided to skip her Thursday appointment with Dr. Deshpande. His story about the little boy was a little bit too macabre for her taste. So, instead of attending her customary Thursday appointment with Dr. Deshpande, Chris had lunch with Beverly at The Ritz. Although, she almost missed the luncheon date due to a bout of nausea and a persistent headache that refused to go away, Chris decided to meet Beverly anyway.

The Ritz was the chic place to be seen in Atlanta. Many of the city's power brokers, blue bloods as well as professional athletes dined there. Although, Chris could have easily blended in, she outright detested the place. The abundance of egos crammed into one place made her sick. Of course, she knew she was just as much a part of that inner circle of elitism and entitlement, exhibited by the next person in the restaurant, regardless if she liked it or not. Nonetheless, Chris knew none of the people in that restaurant were more deserving than many of the children she worked with at the youth center. However, despite her personal opinion, it was Beverly's turn to choose the restaurant and much to Chris' dismay she chose The Ritz.

"So how's your back?" inquired Beverly, detecting a change in Chris' mood. Instead of sipping on her customary Chardonnay, Beverly had decided to go with a Merlot this luncheon.

Chris had not thought about Dr. Deshpande since Tuesday. She had pretty much done the best she could to push him out of her mind. "I'm getting by," replied Chris, not really wishing to talk about the man.

"You're getting by? What is that suppose to mean?" quipped Beverly.

"It means I've been getting by. I've decided to give your witch doctor a rest," responded Chris.

"A rest? Why have you stopped seeing Dr. Deshpande? I thought you said he was the best chiropractor you ever had?"

"Yeah, he's good, but he's just a little bit too far out there for me," insisted Chris.

"What do you mean?" questioned Beverly.

"Well your doctor told me, the reason I was experiencing such chronic back pain was because I was being haunted or possessed by some ghost. I can't particularly remember, whether it was haunted or possessed. Regardless, this spirit is the ghost of some black kid lynched back in 1800's. Can you imagine that? I can not believe he would even suggest such a thing."

"Why is that?" wondered Beverly.

"Come on Beverly, the ghost of some black kid…Couldn't he do better than that? I mean if he is going to sell me a con, he can surely do a better job than that." Beverly simply shook her head and smiled.

"What is it you find so amusing?"

"Nothing really. I was just thinking back to what Dr. Deshpande had told me when I first met him," answered Beverly.

"And what was that?"

"He told me, I was molested by my father as a child in one of my prior lives. That is why I equate sex with love…You shouldn't take what he says so seriously, Chris. I said the guy is a good chiropractor, not mentally stable." Beverly laughed.

"Well, I would feel a lot more at ease if he was a little bit of both," chided Chris. "Besides, I honestly don't see the humor in it."

"Come on Chris, stop being so stuffy—loosen up for a change."

"I don't care what you say. The old geezer gives me the creeps. I've considered going back to Dr. Loewn."

"You rather go back to that quack and be in pain for the rest of your life, instead of seeing a goofy East Indian guy who makes you feel great. That makes no sense to me. I would stick with the goofy guy any day," commented Beverly.

"Well, that is a matter or personal opinion and you're entitled to yours," replied Chris.

Beverly shook her head in disbelief as she stuffed a leaf of lettuce into her mouth. "So, when is Frank getting back home from New York?" she said, once she had thoroughly chewed and swallowed her food.

"Tomorrow night."

"Looks like you have one last evening of freedom, before the task master returns," teased Beverly. "You know, you should really go out with me tonight. It would be good for you. We both know your life practically revolves around Frank. You need to get out more. Do more things on your own, other than shop." As usual Beverly was patronizing her.

Not until Beverly had shut up and taken another bite of lettuce did she notice Russell making his way over to their table. "Oh dear God, here comes Russell," Beverly seethed. Chris turned, to see Russell, coming their way.

"Great, just what I need, to ruin my appetite. You know, I'm never going to forgive you for introducing me to this jerk off," chafed Beverly.

"Please Beverly, he isn't that bad."

"You sleep with him then," snapped Beverly.

Beverly detested Russell, just as much as Russell detested her. Russell and Beverly was the first and last couple, Chris ever attempted to play matchmaker. At the time both, Russell and Beverly, were coming off bitter divorces and Chris figured it would be a brilliant idea to get the two of them together. Little did she know that Beverly had a stringent rule against dating bald men. She claimed seeing a man's shiny, glistening, head only reminded her of how old she was. Yet, Chris felt she was not to blame, she did not know that Russell on occasion wore a toupee. Nor was she aware of Beverly's shallowness when it came to bald guys. If it wasn't for the fact he wore a wig, Beverly might have stayed interested.

Russell waltzed over to the table and gave Chris a peck on the cheek and Beverly a very dry, "Hi," which generated the same response.

"I'm surprised to see you here. Frank told me you guys were not due back until tomorrow...So tell me, how was it? Did you guys do a lot of scuba diving?" asked Russell with excitement. The only problem with Russell's question was that Chris had no idea what he was talking about.

"What are you talking about? Frank is in New York on business," replied Chris baffled.

"Oh, I'm sorry to hear. I'm quite sure you had your heart set on going to Grand Cayman," he said.

Chris gave Beverly a confused look, before replying, "Yes, I did."

Now, Chris didn't have any clue as to what Russell was talking about, however, she decided to play along to see where the conversation lead. Frank had never said anything to her about Grand Cayman and by the way Russell rambled on and on about the Cayman Islands, it was obvious he did not pick up on Chris' reaction to the question.

"Well, hopefully you guys can get there later this year; the Caymans are so much better in the winter anyway," professed Russell.

"Maybe," replied Chris.

"Well, see you later. I got to return to my lunch date. I have a client in from LA, and I don't want to seem rude," said Russell, kissing Chris on the cheek. He purposely ignored Beverly. Now, Chris watched Russell closely as he walked off. She had no idea what he was talking about, but she intended to find out. Once Russell was out of sight, Chris grabbed her cell phone out of her purse and called Frank's office. When his voicemail picked up, Chris zeroed out to get his secretary, Laura.

"Hi, may I speak to Frank Adams please?" demanded Chris.

"Sorry, he's out of town on vacation. Maybe, I can assist you?" Laura replied.

"Hi Laura, it's me…Mrs. Adams."

"Hi Mrs. Adams, how is the Caymans?" she asked. It struck Laura as odd that Chris would be calling for her husband if she were with him.

Chris thought it was peculiar as to how everybody thought she was in the Caymans. Still, Chris did not dare say a word to lead her to think differently. She would have rather continued to live the lie her husband had fabricated, rather than endure the humiliation of telling the truth. It was becoming painfully obvious that Frank had not expected for her to find out. Which only meant…he did not intend for her to know.

"It's great," mumbled Chris, somberly into the phone.

"Wow, what I wouldn't do to be down there getting a killer tan," said Laura, envious.

"Yeah, it's nice," said Chris as her heart dropped.

"Well, what can I do for you?" asked Laura. Little did Laura know, she had already done enough.

"Oh nothing. I have completely forgotten why I even called. You probably think it is silly of me to be calling my husband's job when he is here with me. I think I must have called his number out of habit." She tried to sound jovial but was doing a terrible job at it.

"Don't worry, I understand."

Chris tried fighting back the tears, but it was just too difficult. She was so upset that she was unable to say good-bye. Instead, she simply put the phone back into her purse and wept.

For Chris, heartache was just another reminder of how cruel the world could be. However, unlike the first time when Chris had discovered Frank having an affair, she did not sulk long. This time her heartache quickly turned into rage. She could not believe she had once again been duped into believing Frank was genuinely serious about making their marriage work. Her fury did not let her see pass doing anything, other than avenging Frank's disloyalty. Yet, she had to make certain what Russell had said was indeed true.

Chris and Beverly spent the rest of the afternoon and most of the evening calling every major hotel in New York City. Whenever Frank went out of town, he usually stayed at a W Hotel. When he had to go to New York, Chris knew he usually stayed at the W Hotel in Times Square. However, this time when she called, they informed her there was no Frank Adams registered. Now knowing Frank was a creature of habit, Chris called the W Hotel at Union Square and the one on Lexington Avenue just in case the W in Times Square was overbooked and he attempted to stay at one of the other two hotels. Both hotels informed her they had no guest by the name of Frank Adams registered. After that Chris had pretty much resigned herself into believing Frank was once again cheating on her. She knew how he loved the W Hotels in New York, particular the one in Times Square. So, if he was not in any of the three New York W Hotels, then there was a good possibility he was not in New York at all. Of course Chris did not want to believe it, that is why she talked Beverly into calling every major hotel in New York City. But Chris knew deep down that he was not in New York. When Beverly had finished calling every major hotel and gotten the same response, "Sorry, we do not have a Frank Adams registered as a guest here." Chris could do nothing more than sit next to the telephone and cry.

When the tears had stopped and the burden of truth became too obvious to overlook, Chris went upstairs to her bedroom and began packing Frank's belongings. Seeking for some way to support her friend, Beverly instinctively followed her up the stairs.

This time around there were no more chances. It was over. Once they had most of Frank's things packed they walked his belongings outside and placed it along the curb with the rest of the garbage. Chris could not stop thinking about Frank and some woman relaxing on a beach somewhere in Grand Cayman. Her constant fretting about whether she was wrong and Frank was indeed in New York plagued Chris to the point she began second-guessing whether she was doing the right thing. Even though deep down, she knew leaving Frank was the wisest choice. Beverly watched, Chris pace back and forth trying to come to terms with such conflicting thoughts.

"Look, if you are still uncertain on whether Frank is in New York or not, call his office. I'm certain they know how to get in touch with him," Beverly said, getting tired of watching her pace.

"I can't do that. I've already called there once today. Besides, I'm suppose to be in Grand Cayman with him," snapped Chris.

Beverly grew quiet for a second, before a wicked grin crossed her face. "That is true, you are suppose to be in Grand Cayman…but I'm not," she said.

"What are you talking about?"

"What I'm talking about is, I could play like I'm someone in Frank's family, needing to get in touch with him due to a family emergency." This time Beverly broke into a full fledge smile.

"I don't know if I could let you do that," contemplated Chris.

"Why not?"

"Because, it's just too childish," Chris told her.

"It is, isn't it," stated Beverly.

Beverly seemed to be getting way too much pleasure out of playing such a childish game than Chris thought was humanly possible. However, in her current state, Chris did not see the harm in going along with Beverly's plan.

To have Beverly call Frank's office pretending to be his sister, Emily, made Chris feel pretty juvenile. Yet, she had no other choice in finding out for certain if Frank was in Grand Cayman. The story Beverly gave Laura about their mother being sick was overdone but elicited the desired response. It softened Laura up just enough for her to give Beverly the numbers Frank had left just in case of an emergency. Chris knew Frank always made sure his job knew how to get in contact with him. It was his Achilles' heel. However, Chris found it odd that Laura gave Beverly three phone numbers, instead of one. The first number, Chris recognized. It was Frank's pager. The second number, judging by the number had to be the number to the hotel in Grand Cayman. The third number, however, was a mystery.

Chris decided to call the second number to find out if it did indeed belong to a hotel in Grand Cayman. It did. When the front desk answered the phone, Chris asked to be patched through to Frank Adams room. Instead of being told such an individual was not a registered guest, Chris suddenly heard another phone ringing on the other end. She was frightened to think what she would do or say, once he picked up the phone. However, after several rings a mysterious female voice answered. Chris could do nothing more than hang up. Her suspicions had been confirmed. She could not control the sudden onrush of tears.

After calming down. Chris took the mysterious third phone number and went to her computer, where she attempted to do a search by the number to find out who the telephone number belonged to. She did not want to call the number for caller ID would let Frank know she was on to his little secret, and she did not want him to know just yet. Unfortunately for Chris, she had no such luck for the number was unlisted. Feeling she had no other choice, Chris decided to dial the number.

It took Chris a while to get up enough nerve to go through with it, but Beverly did her part in egging her on. Chris had promised herself that if anyone answered the phone, she would simply hang up. Yet, when she called and voicemail answered the call, Chris decided to stay on the line in hopes of possibly recognizing the voice.

When the recorder said, "Hi, this is Rita," Chris did not need to hear no more. She simply hung the phone up. Chris had thought she had done all the crying she was going to do for one day, unfortunately for her there was more to come.

When the tears had dried up once again, Chris was not the least bit surprised the woman who had came between her and Frank was Rita Thorin. It was Rita Thorin, who had shattered her life once before, and it was Rita Thorin who had shattered it yet again. Chris could not believe that Frank, so brazenly would give his lover's home phone number as an emergency number to his secretary. Chris began to believe that Frank was pretty audacious or extremely stupid, judging by the fact she found out so easily. She was beginning to think he was extremely stupid. Yet, she also began to wonder if Frank wanted her to find out? He knew Chris could have easily gotten Rita's number from Laura. She wondered if he had intended for her to find out about him and Rita all along. By her finding out, it made things a lot easier for him if he sought to get a divorce.

As Chris looked back on it, everything made sense. The countless evenings spent golfing. The supposed long hours spent at work. Those were all signs Chris had chosen to ignore. Frank had succeeded in further humiliating and degrading her and their marriage. She should have seen this coming. Instead, she chose to pretend and turn a blind eye.

While Chris contemplated what to do next, Beverly called her assistant. While Chris waited for Beverly to finish getting her messages and rescheduling her showings, Chris began to feel feverish. The slight perspiration on her forehead was testament to a change in her body temperature. Not only was she dealing with bouts of nausea and headaches, Chris had also been having periods where she experienced the chills, becoming extremely hot one-minute then frigid the next. She was positive she was coming down with a cold. She just prayed to God it was not menopause. She had heard of women entering menopause in their late thirties and early forties. She doubted that was the case, however she could not help but fear the worst.

Chris noticed the plant on the coffee table. It appeared to be close to death. She reached out to examine one of the plant's brownish leaves when it suddenly sprung to life. Right there before her eyes, the leaves of the plant turned from a brownish coloration to a vibrant emerald green.

"What in the hell?" exclaimed Beverly, astonished. "I'm sorry, I was not speaking to you. I was speaking to a friend of mine," she yelled into the phone. "Look, I'm going to have to call you back later this afternoon, okay," Beverly informed her assistant.

"What the hell is going on?" yelled Beverly, hanging up her cell phone.

"I don't know, all I did was barely touch it," shouted Chris, "and it sprung to life." Chris was just as amazed as Beverly.

"Well, it seems to like you," proclaimed Beverly, getting up closer to examine the plant.

"Enough about the damn plant," demanded Chris. Although the plant startled her as much as it had Beverly, Chris did not want it to sidetrack her from the subject of Frank. Besides, the incident with the birds and now the plant was a little too much for Chris to try and comprehend at the moment, especially with everything going on pertaining to her husband.

"I need your advice?" asked Chris.

"Sure thing, but I'm going to let you know, I'm not going to forget what I just saw here," stated Beverly, still watching the plant. "In fact, do you think you can come over to my house and do that? I have several plants I haven't watered in months?" Chris could not help but chuckle. Beverly always had a knack for making her laugh.

"I'm serious, Beverly," Chris replied.

"Me too," chirped Beverly.

"I'm serious. I need to know what I do next?" pleaded Chris.

"Hell, if I was you I would probably start my own gardening show and make a small fortune," said Beverly, cautiously touching the plant.

"Enough with the plant already. I'm talking about Frank," shouted Chris, suddenly becoming irritated.

Beverly picked up the plant and held it up to the light to inspect it. Once she realized that it was simply a houseplant and there was no other mystery to it, Beverly set the plant back down on the coffee table. She looked at the plant and then at Chris for a brief moment before telling her, "Unfortunately Chris, you are going to have to confront Frank."

*   *   *   *

That evening Chris and Beverly finished packing Frank's belongings. The following morning, Frank called and informed Chris his flight from New York would be arriving in Atlanta around 11:15 that evening. Even though she knew he was not in New York, Chris played along. Chris called Hartsfield Airport to find out how many flights flew in from the Caymans that afternoon and found only one. It was a direct flight scheduled to touch down at 3:20 that afternoon. There were numerous other flights that would be routed through Miami but Chris knew Frank, he hated layovers. If it were possible for him to be on that direct flight, he would take it. Chris considered greeting him and his lover at the airport, but decided against creating a scene. If anything, Chris wanted to keep her husband's affair and her humiliation private. So, instead of going to the airport, Chris waited at home. If Frank did not show up at home around the time the direct flight from the Caymans was suppose to touch down, then she would go over to Rita's and confront him there. When Frank confessed to his affair with Rita the first time, Chris had learned she lived in the Occidental Tower—an exclusive condominium in Midtown Atlanta.

Chris kept to herself most of the day. She dreaded having to tell Frank it was over and mean it. Up until the time the locksmith came over and changed the locks on the doors, Chris truly wanted to believe that he was in New York. It was difficult to come to terms with fourteen years of marriage, fourteen years of her life, ending in such a manner. About three thirty the phone rung, Chris silently prayed it was Frank calling to tell her he caught an earlier flight in from New York and was on his way home. Instead, it was Russell looking for Frank. When Beverly told him Frank was not home, he simply replied that he would call him on his cell. He only confirmed for Chris that Frank had taken the 3:20 direct flight out of Grand Cayman.

Up to that point, the day had seemed to move in slow motion. Every second felt like a minute and every minute felt like an hour. It was comparable to her life moving in a succession of still frames, slowly inching towards a climax, she so dreaded to reach. Still, she knew she could not avoid it. The outcome, she was careening towards was inevitable. It did not matter if it was this particular incident or another. Chris knew that their marriage had been building up to this point.

When Chris was certain enough time had lapsed from the time Frank's airplane was scheduled to touchdown and the drive to Rita's condo in Midtown, she gathered up a lone suitcase and headed out the door. Beverly offered to join her, but Chris knew confronting Frank was something she had to do on her own.

CHAPTER II

▼

Rita Thorin would not have recognized Chris from any other stranger knocking at her door. She had attended several of Frank's dinner parties and by chance at one she had a brief encounter with Chris. However brief the encounter, Rita did not feel comfortable meeting her in such a manner. Now that Frank had left his wife, the last person she would have expected to see knocking at her door was Chris. In fact, when she saw Chris standing there at her door, she assumed she was a vagabond begging from door to door judging by her un-kept appearance. She was beginning to get annoyed by the number or vagrants slipping by security. Her floor was only supposed to be accessible by a key, yet she still had to shoo away solicitors and now the occasional bums. However, when Rita opened the door, she had an uncanny feeling that she knew this stranger from somewhere. She just could not place the face.

"Can I help you?" inquired Rita.

"Hi Rita." When Chris greeted her by name, Rita knew they had met somewhere before.

"I'm sorry, but have we met?" asked Rita. The fact she could not place a name with the face was driving her crazy.

"We might have?" Chris, herself, only had a faint recollection of their chance encounter. "It does not matter, I know everything I need to know about you. By the way, how were the Caymans?" added Chris. By Chris making this comment, Rita was able to see beyond Chris' un-kept exterior.

Chris watched as surprise then fear spread across her face. Rita instinctively took a step back, fearful Chris might strike her. For Chris, the urge to lash out was strong. In fact, her hands trembled with desire to be unleashed upon Rita. It took Chris all the energy she could muster to restrain herself, particularly after noticing the bulge beneath her blouse. Just the sight of Rita's protruding belly caused all the rage that had risen to a boiling point inside of her, to dissipate.

"How many months?" asked Chris, fighting back the tears. There was no need for her to ask who was the child's father.

"Excuse me?"

"How many months along are you in your pregnancy?" Chris said, repeating the question.

"Seven," replied Rita, in fear. She could not help, but fear Chris would go into a blind rage and attempt to harm not only her but her baby. In her mind there was no telling what Chris was capable of doing. Just by Chris showing up unexpected at her doorstep, proved to Rita that Chris was not thinking coherently. Rita inched her way back into her condo, hoping to get far enough away where she could make a dash for the phone and dial 9-1-1. At such a close proximity to her, Rita knew she could not escape without Chris catching her in her condition.

"Oh," answered Chris, wiping the tears that know streamed down her face. She had told herself she would not cry in front of Rita or Frank. Chris knew Frank, in particular would take it as a sign of weakness. Yet, no matter how hard she tried to fight them back, Chris could not keep the tears at bay.

At that point, an uneasy silence descended between the two of them. Neither one of them said a word. They simply stood there staring at each other, uncertain of what came next. It was during that awkward moment when Frank yelled, "Honey, who is at the door?" from somewhere inside the apartment. When he saw Chris standing there, he froze.

For Chris to hear Frank refer to someone else as "honey" cut like a knife. She could not recall the last time she had heard him refer to her with such affection. "Hi honey. How were the Caymans?" answered Chris. "Or were you not going to tell me about your little jaunt with your lover here?" remarked Chris.

"Chris…I uh…I can explain," stammered Frank.

"No need to explain Frank! You have made everything painfully obvious to me!" Chris did not want to cause a scene. She simply wanted to tell Frank it was over and leave. However, even that was becoming difficult to do.

"By the way I've brought a few of your things!" yelled Chris, tossing the suitcase at him. Rita had to quickly move out of the way to avoid being struck. "I did, however, forget the most important thing…toilet paper. But we both know assholes like you, Frank, never come clean. Don't we?" Chris paused for a moment to wipe her eyes. "If you want the rest of your things, they'll be outside at the curb like the rest of the garbage!" she screamed.

"I hope the two of you have a wonderful life together," Chris said to Rita before storming off.

"Chris! Chris! Chris, please!" pleaded Frank, running after her. As Chris made her way to the elevators, she realized she still wore her wedding ring. Just the sight of it on her finger repulsed her. She immediately began to try and pry it off.

"Chris please, can we talk about this! It doesn't have to be this way! Chris please, don't do this to us!" cried Frank, catching up with her at the elevator. By that time a few of Rita's neighbors had gathered in the hall to see what the commotion was all about. Although, she had hoped to keep her misery a private matter, it appeared some attention could not be avoided.

Chris had said everything she had wanted to say. She refused to say anymore, fearing she may say something she might regret. An elevator arrived while Frank stood there desperately pleading with her. Unaware that she had pressed the wrong button, Chris realized the elevator was on its way up. She did not care which direction the elevator was traveling as long as it took her away from Frank and that place.

As the elevator doors opened, Chris turned to Frank and screamed, "You know Frank, you should have thought about us before you fucked her!" throwing her wedding ring at him as she boarded the elevator.

Before the doors could close behind her, Frank reached out to her, "Chris, please wait!"

Having grown tired of Frank's games; Chris pried herself free. "Don't you ever, lay your hands on me again!" she threatened

Then the elevator doors shut, leaving Frank there dejected. As the elevator traveled upward, Chris realized Rita Thorin had everything she ever wanted in life, her husband and even her baby.

CHAPTER 12

▼

It was one o' clock in the morning and Chris was wide-awake. She had a migraine headache that had incapacitated her, not to mention a bout of nausea that had her stomach doing somersaults. She was positive she had the flu. It had also become impossible for her to sleep, with the commotion that had suddenly erupted downstairs. Chris got out of bed and trudged over to the bathroom to down two more aspirin before deciding to head downstairs to see what the racket was about.

As she opened her bedroom door she could hear Beverly screaming at the top of her lungs. "I don't care! If you attempt to barge in here one more time, you're going to force me to hurt you! I mean it!"

"God damnit this is my house!" Chris knew by the response, just who Beverly was arguing with. From the sounds of it, Frank had came home and discovered his keys no longer worked.

Chris hurried downstairs only to find Beverly doing her best to keep Frank out. "What is going on here?" asked Chris.

"I caught this jerk trying to break in!" yelled Beverly.

"Will you please call this pit bull off?" bellowed Frank. Beverly slammed the door into his face.

"Fuck you asshole!" Beverly screamed, cracking the door open just wide enough so she could sneak in a knee to his groin.

"Please! That's enough!" shouted Chris.

"You fucking bitch!" gasped Frank falling to his knees clutching his crotch.

"I warned you," said Beverly, strolling past Chris proud of herself.

Frank stayed down on the floor for sometime before gathering up enough strength to stand up on his own two feet again. "I see you've changed the locks," he said, once he was able to catch his breath.

"Yes, I did," Chris assured him.

"God damnit, Chris! Can't we talk this out?" roared Frank. Chris knew, Frank's sudden urgency to talk things out had a lot to do with his fear, she would take him for every penny he had during the divorce proceedings. And if Chris had her way that is exactly what she intended to do.

"That time has passed Frank," said Chris. "Frank, don't come near me," she warned as he gingerly inched towards her.

"Yeah! Stay back!" shouted Beverly, from behind her. "Or this time, you will not just have crushed nuts, but chopped nuts," threatened Beverly. Chris could hear the snipping of shears in her ear.

"So, this is what it has come to? You lock me out of my own house, throw my clothes out in the street, and threaten to castrate me!"

"No Frank, this is how you chose for it to end. Also don't forget my lawyer will be calling yours in the morning," added Chris.

"And whose to say, I'll even be able to find your balls anyway," quipped Beverly.

"Ha, ha...My, aren't we just the comedians tonight!" said Frank flippantly.

"It's over Frank, you've made your choice and I have made mine. Now get out," Chris demanded.

"But I have no place to go, god damnit! Rita threw me out right after you left!" he griped.

"I'm sorry to hear that, but that's not my problem."

"I can't believe this! This is my fucking house, and I can't stay here! Where am I to go?" he screamed, becoming belligerent.

"I don't know Frank, and I really don't care. Now, if you don't mind, will you get out, before I am forced to call the police and have a restraining order placed against you to make sure you stay out."

"Okay, I'll leave but can you at least bring my clothes in from the curb. Russell's car is not big enough to possibly hold everything," he begged.

"They're going to stay right where they are. If they're there when the garbage is collected tomorrow morning, then your belongings will go right along with the rest of the trash to the city dump," insisted Chris.

"I can't believe this!" hollered Frank, storming out the front door.

"And good riddance!" shouted Beverly. Chris slammed the door shut behind him. Chris turned around to find her friend standing there with a gleeful smile on her face and pair of scissors in her hand.

"I don't know what you saw in him in the first place," commented Beverly.

"And just what were you planning on doing with these?" asked Chris, pointing at the scissors.

"Harry may have gotten away, but Frank sure as hell wasn't," Beverly assured her.

"Give me those things," exclaimed Chris, snatching the scissors out of her hand.

CHAPTER 13

▼

Once again, Beverly left early the following morning. She had spent the better part of two days with Chris, and she needed to get back home. Harry was bringing the kids back home after taking them to Yellowstone Park. Besides, Chris understood, Beverly had her own life to tend to. She could not sit around and attend to Chris. So, once again, she was alone. The headache and stomach cramps that had wreaked havoc on her body the night before had appeared to subside. She was about due for her menstrual cycle, so she wondered if that was the reason for the way she had been feeling lately. However, she had never had such severe cramps or migraines before.

Still, despite a reprieve from her physical pain, Chris' emotional distress remained. Being at home alone with no one to help her cope with her feelings, induced Chris to descend into a state of depression. It washed over her in waves. Sometimes she felt fine. She honestly believed she could make it through the day, only to have grief rear its ugly head. For Chris the pain was silent, yet loud. The anguish of the past two days seemed to resonate throughout her.

No longer would there be someone to cook breakfast for in the morning. Instead of Frank complaining about his eggs being over cooked, there will be silence. The feeling of anticipation that consumed her as she waited for Frank to arrive home from work would be no more. No longer was he going to walk through those doors. Everything she had known, everything thing that had existed between her and Frank was now the past. From that point on, Chris' only companion in life would be silence. It would greet her when she opened the door. It will be there when she went to sleep. She was alone.

By all accounts, Chris was a forty-two year-old woman starting over again. She was not exactly in the prime of her life. The last date she had been on was over seventeen years ago. Her biggest concern back then was finding a mate. Now, she was more so worried about living life alone. She had heard the horror stories from single women her age, struggling to find someone to spend their lives with. She had heard of the numerous stories of nights spent alone, and dinner dates for one. She did not have to look no further than Beverly, to see an example of what the single life entailed for an older woman. In Beverly's case it was almost desperation. She clung to anybody or anyone to give her the feeling of companionship. Beverly, at least had her children to keep her occupied. Chris on the other hand had none. And Chris refused to let herself become one of those old ladies with two or three dogs or even worst than that, a house full of cats just to fill the void left by not having the presence of another human being around.

Yet, another dilemma came to mind as Chris contemplated solitude. She did not have the foggiest idea on what to do if she ever did meet someone she was interested in. Thoughts swirled in her head on what to do if a guy asked her on a date. Just the thought of dating another man other than Frank, scared her to death.

As she slipped ever deeper and deeper into depression, Chris realized she desperately needed to hear some words of reassurance that would comfort her and assure her everything was going to be all right. Words that would cause her to believe, she would make it through these trying times. The only person Chris knew who was capable of doing that was her mother.

Chris picked up the phone and dialed her mother's number, hoping she was home. When she heard her mother say, "Hello," into the receiver she breathed a sigh of relief. Although her mother and her did not always see eye to eye on everything, her mother always managed to ease her fears and make her believe everything was going to be all right.

Chris tried her best to maintain her composure as she attempted to speak. Yet, she found it difficult to hold back the tidal wave of emotions consuming her. "Mom, I'm divorcing Frank," were the only words that managed to come out of her mouth.

Chris' mother, Agatha, sat quietly on the phone as her daughter sobbed. She could hear and feel the pain in her daughter's voice. When Chris regained control of her emotions her mother told her, "I'm on my way over."

*   *   *   *

When Agatha arrived at her daughter's house, Chris was distraught. That was apparent by her appearance when she greeted her at the door, in a bathrobe and slippers. It was three o' clock in the afternoon and Chris appeared to have just gotten out of bed. This scared her mother. The last time Chris acted this way was the first time Frank had cheated on her. That time, Agatha, found herself sitting in a hospital waiting room not sure if her only child was going to live or die. She did not want to go through that torture again. Her worst nightmare was that if Chris made up her mind to commit suicide again, she would use something much more lethal than sleeping pills and vodka. Just the thought of life without Chris, frightened her. Not only was Chris her daughter, but also in many aspects her best friend. Agatha did not know if she could survive the loss of a child after suffering the loss of losing her precious husband, Jonathan. That was why when Chris called she rushed to her side. The last thing she wanted was for Chris to do something irrational, and repeat the same mistake she made before.

The first thing Chris said to her mother when she opened the door was, "I'm leaving Frank mother, and that is it!" Agatha could see her daughter was hysterical.

Keeping in mind her daughter's fragile state of mind, Agatha said nothing. She simply listened. It was not the first time she had heard such a proclamation. Instead, she calmly walked inside and headed instinctively for the kitchen. It did not matter whose home she was in, Agatha always felt the most comfortable in the kitchen. She calmly went into the kitchen and began brewing a fresh pot of coffee, while listening to Chris rant about Frank's latest affair. As she took her seat at the breakfast table she listened to her daughter intently. Not until Chris began to calm down did Agatha finally decide it was time to speak, but even then she chose her words wisely.

"Chrysanthemum, I don't think you've truly sat down and thought this out. Are you certain that Frank was even in the Caymans with this woman?" asked her mother.

"Hell, yes!" shouted Chris. "And even if he was not. What in the world was he doing in her apartment, when he was supposed to be in New York preparing to come home? It's over mother, plain and simple."

Not even Agatha could argue with that point. "I will have to say you have a point there. Nonetheless, have you at least spoken to Frank and heard his side of the story?" her mother pleaded.

"I don't need to figure out his side of the story. I caught him red handed," replied Chris.

"But maybe he was—"

"Maybe, he was what mother?" said Chris interrupting her. "Maybe, he was there fixing her pipes?" she said, sarcastically.

"Okay, I know it sounds dumb. I just think you and Frank can work this out. I mean, if you can't what are you going to do?"

"Who knows mom, it is not like that is a question I have not asked myself a thousand times. I do know, I can not continue to go on living like this," answered Chris introspectively.

"You know, you could lose this beautiful house and everything else the two of you have worked so hard to achieve? Not to mention, the effect this may have on Frank's job."

"His job! His job! I don't give a damn about his job! I could care less about this house! What about me mom! Huh, what about how I feel!" screamed Chris emphatically. "This house means nothing to me! I never liked this house anyway! He picked out the house, the furniture, the colors as well as every god damn thing in it! As far as I'm concerned, he can have it! I don't want anything that had to do with him! You sound like you're more concerned about Frank's well being, than you are mine!"

Agatha sat quietly. She had unknowingly said the wrong thing. She felt it was best, she said nothing until Chris once again calmed down. She knew nothing could be achieved while talking to her in such a highly agitated state. Besides, in such an emotional state as Chris was in, her mother knew it was difficult for her to think reasonably. Agatha could smell the freshly brewed coffee. So she decided to get up and pour herself a cup, fixing herself a cup of coffee would give her just enough time to collect her thoughts.

"Where are you going?" Chris questioned.

"I'm going to pour myself a cup of coffee. Do you want a cup?" her mother asked.

"No thank you," replied Chris.

"Well as I was saying—" uttered Agatha.

"Mom, I don't want to hear you defend Frank anymore!" yelled Chris cutting her mother off again. "He left me! He chose to have a mistress! It was his decision! Not mine!...And I haven't told you the worst of it...she's pregnant," she sobbed. "That woman was able to give Frank the one thing I couldn't...A baby! Do you hear me mother? She is going to have his baby.

"Why can't I have a baby? Why must I be tormented like this," Chris sobbed.

"Shush, don't say that. You are not tormented," her mother soothed, placing her arm around Chris.

CHAPTER 14

▼

Agatha stayed with Chris for as long as she could. She was deeply worried about her daughter's mental health. However, she knew she could not stay and watch over her every waking minute of the day, so she reluctantly went home.

Chris' bout with depression lingered with her throughout the week. She refused to answer the telephone and even on occasions she ignored answering the door. Sleep was a luxury she found hard to achieve. Of course, sleeping on the living-room sofa did not help her relax. She was still afraid to sleep in her bedroom. No longer was it because she feared a little boy may surprise her, but because she hated the feeling she got sleeping in bed alone. Plus, her reoccurring nightmare did not make getting asleep and staying asleep any easier.

Beverly and her mother, kept a vigil over her with their periodic dropping by and numerous phone calls. Chris knew their visits were more of a suicide watch, than friendly house calls. Yet, she had no idea how meticulously they had thought out and coordinated their schedules in order to give her very little time alone. To say that Chris did not feel herself slipping into the anguish of depression and had not contemplated suicide would not be true. There was several times during the week, when she had felt herself consumed by distress staring blankly into a handful of painkillers, simply wondering. Yet nobody, including Chris, wanted a repeat of her last suicide attempt. However, all those hours she had spent with a psychotherapist did not prepare her for when despair came knocking on her door again.

Its siren song always came to Chris in the form of self-pity. Why her? What was wrong with her? She often would stand in front of the mirror and stare at her reflection, noticing the effects of time on what had once been a petite frame. The effects of gravity could be seen in the sag of her breast. Her hips that were once pronounced now seemed to blend in with the saddlebags that had mysteriously latched on to her upper thighs. Her once shapely rear-end, which use to sit proudly at the base of her back, slightly sagged now as it expanded east to west. Despite, all of these biological changes taking place none were more painful than the fact she lacked the ability to bring a life into the world.

Chris could not help but think of the countless women enjoying a full life with children, including Rita. It infuriated her that life had left her so feeble, cheating her of the one function that made a woman, a woman. She couldn't help but second-guess that if her ovaries could produce eggs and she could have children, would her life have been any different. Regardless of the torture the answer to such a question would bring, Chris could not resist playing a game of what if.

What if she could bear children?

If she could, would Frank have been faithful?

Of course, she was being critical of herself. Besides, playing such a game only hastened the onslaught of despair, which delved her deeper into depression. Yet, doing such a thing was hard to resist. There was just too much hurt and pain pent up inside of her searching for a means to escape.

If it had not been for her mother calling to remind her about the Founding Father's Day celebration in Jacksonville, Chris might have wallowed in her sorrow for far too long. Possibly succumbing to her morbid thoughts of death. "Hi, snook'ums it's me, your mother," gushed her mother, on the voicemail. "I was wondering, if you still planned on going to Jacksonville this weekend for the Founding Father's Day celebration. If you've had a change of heart, I understand. I'll just tell the mayor neither one of us will be able to attend this year. Call me, when you get home. Bye-bye dear."

The entire ordeal with Frank had caused Chris to totally forget all about promising her mother, she would attend the Founding Father's Day celebration in her place. Chris was really not in the mood for a four-hour drive to Jacksonville, but she felt an obligation to her mother. She did after all promise her that she would stand in for her. Chris erased the message and thought about pretending to act like she had not heard it. Her conscience scolded her for being so insensitive and for even contemplating doing such a thing. Since she was unable to handle the guilt of avoiding her mother, Chris picked up the phone and called her.

Although Chris had originally intended to tell her mother, she was not going to make the trip to Jacksonville. Once Agatha got on the phone, Chris could not bring herself to tell her she was calling to cancel. Of course, Chris' mother was delighted to hear at least one descendant of Clayton Jackson would show up for the annual celebration. So, regardless if she felt like going or not, Chris reluctantly packed a suitcase and headed for Jacksonville.

*   *   *   *

Much to Chris' surprise, the drive to Jacksonville turned out to be invigorating. She let the top on the convertible down and felt the wind blow freely through her hair. As the wind danced around her as she sped down the highway it felt like all her troubles were being blown away. Thus, revealing the new Chris. The farther she got out of Atlanta city limits, the better she begin to feel about herself and life. As it turned out, the drive to Jacksonville was the elixir she needed to clear her mind and gather her thoughts. She did happen to shed a few tears along the way, however they were not tears of despair. Instead it was more of a release, her own way of mourning for the loss of love and her marriage. Chris was not ashamed for crying; in some regards it was therapeutic. It forced her to realize that she had always looked upon someone else to make her happy, instead of depending on herself. Whether it was Frank or her parents, she had always looked to someone else to define the meaning of happiness for her instead of defining it for herself. She knew it was now time for her to define it for herself. She had been gullible enough in the past to give people that power over her, believing no one would abuse it. It saddened her to know the one person whom she trusted the most, Frank, used it against her. Of course, Chris realized she was just as much at fault for her unhappiness as Frank. As she drew closer to Jacksonville, she began to view her trip as a chance to start anew—a chance to focus on her. It was a chance to start all over again.

Jacksonville was a small town in rural southern Georgia. It was roughly an hour and a half to two hours out of Macon, Georgia, going southwest and roughly an hour north of Tallahassee, Florida. It was not far from the Georgia-Florida state line. Although, some cities in Georgia such as Atlanta and to a lesser degree Macon and Savannah, Georgia, had moved into the twenty-first century in regards to race relations. Jacksonville like much of the south remained divided. By all accounts, Jacksonville had not changed much since the Reconstructive Era.

There was only one county road that ran through the town. It divided the town into two sections, both physically and racially. On one side there were The Haves and on the other side there were The Have Nots. The county road was the equivalent of a color line. It split the town right down the middle, with blacks living on one side and whites living on the other. To determine which side of the color line enjoyed a better way of life in Jacksonville was not hard. It was quite obvious by the dilapidated homes that sat on cinder blocks on the black side of town in comparison to the beautiful homes that made up the white side. There were no more than two hundred people living in Jacksonville at one time. Everyone knew everyone quite well. Despite the stark difference the county road in Jacksonville represented, everybody still intermingled with one another. Whites intermingled with blacks, and blacks with whites. Still, that county road showed that relationships, which traveled beyond color in Jacksonville were purely superficial.

Many of the black people living in Jacksonville, pretty much built their homes on the same land where their great-great grandmothers and grandfathers slept in slave quarters. Much of Jacksonville's black population toiled in the same fields as their forefathers, who came to America in shackles and chains. The only difference being instead of cotton the harvest was peanuts, watermelon, peaches and pecans, depending on the time of the year. The reign of cotton in that region of Georgia had ended sometime ago. It had taken the fields surrounding Jacksonville years to replenish the nutrients back into the soil that years of growing cotton had taken out.

As Chris drove into town, a flood of memories came to mind of her first and only trip to Jacksonville with her mother. It was in Jacksonville that Chris remembered seeing her very first 'Whites Only' sign at the local diner. For some reason that sign remained indelibly imprinted on her brain. In that same window right above the sign, she recalled a huge Confederate flag in bright colors of red and blue. The colors were so vibrant, Chris remembered thinking that the flag was brand new. The red was so deep and rich, Chris likened it to the color of blood and the blue was so deep it was darker than any sky or ocean she had ever seen.

It was 1968 and Chris was only eight. It was a full four years after Lyndon B. Johnson, the supposed traitor to the south, signed the Civil Rights Act of 1964 into law. Chris also recalled, that it was two whole months after Martin Luther King Jr. was assassinated in Memphis by James Earl Ray. Despite each one of those events, international in stature, neither one of them changed life for the people of Jacksonville. Life went on as it always did. Although, those events got people talking neither one created much change in town.

As Chris parked her car, she noticed the diner were she had seen the 'Whites Only' sign still existed. The 'Whites Only' sign by the door was gone but the big red Confederate flag still hung in the window. The flag showed its age by its frayed edges, to the faded blue and red, that now looked more like pink and baby blue. Right along side the aging Confederate flag, hung the old Georgia state flag with its huge Confederate coat of arms displayed proudly. Although, the state flag had been abandoned a few years back for a less controversial flag much of rural Georgia still flew the old state flag in defiance to the new more politically correct flag. Further proof of how Jacksonville was still very much apart of the Old South.

As Chris walked inside the diner, she could not help but remember that despite the 'Whites Only' sign by the door the diner did serve blacks. She recalled they were regulated to two small booths in the rear of the diner next to the kitchen, on the other side of a yellow piece of tape on the floor that had "white" painted in big block letters on one side and "colored" on the other. Chris remembered sitting in the front of the diner with her mother and asking her mother, why the blacks that came to eat at the diner came and went through a back door near the kitchen. She could recall how her mother danced around the subject for some time before giving up and not answering her at all. Even some thirty odd years later not much had changed. As Chris stood there rehashing the past, she could see the only difference in the place was that the words "white" and "colored" had been removed from the floor. The yellow tape, although withered, still remained. In Chris' mind, that withered piece of tape was confirmation to no matter how much things changed beyond this small town, things would always remain the same in Jacksonville.

Jacksonville was not some big city where Chris could readily find a hotel or motel. So, finding a place to sleep that evening was a dilemma Chris needed to resolve quickly. Her mother had simply instructed her to check in with the mayor when she arrived and he would take care of everything. The only problem was, Chris did not know where to find him. Still, she figured it could not be that hard finding the mayor since Jacksonville was a small town. Chris took a seat at the counter and ordered eggs over-easy with a side of bacon and toast. Although it was after noon, Chris was in the mood for breakfast. As she sat there waiting on her order, she could feel the eyes of the diner's local patrons on her. In small towns such as Jacksonville, spotting a stranger was easy. The hard part was trying to figure out why they were there.

When the waitress returned with her eggs and bacon, Chris nonchalantly asked her, "Do you know, where I can find the mayor?"

"Who's askin'?" snapped the waitress; common courtesy was not a virtue wasted on strangers in rural Georgia. If you were not a local, they took you for uppity city folk.

"I'm sorry," apologized Chris, turning on the southern charm. "My name is Chrysanthemum Jackson-Adams. I'm the great-great granddaughter of Clayton Jackson. I'm in town for the Founding Father's Day celebration."

"Well huney, why didn't chea say dat ta begin wit? Ya should be able ta fine Roy in da town store next door; he runs it ya know," claimed the waitress, loud enough so everyone could hear. Once it had been determined, who Chris was and why she was there, the entire diner seemed to breath a collective sigh of relief.

"Thank you," said Chris smiling.

"Sure thang," replied the waitress, hurrying off to the kitchen to tell the cook. Chris was quite sure that is what she had done judging by the way he came out from behind the grill to take a peek at her.

Since everybody in the diner now knew Chris was the great-great granddaughter of Clayton Jackson, people instantly began to warm up to her. Chris found it difficult to eat, due to the numerous people who wanted to converse with her, or shake her hand while she ate. Even a pair of elderly gentlemen interrupted her meal in order to have their picture taken with her. She obliged them, but found the sudden fuss everyone was making over her quite odd.

As she finished her breakfast, Chris noticed an elderly black woman sitting in the rear of the diner watching her closely. When she looked over at her, their eyes instinctively met. The elderly woman politely smiled her way, before placing her money on the table and walking out the back door. Chris watched her as she left. She could not explain what it was about her, but there was something about the old lady that stirred something inside of her. She had never seen the woman before, yet, something about her seemed familiar. Chris did not know why, she felt as if they had met somewhere. After racking her brains trying to figure out where she recognized the elderly woman from and drawing a blank, Chris decided to let it go.

Chris finished breakfast and proceeded to pay for her meal, when the waitress came over to where she sat and asked her, "Wat are ya doin'?"

"Excuse me," replied Chris, unsure of what she was referring to.

"I says, wat are ya doin'?" repeated the waitress.

Chris, looked at the money in her hands and said, "I'm paying for my meal."

"Huney, yar money iz no good here. Yar the daughter of da great Clayton Jackson, ya don't pay fo' a damn thang in Jacksonville. Now, go on befo' I gits offended," insisted the waitress.

"It's only right, I pay," Chris told her.

"Wat did I tell ya? Yar a Jackson, and no Jackson pays aroun' dese heah parts. So, go on an put ya muney up," she told Chris.

"Okay," stammered Chris, reluctantly placing her money back in her pocketbook. "So, you say I can find the mayor next door at the town store?" she asked, still somewhat confused.

"Yep, he should be right nex' door," proclaimed the waitress, watching her go.

"Thank you," said Chris, heading out the door.

"Huney chile, ya do not have ta thank me," the waitress answered as Chris walked out.

Chris walked out of the diner and over to the town store as the waitress had instructed. She passed two elderly gentlemen, who had made a table and chairs out of empty crates, playing a rather loud game of checkers right there on the sidewalk. They became as quiet as field mice as she passed, only to once again become loud and boisterous the moment Chris stepped inside the store. In the store, a young girl with a bad case of acne, who looked no older than fifteen, greeted her.

"Hi, I'm looking for Mayor Roy Wilks?" said Chris, walking up to the cash register.

"Dad's at home workin' on da truck?" said the girl. She blew a fresh pink bubble from a huge wad of bubble gum stuffed in her mouth. For Chris her constant chomping on that wad of gum reminded her of a cow chewing a cud.

"Well, do you know how I can reach your father? I was told, I would be able to find him here."

"Is dis police biz'ness or mayor biz'ness?" questioned the girl, rolling her eyes. "Neither…My name is Chrysanthemum Jackson-Adams, and I was told I should locate your father if I needed a place to stay while I was here for the Founding Father's Day celebration."

"Are ya dat founder's gurl?" she asked. She blew another pink bubble that burst, splattering a sticky pink film over her cheeks.

"Yes, I am."

"Well, he told me ta tell ya to meet 'im out at da haus," she said, attempting to peel the gum off her face.

"Okay, how do I get there?"

Finding the mayor's house was a lot harder than Chris had imagined. After traveling down a few lonely dirt roads that went nowhere, Chris finally was able to find the mayor's house at the end of a dead end road. Chris blamed her long adventurous journey on the mayor's daughter's southern drawl, which made her directions hard to decipher. Although, Chris knew she had a slight accent herself, her diction was nothing compared to the mayor's daughter. Nonetheless, after a brief detour Chris was able to find the mayor's place.

Now judging by the numerous automobile husks that littered the mayor's front yard, Chris quickly assumed that not only was the mayor, the mayor and the chief of police of Jacksonville, but also the town's mechanic as well. A radio sat on the front porch of a house, badly in need of repairs, blaring country-western music. The home appeared to be on the verge of collapsing judging by the way it leaned to one side. The tune on the radio was not a song Chris recognized. It was not like she would have known anyhow. She was not a big country-western fan. Other than a few country artist that made it into mainstream music such as Garth Brooks, Shania Twain and the Dixie Chicks, she could not tell one country singer from the next. The only reason she knew anything about Shania Twain and the Dixie Chicks was because Frank lusted after them. Besides that, the closest Chris ever came to being an urban cowgirl was during the line-dancing craze, when she took line-dancing lessons to learn how to do the Tush Push. That was about as close as Chris came to being a cowgirl.

As she got out of her car and waded through the cars that sat about the yard like old dinosaur relics, Chris could hear someone singing along with the tunes on the radio. The only problem was she couldn't tell from which car the singing was coming from. Not until she stumbled upon a pair of cowboy boots sprawled out beneath a pick up truck did Chris find the esteemed mayor of Jacksonville.

"Excuse me?" The guy under the truck kept on singing. He obviously could not hear her over the tapping of his steel tipped boots. "Excuse me?" Chris repeated, this time a little louder. Still, he kept right on singing.

"Excuse me!" Chris screamed, this time nudging his foot.

Suddenly startled by the fact he was not alone, the gentleman hit his head on the belly of the truck. There was a loud, hollow sounding, metal pang followed by an uncontrollable howl of, "Gawd damnit!"

When he managed to wiggle his way out from beneath the pickup to see who had kicked him, Chris was blessed with the sight of a true 'good ole boy.' The mayor was adorned in not only cowboy boots but also a baseball cap embossed with the Confederate flag that he tossed on to his hand once making his way out from beneath the truck. His shirt barely covered his beer belly that extended well beyond the lip of his pants. There were spots of oil littered sporadically throughout his shirt, along with what appeared to Chris to be gravy stains of some sort as well.

"Gawd damnit Missy! Ya can't be sneakin' up on folk like dat! Ya liable ta git someone kilt!...Now wat can I do for ya?" he shouted, reaching into a nearby cooler and pulling out an ice-cold beer. He immediately began to use the beer as a makeshift ice pack to ease the swelling on what was shaping up to be a nice size knot on his forehead.

"I'm sorry," said Chris, fighting back her laughter. But I'm looking for the mayor."

"Well ya foun' 'im. Wat can I do fo' ya?" the mayor replied, obviously annoyed.

"I'm Chrysanthemum Jackson-Adams," answered Chris, extending her hand. "My mother informed you, I would be coming in her place this year for the Founding Father's celebration."

"Well, I'll be damned. If I would hav' known ya waz a Jackson I would hav' been a bit more hospitable ta ya," said Mayor Wilks, struggling to his feet to shake her hand. "I thought ya waz one of 'em Jay-hovas witnesses. Even though I live out 'ere in da sticks, dey always seem ta fine me," he said, laughing. "And don't chea worry none 'bout da noggin, I bumps it all da time."

"Well, I am very sorry."

"Like I says, it's nuttin. If yar ma had not called me, I wood hav' figured ya'll be comin' in tamorrow," said Roy, suddenly turning on the charm.

"I thought I would come down a day early. Possibly, reacquaint myself with the town. The last time I was here, I was too young to remember."

"Hell, ya can git mighty friendly wit everythin' in jus' 'bout fifteen minutes. Ya sure don't need a whole day. Dis town aint nuttin but a thimbleful," he said, finally popping the top on his can of beer and taking a swig.

"Dat dere sure iz a fine piece of machinery ya gat dere. Iz dat yars?" he said, belching. Before Chris could reply, he had already moseyed down towards her Saab. If the beer belly and the Confederate cap wasn't enough, the mayor's pants had slip halfway down his butt revealing a good portion of his ass to Chris and the rest of the world.

'Southern hospitality at its finest,' Chris thought as she followed him down to her car. "Yeah it's mine," she said, in response.

"Dis sure iz a fine piece of steel. We don't see ta many of des foreign jobs down heah. She mus' hav' cost ya a pretty penny. Ya goin' ta hav' ta let me take a look up underneath da hood befo' ya go."

"Sure, no problem," said Chris just to appease him. In actuality, she was not going to let him come within ten feet of her car. "I would love to talk about cars with you, Roy, but I was wondering where can I get settled in at around here?"

"Dere isn't no motel in dez heah parts, strangers usually shack up wit Ethel. She runs a boadin' haus in town. She's also da town historian. Although, tek'nically she's really not da historian, it'z jus' a title we giv' ta da oldest geezer in town. Anyhow, Ethel usually rents out a couple of rooms a night ta those willin' ta pay. She's a real sweet ole' lady. I figure since yar Clayton Jackson's great-great granddaughter, she might let ya stay dere fo' free. She usually let ya mother, stay dere fo' free. But hell, if ya want ya can shack up out heah wit me," he said, with a devilish grin on his face.

"Thanks for the offer but no thanks. I think I'll stay at Ethel's," Chris replied. Chris was thankful she had not reached that level of desperation yet.

"Suit yarself. I would let ya follow me in ta town ta her place, but on account I'm a fixin' up yar heah float, I can't."

'Great the grand marshal's vehicle is an ancient pickup with a gun rack,' was the comment that floated through Chris' head. "No problem, I'm sure I'll find it. It isn't like I could get lost. Like you said this town is nothing but a thimbleful."

"Yeah, ya sure right 'bout dat," he said, finishing off his beer.

*   *   *   *

Unlike the mayor's house Chris had no problem finding Ethel's home, and since Chris was the great-great granddaughter of Clayton Jackson, Ethel did indeed offer to let Chris stay there for free just as the mayor had suggested she would. It was a generous offer, but Chris intended to pay her for her hospitality.

After settling in and changing out of a pair of uncomfortable jeans, Chris slipped into a sundress that was more suitable for the weather. Once she was dressed, she decided to relax a bit with Ethel out on the porch. Ethel had made a pitcher of sweet tea, so Chris felt it was only fitting that she enjoyed a glass with her. As the town bustled with activity, everyone getting ready for the Founding Father's celebration that weekend, Chris and Ethel talked and watched the town's growing anticipation for its gala event. They didn't pride themselves on much in Jacksonville. About all the town did have was its Founding Father's Day celebration. For most of the people in town, it was the Fourth of July and New Year's Eve all rolled up into one. Just like New Orleans had Mardi Gras, Jacksonville had the Founding Father's Day celebration. It was Jacksonville's very own mid summer Mardi Gras.

For the first time in a long time Chris felt at peace. For her, it felt good to just be able to breathe freely, after feeling suffocated for so long. Sitting there on the porch was the first time since leaving Atlanta that she did not think about Frank.

'Maybe being alone, isn't all that bad,' she conceded, running her feet along the wooden planks of Ethel's porch. To Chris this was what life was all about, open spaces, unadulterated skies and sipping sweet tea while sitting in a porch swing on a hot summer day. When she thought about her life, this was how she envisioned it, relaxing and simple.

It was a little bit past three in the afternoon, when Chris decided it was time she paid her respects to her late great-great grandfather. She felt it was the least she could do while in Jacksonville. Chris could not recall the last time she had seen the plantation other than in pictures. Yet, before she headed out Ethel felt it was necessary to give her a few words of advice about life in Jacksonville, particularly when it came to the town's "colored folks" as she put it.

"Dere preddy docile folk. Not like 'em niggers back up in da city. Da colored folk aroun' heah know dere place. Still, if dey are provoked dey can turn on ya like a rampant dog," warned Ethel.

Now Chris didn't want to seem disrespectful or even ungrateful for Ethel taking the time out to speak with her, so she did nothing more than smile and tell her 'thank you' before heading off to the mansion. The only reason Ethel felt inclined to give Chris such advice was because the only way to get to the plantation was through the black part of town. At first Chris did not think much of it. In her mind walking down one lonely road to get to her late great-great grandfather's plantation was nothing in comparison to walking down the street in Atlanta. Yet, while many of the people whose ancestors were probably slaves to her great-great grandfather watched as she walked along that gravel road to the plantation, Chris could not help but feel a little intimidated. Many of the people, who were sitting on their stoop attempting to escape the summer heat, grew quiet as she walked by. Children rode their bicycles beside her, simply to gaze in her face. They looked at her as if they were searching for something recognizable. Chris could not help but feel she was being viewed as some kind of oddity amongst them.

When Chris made it to the mansion, an elderly gentleman by the name of Emmett greeted her on the mansion grounds. It appeared Ethel had called ahead and informed him of her pending visit. Emmett claimed to be the caretaker of the place, doing whatever was necessary to maintain the up keeping of the mansion. He also claimed to be a direct descendent of one of Chris' great-great grandfather's slaves, a fact Chris found to be interesting. As Emmett led her inside, a huge portrait of her great-great grandfather, Clayton Jackson, and her great-great grandmother, Emma Jackson, greeted her in the foyer. It amazed her, how the town had managed to take such immaculate care of the place over so many years. The place seemed frozen in time.

Emmett gave Chris a guided tour of the mansion, telling her stories related to the plantation that had been passed down from generation to generation. Although the town had managed to keep the place in marvelous condition, they did however, neglect to update the mansion with the pleasantries of modern technology such as air conditioning. Fans were placed throughout the mansion; however, they did very little in giving Chris relief from the heat. She decided to cut her tour short in hopes of escaping out back to catch a refreshing breeze. As she stepped outside into the setting sun, Chris was caressed by a soft gentle breeze that managed to blow through her dress and cool her moist skin. She looked out on to the acres upon acres of overgrown fields that at one time in history harvested bounties of cotton that in turn made her great-great grandfather a wealthy man. Now those same fields were choked with weeds. As she stood there gazing out upon the land, Chris noticed a small trail that ran along the fields' edge into a small thicket of trees. Judging by how worn the path was it was obvious that someone still traveled it. Chris' curiosity got the best of her. So Chris removed her shoes, so she could feel the earth beneath her feet as she followed the path.

Chris walked along the trail, enjoying the feel of the dirt in between her toes. She could not help but watch in wonderment as each cloud of dust rise and fell with each footstep she took. As the dust lightly dusted the tops of her feet, she could not help but smile from the joy she received from feeling so free. It did not take long before the trail diverged into two separate paths, one trail continued along the outer-limits of the fields, while the other strayed into the woods. Chris couldn't explain why she chose the path leading into the thicket of trees. For some reason she felt drawn to it. Her curiosity was ultimately rewarded, when the trail emptied into a small clearing occupied by a beautiful garden.

There was an assortment of flowers emanating vibrant pastels and beautiful bright hues that radiated. There were lilacs, jasmine and clover, but the one flower that was prominent throughout the entire garden was chrysanthemums, a fact that was not lost on Chris. Numerous oak trees, draped in moss, encompassed the clearing, giving it the feeling of an inner sanctum. The moss gave the trees an ominous presence. One oak tree in particular, a large majestic oak, resided at the base of the garden. It reminded Chris of sentry assigned to guard a post. Although, it was nothing more than a tree, it appeared menacing. Judging by how well kept the garden appeared, Chris deducted the garden was tended to regularly. As she stood there admiring the garden's beauty, a flock of sparrows in the nearby trees set the countryside abuzz with their chatter. She wondered if they were alerting the garden's caretaker that the sanctimony of the secret garden had been breached.

Realizing she had trespassed on someone's secret hideaway, Chris decided it was time to leave. Yet, when she turned to leave, she suddenly became nauseous and the world around her began to spin viciously out of control. The world seemingly turned from day into night in an instant.

"What is happening to me?" Chris asked, trying her best to get her world to stop spinning.

It was then when Chris turned back around towards the garden, when she realized the garden was gone. Just like that it had vanished. Instead, in its place were smoldering remains of a building, and from the menacing oak tree that had stood sentry over the former garden hung a little boy.

Suddenly it dawned on Chris that she was dreaming. She was once again inside her nightmare. The only difference was this time everything felt real. The grass beneath her feet felt real. She could feel each individual blade of grass upon the soles of her feet. Not only that, the suffocating smell of the smoke that billowed from the charred remains of the cabin seemed real to her sense of smell. She could even smell the scent of death that seemed to be carried on a light wind throughout the small clearing. She could not resist questioning, if she really was asleep judging by how vivid the sights, sounds and smells were to her senses. She suddenly heard the piercing sound of someone screaming. It took her a moment, but she realized the person screaming was none other than her. She could hear herself screaming, pleading with herself to wake up, to take her away from there. Yet, regardless of how loud she cried, her body refused to awaken from its slumber. For Chris the more she screamed, the more her world spun violently out of control.

CHAPTER 15

▼

Chris woke up screaming.

"It'z a'right chile. Everythang is goin' ta be a'right," someone said, trying to soothe her. It was a voice Chris did not recognize.

When Chris opened her eyes, she found herself in a room with an elderly black woman hovering over her like a doting mother. The woman was the color of molasses. The silver mane that crowned her head was in stark contrast to her jet-black skin. The weathered look of time shown on her face in the furrows that graced her brow and the engraved creases along her cheeks. As she stood over her, Chris could see she had a slight hunch in her back. After closer examination, Chris quickly realized she was the same old woman she had seen at the diner earlier that afternoon.

As Chris' life phased in from dream to reality, the old lady looked at her and smiled before saying, "Glad, ta see yar awake?"

"Where am I?" asked Chris, bolting upright in the bed.

"Aw, don't ya fret none chile, yar at my haus, so yar safe," the old lady said, folding the blanket she had used to cover Chris.

"But I was outside in a field when," Chris' voice trailed off. She suddenly remembered seeing the little boy hanging from that huge oak tree.

"Wat's da matter chile? Ya acts like ya done seen a ghost," exclaimed the elderly woman, noticing Chris' face go flush.

"I don't know. I saw something out in that clearing today," stated Chris.

"Well, wat ever it waz ya don't have ta worry 'bout it no more. Yar at Annie Mae's haus now, and I'm goin' ta take care of ya."

"You brought me here all by yourself?" asked Chris in amazement.

"Ah, no chile. I'm too old ta be draggin' folk aroun' town. My grandbaby, Hope foun' ya passed out in da clearin' behind da Jackson place. She came an' gat Buford ta carry ya back heah. I think da heat may hav' caused ya ta pass out like dat. Ya know, ya should drink plenty of water when it gits hot like dis," said Annie Mae, placing the blanket at the foot of the bed. Chris winced in pain as she attempted to get up. It appeared that somewhere between Annie Mae's and the plantation, she had re-aggravated her back.

"Are ya a'right?" questioned Annie Mae, noticing her pain.

"Yeah, I'll be fine."

Annie Mae smiled and said, "Ya know, ya looks jus' like her."

Chris was not sure what she meant by that, but instead of trying to figure it out, she simply smiled and said, "Thank you." She figured the less conversing she did, the sooner she could get out of there.

"Hope iz goin' ta be glad ta see yar a'right," Annie Mae told her, just before screaming her granddaughter's name. "Hope! Hope! She's awake!"

"So tell me, how's yar mom doin'?" inquired Annie Mae, taking a seat in an old rocking chair across the room

"Excuse me…My mother?" replied Chris.

"Yeah, how's Agatha doin'?" reiterated Annie Mae. Just as Chris was about to ask how is it she knew her mother, another woman entered the room.

"Well, I'm glad to see you're all right. I was beginning to get worried about you," the woman said.

"She looks jus' like her, don't she Hope?" said Annie Mae.

Hope stared at Chris for a moment before saying, "Yeah, she sure does Gran." Now when Annie Mae had told her that her grandbaby, Hope, had found her in the clearing, Chris was expecting Hope to be a little girl not a grown woman. Chris was suddenly very confused. What had started off as a good day had gone totally wrong, frightfully wrong. Chris could not help but imagine it was the sort of feeling Alice had after falling down the rabbit's hole.

"Wait a minute. What is going on here? The last thing I remember before waking up here was standing in a clearing next to a flowerbed. Then all of a sudden everything changed. Day suddenly turned into night. There was a garden where I was at and then all of a sudden there wasn't. The worst part about it was that there was this little boy hanging in the tree. It was just like my dream.

"Now, I wake up here in a house with a bunch of strangers, whom I do not know but they know my family…Can somebody please explain to me what the hell is going on?" pleaded Chris. Both Hope and Annie Mae gazed at each other for a brief moment, before turning their gaze back towards Chris.

"Well, if it makes ya feel any better when I found ya I did not find no boy lynched in those trees," Hope informed her.

Realizing she was not going to get a straight answer from neither one of them, Chris struggled to her feet while informing them, "I got to be going."

"Wat's da rush gurl? I jus' finished makin' supper," exclaimed Annie Mae as Chris hurried out the room.

"I'll walk with you to make sure you don't get lost on your way back to old lady Ethel's house," said Hope.

"That is all right. I can find my own way back," stated Chris, definitely not in the mood for company. "It is not like this town is that big. Besides, how did you know I was staying at Ethel's house anyway?" snapped Chris, storming out of the front door and out onto the gravel road outside.

"She's the only person in town with a boarding house and your mama stays there all the time she is in town. Besides, you need to go the other way if you plan on getting to Ethel's anytime tonight," said Hope following her out the door.

"Thank you," snapped Chris, changing direction.

"Sure thang," said Hope quietly walking along side her.

They walked for sometime in silence, neither one of them saying a word. When they reached the county road that split the town in two, Chris realized she had not heard Hope speak with the same thick southern drawl as Annie Mae or anyone else in Jacksonville.

"Why is it you talk so proper?" asked Chris, breaking the silence.

"Excuse me?"

"You don't talk with a heavy southern accent, like most of the people here in Jacksonville."

Hope smiled. "That's because I'm not. I live in Atlanta. I am just down here to visit my grandmother."

"Annie Mae?" questioned Chris. She was not sure if Annie Mae was indeed Hope's grandmother.

"Yep."

"Oh…How is it that you and your grandmother know so much about my mother?"

Hope smiled. "Because your mother usually came down for the Founding Father's Day celebration. We were kind of surprised to hear you were coming in her place this year."

"Oh," Chris replied, once again becoming silent.

It was not until they were almost to Ethel's when Chris asked Hope another question, "What did your grandmother mean by 'I look just like her'?"

"She was referring to the fact you look just like my great aunt Celia."

"Celia?" remarked Chris, in amazement. "That's such a coincidence."

"What is?" replied Hope.

"That your great aunt's name is Celia. My great grandmother was named Celia."

"I know," answered Hope. "They're one in the same person."

Chris stopped dead in her tracks and looked Hope dead in the eyes. "If that was meant to be a joke, it was not funny," she replied.

"It was not meant to be a joke," Hope assured her.

"So, you're trying to tell me, your great aunt is my great grandmother," stated Chris.

"I'm not trying to tell you…I'm simply stating a fact," stated Hope.

Chris could not help but respond with a nervous chuckle. "That is impossible. You're…" replied Chris, her voice suddenly trailing off.

"What…black?" responded Hope, finishing Chris' sentence.

"Well, yeah."

"Don't be ashamed to say it. I'm not," Hope informed her. "Besides, why is it so hard to believe that your great grandmother was possibly black. Is it much easier to conceive that black people has someone white somewhere along their family tree, but it's harder to see it the other way around?" inquired Hope.

"No, I'm not saying that," stated Chris, suddenly feeling she had to defend herself. "What I'm saying is that my great grandmother is white and I am quite sure your great aunt is black. So, you can see that is genetically impossible."

"Is it?" asked Hope, smirking.

"Look, I don't know what happened to me today? Nor do I know how I wound up in your grandmother's house either. But I am starting to believe, you and your family has got a few screws loose," said Chris.

"Well in regards to my family, we have always been a little nutty. However, in regards to what I told you about your great grandmother, I know it's hard to believe but believe me Chris when I tell you it is true. Just ask every black person here in Jacksonville. Better yet, why don't you ask your mother," Hope challenged.

Chris grew silent. She had no idea how a day filled with so much promise had ended up with her listening to a crazy woman claim they were distant cousins. "Look, I know my way to Ethel's from here. I wont need your assistance any further," exclaimed Chris, obviously having taken offense to Hope's remarks.

"Suit yourself," said Hope, watching her go.

CHAPTER 16

▼

That night Chris had a hard time sleeping. What Hope had said had really disturbed her, not to mention the nagging backache that also troubled her throughout the night. The following morning Chris awoke in pain, and feeling ill. She spent the majority of the day milling about Ethel's, mainly sitting on the porch watching the Founding Father's Day pre-celebration preparation. She hoped taking it easy would ease the nausea. The events of the day before had made her a little reluctant to wander off too far from Ethel's. Although, Ethel's house was not home, it was as close as she could come to it in Jacksonville. The last thing she wanted was to blackout and wake up in another stranger's bed again. Although, Ethel had questioned Chris as to why it took her so long to get back to her place after leaving the plantation, Chris refused to tell her the truth. She rightfully could not expect Ethel to believe her story for she was having a hard time believing it herself. Despite, the surreal feeling of the day before, Chris could not shake what Hope had said to her on their way to Ethel's. Her words seemed to eat away at her all day long.

If Chris had known a great deal more about her great grandmother, she might have been able to refute Hope's claims with a little more confidence. Honestly, the only thing she could say about her great grandmother with any great deal of assurance was that she was the only child of her great-great grandfather, Clayton Jackson. Of course, she knew her great grandmother was white because her great-great grandfather, Clayton Jackson, and great-great grandmother, Emma Jackson, were both white. So, being that her great-great grandparents were white there was no question that her great grandmother, Celia, was white. However, Chris did not know much about her great grandmother beyond those facts. Yet, even though she could disprove Hope's claims to her great grandmother's race, Hope had nonetheless sparked a sense of curiosity as to how Hope and Annie Mae even knew about her great grandmother.

By that evening, Chris' curiosity had piqued. She had to find Hope, in hopes of trying to clarify what exactly she meant by implying Chris' great grandmother, Celia, was black. So, about the time the Ferris wheel was complete and going through a few test runs and the kissing booth had opened for business, a line had already gathered of both young and old men willing to pay to kiss one of the town's maiden whom Ethel quickly denounced as the town slut, Chris had decided she must speak with Hope. Of course, Chris knew it could have all been just a joke. Everybody in town knew her family history. The town was named after her family. The Jackson family name was synonymous with the town itself. Still, Chris felt she needed to find Hope and get her to explain just exactly what she meant by her comment the night before.

Chris informed Ethel she was going for a walk, right before dinner. She left the house before Ethel could ask her the inevitable question of "Where she was going?" If Ethel had any idea she was crossing the county road into the "dark-side" of town again especially during dusk, Chris would have been subjugated to a rash of questions. She felt better avoiding the cross examination for the time being. She felt it was best to keep her destination a secret rather than reveal it when she was not prepared to. As she ventured across the county road, a few towns' folk caught a glimpse of her walking up the gravel road towards the plantation in the fading sunlight. Those that saw her did not think much of her evening stroll. They figured she was heading up to the plantation once again.

When Chris had left Annie Mae's the day before it was dark, so, she had no recollection of which house along that lone gravel road was Annie Mae's. Not wanting to embarrass herself by knocking upon the wrong door, Chris stopped a little boy she saw riding his bicycle in the road and asked him, "Excuse me, can you tell me where Annie Mae lives?"

The little boy stared at her in bewilderment and a hint of fear before telling her "Ms. Annie Mae lives two doors down," pointing in the general direction. Before Chris could thank the child for his help, he had scurried off on his bike hollering for his mama, leaving only a dust cloud in his wake. Chris watched as he left in haste, before continuing on towards the house the little boy had pointed out.

As Chris walked up to the front yard of the home, the young boy had claimed to be Annie Mae's, she saw a gentleman sitting on the front porch. Like many of the houses on that side of town, cinder blocks, at each corner of the house made up the home's foundation. Quite different from the homes on the other side of town that at least had a foundation. Not only that, the house appeared to be in desperate need of a paint job. Underneath the home resting in between the crawl space between the earth and the home was a dog. The dog had a yellowish-brown mangy coat caked with dirt. It seemed to be in desperate need of a meal. The dog glanced at Chris for a moment as she drew near, but realized she was not a threat and went back to its nap. Due to the setting sun, Chris found it hard to make out the gentleman sitting on the porch. She was forced to squint in order to tell if he was sipping on a soda bottle. She figured the boy had led her in the wrong direction for she did not recall seeing any gentleman at Annie Mae's house the day before. Still, she was certain if she was at the wrong place, he could send her in the right direction.

"Excuse me, is this Annie Mae's house?" Chris asked.

The man squinted. He was not sure he was not seeing things in the day's fading light. He had sat out on that porch many of times during dusk before and believed the setting sun was playing tricks on his eyes, causing him to see things that were not there. He often thought he saw ghosts trudging back and forth on that gravel road. That path up to the plantation had seen plenty of sorrow and pain over the years, so such visions would not have surprised him. He tended to think of those visions as haunts that found only a brief moment of respite in their pain and suffering in the waning sunlight. However, once he was sure that Chris was an actual person standing there, the gentleman lowered his soda bottle from his lips and stared at her bewilderingly before answering her.

"Dat dere depends on who's askin'?"

"My name is Chrysanthemum Jackson-Adams. I was here yesterday," Chris responded. The man squinted once again, this time putting the soda bottle down next to him on the porch.

"Dere aint no Annie Mae Bedford here," he exclaimed. Suddenly there was hostility in his voice. The fact he gave Annie Mae's last name, let Chris know she was more than likely at the right place.

"Sir, are you sure this is not Annie Mae Bedford's home?" stated Chris.

The gentleman hesitated before getting up and walking over to where Chris stood and sternly saying, "Ya deaf or sumthin'. I says, Annie Mae Bedford does not live heah." He looked Chris dead in the eyes before adding, "Y'all ofays always cumin aroun' heah startin' trouble. Like I says, we don't need wat ya sellin' and we don'ts want wat ya gat'." Upon finishing the statement, he stepped a little closer towards Chris, so he could look down upon her. Although, he was slightly overweight, he still was an imposing figure close up. Yet, despite his attempt to scare her, Chris was not going to be denied entry into that home if it was indeed Annie Mae's. She had walked over there, not to simply be turned back. Chris wanted to see Hope and she refused to leave until she did.

So, Chris asked him once again, "Sir, I have been having a rough day. If you can just direct me to Annie Mae Bedford's home, I will leave you alone. It is important that I see Annie Mae or Hope," said Chris, defiantly. The gentleman stepped even closer, this time breathing right down on top of her. Chris feared he might harm her for not heeding his first warning. She suddenly wondered if trying to find Hope was worth being accosted.

Just when she feared the worse, Chris heard a familiar voice, "Buford, git yar tail in dis haus boy…supper is ready." It was Annie Mae. "I told Hope ya wood be comin' back," Annie Mae yelled, when she noticed Chris standing there. "Buford, I said git on in heah and fix yar plate. Chrysanthemum, ya might as well cum on in heah an' eat too," Annie Mae added, turning around and heading back inside. Buford glared at Chris for a brief moment before doing as he was told. Chris was unsure if she should follow him inside, but after giving it some thought she realized she had nothing to lose by doing so.

Inside Annie Mae and Hope were setting the table. Hope immediately lit up when she saw Chris walk in. "I didn't think I would ever see you again," she said taking her seat at the table.

"If ya wouldn't hav' gone fillin' dis ofay's head up wit talk bout how we're family an all, she'd woodn't be back heah," complained Buford.

"Now Buford dat's enuf!" Annie Mae said, giving him an icy cold glare.

"But Mama!" Buford protested.

"Boy, don't but Mama me! Ya heah me! I says dat iz enuf. Now Chrysanthemum iz family, an ya will treat her as such," insisted Annie Mae.

"Mama dis ofay iz no family of mine. Her so called great-great granddaddy did nuthin for us—"

"Boy did ya heah me!" shouted Annie Mae, cutting him off. "I says she iz family, no matter how many times removed or wat happ'in in da past. Do ya heah me?"

Buford grumbled a reluctant "yeah" under his breath before shoving a fork full of black-eyed peas down his throat. Annie Mae cut her eyes at him one last time, to make sure her point had been made.

"I hope ya like chitterlins wit black-eye peas an' rice fo' supper," said Annie Mae, placing a plate of the delicacy in front of her. Hope could not help but chuckle to herself at Chris' expression when she caught a whiff of her meal.

"Don't worry it takes a little getting use to," Hope teased.

Chris was silent through pretty much most of the dinner. It was hard for her to be very talkative when it was just as hard for her to fathom how she was sitting there eating dinner with a bunch of strangers, who called themselves family. Sure they claimed to be related to her, however, Chris was not sure their claim to being a long lost limb to her ancestral tree was true or some kind of sham. Hope and Annie Mae did most of the talking during dinner, while Buford occasionally snarled at Chris from across the table. Needless to say Chris did not eat much. The sight of pig intestines on her plate was not something she was accustomed to seeing at the dinner table. None of the restaurants Beverly and her frequented, ever served such a meal as the one sitting on Annie Mae's table.

After dinner, Chris felt it was only appropriate that she help Hope and Annie Mae clean up. When they had finished Hope told her, "Come on outside and sit on the porch with me. There is something I want to ask you."

Annie Mae gave Hope one of those icy glares she had reserved for Buford. "Hope Bedford, ya jus' remember wat I told ya?" she admonished.

"I remember Gran," Hope intoned, sounding disappointed Annie Mae had overheard her.

Hope led Chris outside onto the porch where they sat down on the steps. A hint of curiosity ran through Chris as to what it was Annie Mae had exactly forewarned Hope about. After pondering whether she should ask Hope as to what Annie Mae was referring to, Chris decided what was the harm.

"What is it that she told you to remember?" inquired Chris, trying not to pry.

"Oh nothing, she just wants to make sure I don't scare you off again," she stated. "Also, don't pay no mind to Uncle Buford, it's hard for him to let go of the past. It is hard for him to let time heal old wounds."

Now, Chris could not understand why her uncle would have a grudge against her. She had not met him until that day. The only thing she could deduct from her comment was that he was not too kind to strangers or even worse that he was prejudice. Chris considered asking her if that was the case, but decided against it realizing that was a loaded question and there was no telling how it would be received. So, she let it go.

When Chris had told her mother she would attend the Founding Father's Day celebration in her place, she never would have imagined she would be sitting on a porch with people she did not know, who claimed to be her relatives. At the time she left Atlanta, Chris' main goal was to forget about Frank. Up to this point she could say with confidence that she had achieved that goal. The only problem was that she had now replaced concerns about Frank with questions about her lineage. As she sat there with Hope looking into the night sky, Chris could not help but wonder how much of this her mother already knew and why she never bothered to tell her.

"They're beautiful aren't they?" asked Hope, looking up into the sky.

"I'm sorry?" answered Chris, not sure what she was talking about.

"The stars," said Hope, pointing up.

Chris looked up at the shimmering slithers of light. They seemed to sparkle like diamonds. "Yeah, they are beautiful." In the city, the stars never seemed to radiate so bright.

"They contain so many secrets," muttered Hope.

"Like what?"

"You know like…where are they at? Is there life on any of their planets? And do they even still exist? We could just now be seeing a star that had burnt out ages ago…Sometimes, I wonder will we ever be able to fully grasp the stars meaning or their power. It's sort of like our past. We see pictures and hear stories about our ancestors or relatives that came before us, yet, since we were not there, we often find ourselves questioning how much of the stories is fact and how much of it is folklore, passed along from generation to generation. We, also, find ourselves trying to understand just how the events that took place in our past shape our very lives now as well as our future." Chris stared at Hope in bewilderment. She failed to make the connection between family and astrology.

Before Chris could ask Hope to explain, Annie Mae came outside and took a seat in a rocking chair on the porch. She appeared to have a book in her hand. "Hope, go inside an' git a couple of chairs. I want ta show y'all sumthin'," instructed Annie Mae. Hope went inside and brought out two chairs, placing them next to Annie Mae's rocker.

"Cum on up heah an' sit next ta me chile," Annie Mae beckoned to Chris, rocking back and forth. "I want ta show ya sumthin." Chris did as she was told and took a seat next to Annie Mae. Once sitting next to her, Chris could see that she held a photo album in her hand.

"Dere iz a lot of history in dis heah book," said Annie Mae as she opened the photo album.

Annie Mae flipped through the pages, occasionally telling a story or two to go along with a particular picture. All the photos Chris had seen were of people and places she knew nothing about. Hope and Annie Mae mainly discussed the particulars of each photograph amongst themselves. The whole affair of sitting there and listening to them talk made Chris feel uncomfortable, like she was eavesdropping on their most intimate family secrets. That was of course until Chris recognized a familiar face amongst the photos.

"Do ya remember dis day Chrysanthemum?" said Annie Mae, holding a picture up for her to see. "Probably not, it waz such a long time ago. That waz da first and only time yar mother brought ya ta Jacksonville."

Chris stared at the photograph in disbelief. There was no doubt in her mind who that little girl with the pigtails was. Her mother always made her hair up that way, whenever she took class pictures or for special occasions. Chris could point to a half a dozen class photos where her hair was made up in the exact same fashion. It was without a doubt her mother's favorite hairstyle for Chris as a child. However, Chris did not recall ever taking that picture. Yet, there was no doubt in Chris' mind that was her. Besides the recognizable pigtails, Chris bore a huge smile that revealed two missing front teeth. She stood in front of her mother holding another little girl's hand. The little girl was standing in front of a lady as well, which only led Chris to believe that was her mother too.

"I tell ya, when yar mama brought ya over heah fo' da first time Chrysanthemum, ya and Hope took ta each otha like beans and cornbread. Da two of ya jus' ran a aroun' heah causin' trouble fo' folks," spouted Annie Mae, laughing. "It warmed my heart ta see da chirren of Nettie back tagether again." Chris forced a smile on to her face, not knowing who Nettie was or how Annie Mae got that picture. However, what truly baffled her was that she had no recollection of ever taking that picture or that day. Chris could remember the diner and the yellow strip of tape on the floor, but she could not remember standing there and posing for that photo.

Hoping to jog her memory in some way, Chris asked Hope, "That is you?"

"Yep," said Hope, smiling. "I must've been the biggest tomboy in the state of Georgia, at the time."

"Who is that woman standing behind you?"

"That is my mom," replied Hope, in a somber tone.

"If you don't mind me asking, where is she now?" Chris did not immediately pick up on the change in Hope's mood when she answered her. Yet, by the sudden somber looks on both Hope's and Annie Mae's face when Chris inquired as to her whereabouts, it was clear the answer to her question was not good.

"My mom passed away last year of breast cancer," murmured Hope.

"Oh, I'm sorry to hear that." Chris suddenly felt embarrassed for asking such a question.

"Thank you," stated Hope.

"Yeah, my baby gurl, Josephine, haz already gone unto da Lawd," interjected Annie Mae. It was obvious the grief from Hope losing a mother and Annie Mae losing a daughter was still fresh.

The fact that Chris' mother knew Hope's mother, Josephine, and never mentioned it to Chris troubled her. She wondered, why her mother would hide such a thing. If the two of them were indeed friends at the time of the picture and remained friends up until the time of Hope's mother death, it meant they knew each other for over thirty years. That would have made Hope's mother, one of her mother's oldest friends.

It took Annie Mae a moment to regain her composure before continuing to flip through the photo album. She once again began describing people and places Chris knew nothing about. Not until Annie Mae came to the last page of the photo album did she pause for moment and smile, "Heah she iz," she beamed.

The picture on the last page was rather old. It had a sepia-toned look to it, resembling many photographs taken before the 1920s. The woman in the photo stood regally for the camera. She stood there proud, yet, sad. However, the one thing that grabbed Chris' attention was the striking resemblance she shared with the woman in the photo. She had always prided herself on the fullness of her lips and her high cheekbones; these features were the epitome of beauty. As she gazed into that photograph, there was no mistaking whom she had inherited those features from.

"Who is that?" asked Chris in wonderment.

"Dat right dere iz yar great grandma and Hope's great auntie Celia Jackson." Chris recalled seeing a picture similar to that one as a child growing up, her mother use to keep it out in the open around the house until one day it simply disappeared. It had been so long since Chris had feasted her eyes on that photo. She had forgotten what her great grandmother even looked like.

"What do you mean, my great grandmother and Hope's great aunt?" questioned Chris, glancing at Hope then back at the picture. Although the photograph was old, it appeared the woman was white.

"I means exactly dat," Annie Mae assured her. "Ya know dat dere garden ya foun' yesturday?"

"Uh huh," replied Chris, nodding her head.

"Well, yar great grandmother planted dat dere garden a long time ago. Thru da ages, all da descendants of Celia and Nettie tended ta dat garden at one time or another. Right now, it iz my turn ta keeps it up, but I'm certain dere will cum a day either ya or Hope will tend ta dat garden. Dat iz why she founs' ya yesturday, cuz I tolds her ta go look afta da garden fo' me. Dat plot of dirt iz older than all of us put tagether."

"I don't understand," said Chris, confused.

"Yar mama had said da same thang ta me when yar grandma brought her down heah ta see me," replied Annie Mae, with a big smile. "Wat if, I waz ta tell ya dat Celia waz not da only chile of yar great-great grandfather Clayton Jackson?"

"Oh, I would say that it can't be so and that you was a liar."

"Oh, it can be so chile, an' believe me when I tell ya it iz."

"But how?" Chris demanded.

Annie Mae hesitated a moment before telling her, "Well chile, it iz a complicated story an' one dat requires ya ta follow along closely, but I'll take my time tellin' it ta ya, so's ya can understand." Annie Mae paused for a moment to collect her thoughts on how to explain to Chris, how her lineage traced back to a slave named Nettie. Annie Mae knew telling someone white they were related to someone who was black was much more difficult than telling a black person they were related to someone white. For a white person that was traumatic, often a shock to their system. It was usually hard for their mind and soul to digest such information at the same time. So, Annie Mae knew it was a topic to be approached with extreme caution.

"Well, I sees yar mama has not told ya any of dis...probably her way of protectin' ya. It matters no how, cuz wat I'm 'bout ta tell ya iz da truth," stated Annie Mae, looking Chris squarely in the eyes. "Yar great-great granddaddy had several chirren, most of 'em by da slave women he kept. Not ta mention, he had two by Mrs. Emma, Timmy and Jane."

"That is not true, my great grandmother is my great-great grandfather's only child," insisted Chris.

"Ya can call 'em lies all ya want ta chile, but look aroun'...sum of da black folk aroun' here is almost as pale as ya. Now, how can dat be when dere mama an' daddy iz as black as night...I tells ya why...cuz of Clayton Jackson dats why. He liked him sum colored women an' made no bones 'bout it."

"If that is the case, why is it I have never heard of Jane or Timmy?" protested Chris.

"Well, dat iz a little harder ta explain, but I'll do my best...Ya great-great grandma waz not Mrs. Emma, it waz a former slave turned sharecropper afta da Civil War by da name of Nettie. She iz also my grandma an' Hopes great-great grandma. She waz ya great-great grandpa's favorite. Ya knows wat I means when I says favorite, doint ya?" remarked Annie Mae. Chris nodded her head solemnly, stunned by what she was hearing. Her first reaction was to get up and run away, but something inside of her forced her to stay.

"Anywayz, she had two babies by Mista Jackson, Celia an' her older brother Cletus," Annie Mae continued.

"Lies! These are all lies! I will not sit here and listen to this!" proclaimed Chris, refusing to listen any further. For some reason at that point she had heard enough. The thought of her being the great-great granddaughter of a slave, she found to be too hard to grasp. She had listened to their lies long enough. The accusation that her great grandmother was the daughter of a former slave, Chris felt was down right despicable.

Chris got up and stormed off the porch, getting as far as the end of the walkway before Annie Mae shouted, "Stop right dere! Yar goin' ta lissen ta dis cuz ya've gon' long enuff witout it!" Up to that point, Annie Mae had been a pleasant, almost endearing woman. Yet, when Chris turned around to face her, all the pleasantries that had once graced her face were gone. There was now a defiant woman in her place.

Sensing her grandmother's sudden outburst would only push Chris further away, Hope walked over to Chris and pleaded with her, "Please Chris…stay."

"I knows wat I'm tellin' ya iz a jolt ta da system, but I swear ta ya chile, dat it iz da truth. You an' yar ma are family. I would never tell ya anythang like dat, if it waz not true. I know it's hard ta believe, but sumtimes ya hav' ta take wat I call a leap of faith. Now, cum on back up heah an' sit down," urged Annie Mae. Chris looked at Hope then at Annie Mae, before returning to her seat.

Annie Mae smiled, and placed her hand on Chris' knee when she took her seat. "Trus' yar heart chile, it will never steer ya wrong," Annie Mae told her. Annie Mae had not said anything insightful. It was just that she was capable of saying the right thing that had a soothing effect.

"Now becuz she waz da massa's favorite," Annie Mae continued. "Nettie was shunned by da other Negroes. She was called da massa's whore. No colored man fo' miles aroun' would even look at her, cuz she rather bed down wit da massa than one of her own kind. Her cabin use ta be in yonder field were ya foun' da garden. Dere cabin waz burnt down, but dat's getting' ahead of myself.

"Ya know when da Civil War came yar great-great grandfather went off ta fight da North. Many of da Negro, men, women and chirren who worked out in dem dere fields, picked up an ran fo' dere freedom like da sun chasin' da moon across da sky. A lot of dem had no idea were dey waz goin', but dey knew dey had a chance ta be free, 'cept fo' Nettie. Nettie refused ta believe any army filled wit a bunch of ignorant colored folk waz goin' ta whip da South, but dey did.

"Now, ya can figure da sentiment tawards black folk at da time down heah waz down right nasty. Black folk were takin' office, while da South stayed up under da Union's boot. Dere were sheets runnin' wild jus' a lynchin', beatin' an' rapin' black folk. An' thoz who went off ta fight, like yar great-great granddaddy, Mista Jackson, came back home wit nuttin but dere dignity. Yar great-great granddaddy's ego wood be hurt further, when he foun' out Miss Emma waz da mistress ta a Yankee general in order ta spare her family wat little yar great-great grandpa had left. Befo' yar great-great grandpa made it back home from da war, she bore dat general a chile, but story haz it she took it in da woodz one day an' came back empty handed. No one ever 'new wat happened ta dat chile nor asked.

"See, back in dose dayz white folk down heah hated da Yankees more than dey hated black folk, an' fo' a Southerner ta be a Yankee's mistress waz worse than hav'in a Negro's baby…No how, other than his home, Mista Jackson had nuttin'; no slaves and no cotton ta pick. Wat the North could not steal, dey destroyed. All he had left waz Nettie an' a few other Negros who didn't or couldn't runaway. An' in all dis mess Nettie's boy, Cletus, began makin' trouble an' drawin' da attention of da wrong kinda folks. If ya know wats I mean?"

"Why?" Chris questioned.

"Let's jus' say Cletus waz doin' thangs not looked upon too favorably by da town's white folks. An' sum of the town's folk let Mista Jackson know 'bout it. Yar great-great grandpa tried his bes' ta control da boy, but he jus' couldn't. Cletus waz wat ya called a free spirit. Nobody could control dat boy, not even Nettie. So, da Klan took it upon demselves to put Cletus in his place. So, in yonder field where Hope foun' ya at yesterday, dey burnt down Nettie's home and hung Cletus, he waz only ten years old. Dis sent my grandma Nettie, inta a bout of despair equaled ta none otha, on account of Cletus bein' her favorite. She swore Gawd waz goin' ta punish those dat done dat ta her boy.

"Da next year while Nettie waz still in mournin' over Cletus' death, a plague swept through town killin' many of da town's chirren. Celia waz spared. Unfortunately, Timmy an' Jane, yar great-great grandpa's an' Emma's two chirren, were not. Afta dat, dey tried ta hav' other chirren but couldn't. Many of people back den believe she waz cursed fo' wat she had dun ta dat Union general's baby. So, feelin sum guilt over wat happened ta Cletus an' da fact that his blood did course thru Celia's veins, yar great-great grandpa, Clayton Jackson, an' Emma decided ta take Celia in as dere own. At dat time my grandma, Nettie, waz still hurtin' over Cletus an' had been neglectin' Celia fo' sum time.

"It took Nettie a while, but she waz able ta git over her grief. She waz even able ta love again. She fell in love wit my grandpa, Jessup P. Bedford. An' from dere union dey had twelve chirren, one of 'em bein' my daddy Esque Bedford. Nettie often thought 'bout getting' Celia back, but decided ta let her be where she waz, when she realized Celia waz livin' a life she could never provide fo' her. Although, she missed her daughter terribly, she wanted her ta hav' da finer thangs in life she 'new she could not giv' her. So, she let her stay wit da Jacksons, settlin' fo' an occasional visit heah an' dere." Annie Mae paused for a moment to let her words sink in.

"Celia grew up simila ta any otha white chile. Her skin waz almost as fair as yars, so, she could easily pass fo' white. She went ta all da white schools, attended white folks parties, an eventually married a white man. Otha than da Jacksons, who loved her as dere own, most of da folks aroun' dese heah parts thought she waz white. I'm certain dat afta a while, even she believed she waz white and dat is how she lived her life—a black woman masquerading as a white woman."

Chris was silent. She tried her best to believe such a farfetched story. Nonetheless, if what Annie Mae said had just a hint of truth to it, Chris could not fathom the implications of what it meant to her.

Annie Mae saw the dazed look on Chris' face and told her, "Take yar time chile an' lit it sink in slowly."

The only response Chris could mutter was, "It's late I need to be going." Of course, Chris could have stood up and screamed liar once more, but she decided it was best to say nothing at all and simply leave.

Annie Mae looked at Chris somewhat perplexed, before glancing over at Hope who suggested, "Why don't you stay the night here. I can sleep on the couch in the living room and you can stay in the spare bedroom." Chris thought about it for a moment. It was late and she was not feeling so good. She did not know if she became sick from Annie Mae's cooking or from her story.

"That is fine," uttered Chris, walking inside without saying word. Hope and Annie Mae both watched as Chris wandered inside the house and into the bedroom she had occupied the day before.

CHAPTER 17

▼

Once again Chris found it hard to sleep. The tale Annie Mae had spun for her the night before had left her in a daze. What was she suppose to think? What was she suppose to believe? Everything she knew, everything she believed in had been turned upside down...placed in doubt.

She could not help but wonder, 'What if Annie Mae was telling the truth?'

By uncovering such a family secret, Chris could not help but question every facet of her life. As she lay there on the cot, she ran through her childhood memories, memories she had of growing up, trying to figure out if she remembered anything out of the ordinary. Anything she may have purposefully forgot. As far as she knew, nothing stuck out in her mind as unusual. Of course, she knew she could have dismissed everything that Annie Mae had said as hearsay, but that was hard to do when it was obvious some of it was indeed true. Chris wanted so desperately to dismiss here stories as lies, but she couldn't. Besides, what did Annie Mae have to gain by lying to her?

Chris got out of bed sore. The coils of the mattress could easily be felt through the fabric not to mention a few had even broken through and scratched her in several places. It didn't surprise her after what she had ate the night before that she felt ill. She could hear someone milling about the house as she struggled to her feet. She quietly got dressed before walking out into the living room to find Hope making up her make shift bed on the couch.

"Good morning," said Hope, noticing Chris standing there.

"Morning," muttered Chris.

"And how did you sleep last night?"

"Fine," Chris lied.

"Good, that's good to hear. I know that bed can be a monster to sleep on at times. Sometimes, I wonder if I just might be better off sleeping on the floor," professed Hope with a grin. Chris could not have agreed with her more.

Chris spied the suitcase by the door and asked, "Are you leaving?"

"Yeah, I'm going to head on back up to Atlanta. I want to spend sometime with my boys. Their dad has had them long enough. Besides, I miss them."

"I think, I need to be heading back over to Ethel's myself, so I can change out of these clothes," added Chris.

"That's right today is the Founding Father's Day parade. Well, I need to give you my phone number and address back home, so we can stay in touch. Maybe, we can get together and have lunch or something," Hope insisted.

"That sounds nice."

Just then Annie Mae walked into the living room complaining. She had an empty carton of eggs in her hand and it was obvious her anger stemmed from a lack of eggs. She quickly noticed Chris standing there and said, "Good mornin' baby. How did ya sleep?"

"Okay." Chris figured she might as well continue the lie since she had started it with Hope.

"Good...I know dat old bed can be tuff on a body," Annie Mae proclaimed. "Dere haz been plenty of mornin's, when dat damn bed dab near put me in traction." Chris wondered why, if everybody knew the bed was no good did they let her sleep on it.

"I waz goin' ta cook us breakfast dis mornin', but it appears Buford ate up all da damn eggs an' put da empty egg carton back in da refrigerator... Buford!...Buford! Ya heah me callin' ya boy." Since the brief time she had known Annie Mae, Chris had never heard her curse. So, to hear damn come out of her mouth twice was a total surprise.

"Yeah Mama," said Buford, making his way into the living room.

"Boy, did ya eat all da eggs?" demanded Annie Mae.

"Yeah, I had myself an egg sandwich yesturday."

"Boy, now wat am I goin' ta hav' ta go wit des heah grits, I already started cookin'. I wanted ta make breakfast dis mornin' fo' Hope befo' she gits on da road, an' Chris befo' she head back over ta Ethel's house." Buford glanced over at Chris and rolled his eyes.

"Ya shouldn't be worrin' 'bout dis ofay no how," he huffed.

"It's all right Gran, I'll get something to eat along the way," Hope told her.

"Dat is no way ta start yar day off gurl," exclaimed Annie Mae.

"I will be all right Gran."

"Yeah, don't worry about me either Annie Mae. I can get something to eat at the diner," added Chris. Besides, she didn't want to take the chance of eating something else that would only upset her stomach further.

"Well, it looks like we're goin' ta hav' ta eat at da diner too. Since we don't hav' no eggs," snapped Annie Mae, glaring over at Buford. "Dey don't know how ta fry no eggs down dere. I always tell 'em I want my eggs scrambled hard, an' dey always bring 'em back ta me runny," she complained, grabbing her purse.

"Well den we don't hav' ta eat dere. I don't know why black folk go in dere any way. Everybody knows Old Man Cooper had sumthang ta do wit Delilah's place burnin' down."

"Now Buford, ya know dere aint no truth ta dat," stated Annie Mae.

"Wat do ya need Mama, Old Man Cooper holdin' da match. He let it be known he didn't want no competition in town, especially from black folk."

"Well, if ya woodn't hav' ate all da eggs we wood not be goin down ta da diner ta eat breakfast, now wood we." Buford decided to wisely keep his mouth shut. It was humorous to Chris how Annie Mae treated Buford as if he was an adolescent. Chris assumed Buford had to be in his late forties to early fifties. Chris took Burford's inability to respond as her cue to leave. She had already seen him humbled before and did not care to see him humbled again. "Well, maybe I'll see you guys down at the diner?" Chris said, walking towards the door.

"A'right chile. I cant's go no where till I find my shoes," said Annie Mae, in disgust.

"I'll leave my phone number and address with Gran," Hope informed Chris as she made her way out the door.

"That would be great," replied Chris. She wasn't sure she really wanted Hope's phone number or address at all.

The walk back to Ethel's place seemed longer than usual that particular morning. Chris didn't know if it was because she didn't feel well or because the walk was even worse on her back. Despite the pain, Chris made it back without much trouble. She was surprised to find the truck the mayor had informed her was the grand marshal's vehicle parked outside. If Hope had not reminded her about the parade that afternoon she would have totally forgotten.

"Dear Lawd, dere ya are! We were worried sick 'bout ya," exclaimed Ethel, greeting Chris at the door.

"I'm glad ya showed up. I waz 'bout ta send out a search party ta find ya," the mayor exclaimed, walking up to greet her as well. "Ya know we gat da parade tuday?"

"I know...I'm fine. I just stayed over at a friend's house for the night," explained Chris.

"A friend's house? Here in Jacksonville?" the mayor said, giving Ethel a suspicious glance. Ethel could only respond with a shrug of her shoulders.

"Yeah, a friend," reiterated Chris.

"Well, it doesn't matter, yar okay. We jus' couldn't 'elp but not git worried, when sumone named Beverly called from Atlanta, tellin' us ta tell ya to call home as soon as possible. She said it waz a emergency," Ethel informed her.

"She said it was an emergency?" said Chris panicking. The first thought that crossed her mind when she heard the word 'emergency' was her mother.

"She sure did," answered Ethel. By the time Ethel had finished her sentence, Chris was already up the stairs to retrieve her cell phone.

*   *   *   *

The good news was that her mother was fine. The bad news was that Frank had broken into the house and ransacked the place. Thus, bringing her stay in Jacksonville to an abrupt end. She also surrendered what little of Annie Mae's dinner she had ate of black-eyed peas and chitterlings into Ethel's toilet. Although it was quite painful, she did feel much better in the end not to mention hungry. Chris liked to think, she got sick at the thought of Frank.

Both the mayor and Ethel were disappointed to hear she had to go, but they understood. She had more pressing needs back home that required her attention. The mayor took the news in good spirits. He claimed he could find someone else to be the grand marshal, which made Chris feel a little better leaving on such short notice. However, there was still one last thing, Chris needed to do before leaving. Since Ethel was the oldest person in town, Chris figured she would be the best person to ask a question that nagged her since last night.

"Ethel, may I ask you something?" inquired Chris, putting her suitcase in the car.

"Sure wat iz it?" Ethel replied.

"Was there ever a plague in Jacksonville?" she asked.

"Not dat I know of. Who told ya dat? Have ya been talkin' ta Annie Mae Bedford? Did Annie Mae Bedford tell ya dat?" she quizzed. Chris did not answer. "Lissen ta me. I don't know why yar ma an' ya are so bent on lissenin' ta anything dat old coon has ta say becuz she iz plum crazy. Plum crazy! Do ya heah me!" fumed Ethel. Chris could tell by her response, that she did not care too much for Annie Mae.

"Thank you," said Chris, getting into the car.

After getting rid of last night's dinner, Chris was starving. So, she decided to stop by the diner and grab something to eat before getting on the road after all. When Chris walked inside, she spotted Annie Mae and Buford sitting in the back, near the kitchen. She put her order in at the counter with the waitress and walked back to join them. Of course, she could've just ignored them like everyone else, but that would have been rude especially after staying the night at their home. Still, Chris had no idea how much trouble she would cause simply by crossing that weathered yellow line.

"Is it all right if I join you guys?" asked Chris.

"Hell no ya cain't join us! Ya aint doin' nuttin but bringing us trouble!" exclaimed Buford. He quickly noticed the unwanted glares they were receiving by Chris venturing over the yellow line.

By the way Annie Mae whacked him upside the back of the head over that comment, it was obvious she was still sore at him over the eggs. "Boy, how many times do I hav' ta tell ya, Chrysanthemum is family!" Annie Mae scolded. "Chrysanthemum go right ahead an' sit down gurl. An' Buford, ya need ta jus' keep yar mouth shut. Ya keep talkin' like dat an hell is exactly were ya will be goin'." Chris could not help but smirk from the chastising Annie Mae delivered.

"Oh befo' I fo'git, Hope gave me dis heah letter ta give ta ya," Annie Mae said, reaching into her purse and producing an envelope. Chris opened the envelope and pulled the letter out to read, when the waitress interrupted her to inform her that her breakfast was ready.

"Yar breakfast iz dun," she said, standing there.

"Thank you…Where is it?" inquired Chris, noticing she stood there empty handed.

"It'z at da counter," she said, pointing towards her plate. Chris turned to see her plate resting on the counter.

"Can you bring it over here? I decided I'm going to eat here." It had not dawned on Chris until the waitress did not move that she had broken one of Jacksonville's cardinal rules. She had crossed the color line. Chris glanced over at Annie Mae, who seemed to have understood the seriousness of the situation. Chris knew that if she went back to the counter, it would not only be an insult to Annie Mae and Buford, but acknowledgement of the underlying rule of separate but equal that still permeated through Jacksonville.

Sensing the predicament Chris was in, Annie Mae told her, "Go on chile, it aint no big thang." But to Chris it was a big deal. She could not insult a woman who had for the pass two days treated her like family. It would be wrong for her to take that seat at the counter and Chris knew it.

So, she turned to the waitress and said, "I'm going to eat my meal right here, thank you."

The waitress looked over at Annie Mae and then at Buford before sneering at Chris and giving her a crass, "Suit yourself," and storming off. She retrieved Chris' plate and nonchalantly tossed it in front of her, along with the tab. It seemed that her money was all of a sudden good there. Not wanting to make a scene, Chris paid her no mind. Feeling the situation had been defused; Chris returned her attention back to Hope's letter.

Dear Chris,

Ever since the day I met you and we played together as kids, I knew we shared a special bond. I know this may sound strange, since up until this weekend I was a total stranger to you. I have always believed we shared in a "gift". Unfortunately, I was unable to determine if such a gift still dwells among us while I was here in Jacksonville. Nonetheless, I was glad to have seen you once again. I hope we can keep in touch when you get back to Atlanta.

Hope
404-555-1671 (h)
404-555-3419 (w)

P.S. Please, don't mention the "gift" to Gran. Although, she is blessed with it herself, she refuses to talk about it.

'Gift? What gift?' Chris wondered.

"What did she say?" questioned Annie Mae, curious to know what Hope had written.

"Oh, nothing…She just gave me the phone numbers of where I can reach her, when I get back to Atlanta," said Chris, rushing to put the letter in her back pocket. She did not want to give Annie Mae the chance to ask to read it. Although she did not know what the "gift" was, she was nonetheless going to honor Hope's request to keep it a secret.

"Wow, I'm starving. I hope you don't mind if I dig in?" commented Chris, stabbing at her eggs with her fork. The sooner she could get past the subject of Hope's letter the better.

"Go on ahead…Da sooner yar done, da sooner ya can git out of my face," insisted Buford.

"Boy, if ya don't shut up," Annie Mae threatened.

As they ate, Annie Mae and Chris preoccupied themselves with idle chatter. Chris informed her that she was heading back home. However, she neglected to tell Annie Mae the reason why. Although, she was beginning to feel comfortable enough around them to eat without feeling uneasy, Chris still did not feel comfortable sharing her personal life with them. Annie Mae was disappointed by Chris' announcement, but she understood. When they had finished their breakfast and paid the waitress, it indubitably came time to say their good-byes.

"I should get going, so I can get into Atlanta at a decent hour," proclaimed Chris, getting up from the table.

"Yeah, we need ta git goin' too. Although, I needs ta stop by da store an git sum eggs first," said Annie Mae, giving Buford the evil eye.

Annie Mae got up to leave, instinctively heading towards the backdoor out of habit. Before she could get to the kitchen, Chris grabbed her by the hand and informed her, "My car is out front. I would like it if you saw me off." Chris figured since she had already broken one of Jacksonville's unwritten rules, it was time for Annie Mae to break another.

"I can meet ya out front," said Annie Mae, trying to make her way to the kitchen. It was to no avail, Chris' grip was tight and she was already leading her over the yellow tape.

"Come on its quicker if we just go out the front," stated Chris, dragging her along. Of course, such a thing as Annie Mae and Buford walking out the front door of a diner would not have garnered any attention anywhere else. However this was Jacksonville, and the shock and fear of just what that meant was written all over Annie Mae's face and the faces of the people inside the diner.

"I've been tryin' ta git her ta walk out da front door fo' years!" shouted Buford, once they were outside. "Dere waz no need fo' her ta be walkin' out da back like she waz da 'elp or sumthang."

"Hush boy, sumtimes ole habits iz hard ta break. Besides, I didn't want any trouble," insisted Annie Mae.

"Well, we gat dat," exclaimed Buford, laughing at the countless faces pressed up against the diner's glass window.

Annie Mae just smiled, before turning to give Chris a hug, "Ya drive home safely ya heah. An' tell ya mama I said 'hi'."

"I will do that," said Chris, fighting back the tears. She could not explain why she had become so emotional. She had only known Annie Mae for a short period of time, and in that short period of time she had told her a story that Chris figured did not contain one ounce of truth. Yet, deep down, Chris felt a bond with this woman. There was something that made her feel like they shared something special. Chris could truly say she was glad Annie Mae had come into her life.

"Oh chile, dere is no need fo' all dat. Ya cum on back down heah soon an' see yar Auntie Annie Mae," stated Annie Mae, wiping away a few tears of her own.

"I'll do that," sniffled Chris.

Before turning to say good-bye to Buford, Chris heard a tuba blow down the county road. She glanced up the road to see a local high school marching band practicing for the parade. People were mingling in the street, trying to make sure they found a good spot to watch the parade. Children smiled and begged their mothers for cotton candy or a last minute ride on the Spider, before they would be forced to sit still and watch the grand marshal drive by in an antique '57 Ford pickup. Chris was kind of sadden by the fact she was going to miss the festivities, and even contemplated staying. Unfortunately, she had a mess at home she needed to clean up, and as always it centered around Frank.

As she got into the car she looked over at Buford and told him, "Buford ya take care of Annie Mae for me."

He nodded his head and told her, "I gat dat covered. Ya jus' drive safely." Chris couldn't believe it, but it appeared she had won over Uncle Buford.

CHAPTER 18

▼

The drive back to Atlanta was a stark contrast to the drive to Jacksonville. The drive to Jacksonville felt rejuvenating while her trek back to Atlanta felt repressive. She felt like she was being smothered. She had expected such feelings to accompany her back home. However, she was unprepared for her other travel companion who had decided to join her on her return trip. Her memories. With so much time on her hands to think, Chris was able to unlock a door in her mind, which housed memories she had repressed for years. It was during this time of self-reflection; this sea of memories came rushing in. She remembered how her father, forbid her to ever mention Jacksonville again. How he refused to allow Chris to accompany her mother on subsequent trips to the town. Chris even recalled how her father had threatened to burn her mother's Jackson Family album, and how her mother hid it to avoid his wraith. It became painfully clear to Chris, why she did not remember ever meeting Annie Mae or Hope…She was conditioned not to.

Although Chris was in a rush to get home and survey the damage Frank had left behind, she was more concerned with getting the answers to the sudden deluge of questions that filled her head. She knew there was only one person who could answer her questions…her mother. So, Chris bypassed going home and instead headed straight to her mother's house.

Upon pulling into her mother's driveway, Chris noticed her car was gone. Fortunately for her, she had a spare key. Inside a sole light in the kitchen, illuminated the home. There was a deafening silence about the place that made her feel uneasy. She was there to unearth ghosts from the past, buried for so many years by hatred and shame. Since her mother was gone, Chris took it upon herself to find the answers to the questions that now plagued her.

Chris went into the living room where she was greeted by the stale smell of cigars, permanently baked into the furniture. It had been so long since she had been in the living room; she had forgotten the wretched stench cigars left behind. It was her father's undying love for cigars, which led to the throat cancer that eventually killed him. The walls in the living room were adorned with countless photos of her father fraternizing with local politicians. Still, there was not one black face among them. Out of the numerous photographs cluttered along the mantel none of them resembled Anne Mae or Hope. Most of the photographs were of Chris, her mother and father as well as her grandmother, from her father's side of the family. There were pictures of aunts and uncles that Chris may have seen only once or twice in her life or just around the holidays. The thing about it that did not strike her as peculiar until that very moment was that all her relatives in the photos was from her dad's side of the family. There was not one photograph of any of her mother's relatives, not even her mother's father or mother. The more Chris thought about it the more she realized, other than her grandmother and grandfather, Chris had never met anyone else from her mother's side of the family, except during that one trip to Jacksonville. Of course, Chris now knew why her father had so much disdain for her mother's parents and why there were no pictures of aunts and uncles from her mother's side of the family scattered throughout the house.

Growing up Chris used to think of the attic as a place where things went when they were no longer welcomed. It was a place where undesirable items went only to later be thrown out with the trash, or given to someone considered less fortunate. As an adult Chris could not believe, how much truth could be derived from a little girl's childhood imagination. A sense of anticipation overwhelmed her as she walked up the steps to the attic door. An un-abating sense of uncertainty at what may lie behind the door greeted her as she reached for the doorknob. She stood there for what seemed like an eternity with the doorknob in her hand, contemplating whether she should open the door or run. When she finally did open the door, the smell of stale air and memories long forgotten welcomed her.

Chris turned on the lights and slowly walked up the steps to see a slew of boxes strewn about the room. There was an antique sewing machine shrouded in dust in the far corner, along with a box labeled Christmas. However, what Chris came looking for sat in the middle of the room in plain view. It seemed to have been waiting for the day, when she would come seeking to know the truth. In bold red letters written on its sides the words "pictures" were inscribed. The bright red handwriting, along with the huge block letters called out to her like a neon sign.

Chris walked over to the box and stared at it for a moment, still, unsure if she wanted to go through with it. Yet, after calming her fears and getting over her initial reaction to turn and leave, Chris emptied the box's contents on to the floor. A bounty of pictures spilled forth. There were baby pictures, pictures of family vacations, and more pictures of uncles and aunts. There were even pictures of her with old childhood friends. However, all those photos were irrelevant when it came to her mother's revered Jackson Family photo album. As a child growing up, the Jackson Family photo album use to be more prevalent about the house, her mom use to place it out on the coffee table for everyone to see. It was after the family trip to Jacksonville, when the photo album mysteriously disappeared. No one ever asked about it or seemed to care what happened to it after they returned home from Jacksonville that year, almost thirty years ago.

The photo album had collected an ample amount of dust and the pages had turned a tarnished yellow from the passing of time. Inside the album, there were photos of her great-great grandfather, Clayton Jackson, wearing his Confederate uniform in front of the mansion in Jacksonville. Judging by the sense of pride displayed on his face, Chris assumed that particular picture had been taken prior to him enduring the ravages of war. A picture of her great-great grandmother, Emma Jackson, in the parlor of their home graced the opposite page. However, there were no pictures of Celia, Annie Mae or Hope.

Chris traversed the pages of the book, frantically searching for any photo that resembled one of the photos she had seen at Annie Mae's. She had thumbed through the entire book, without finding one picture of Annie Mae, Hope or Celia. Instead most of the books pages were blank. However, fate would have it, a lone picture slipped out of a sleeve in the cover. It was a picture of her and Hope in front of Annie Mae's house in Jacksonville. It was almost identical to the one Annie Mae had shown her in Jacksonville. As she searched the hidden pocket further, she found dozens of pictures tucked away. There was a picture of what appeared to be a much younger Annie Mae, a picture of Josephine with her mother, but most important of all, there was a picture of Celia. It was the same photo Annie Mae had shown her. Chris paused for a moment, realizing that everything Annie Mae had said; every date, every face and every story behind them were indeed true. All those unidentifiable faces in Annie Mae's photo album undeniably shared with Chris one common bond, blood.

Chris continued to rummage through the photo album, hoping to find more photographs. Her search produced more photos of people she did not know, but recognized from Annie Mae's photo album. There were more photos of her mother and Hope's mother, Josephine. There was a picture of her grandmother from her mother's side of the family sitting on a porch with Annie Mae and plenty of people Chris did not know. She was devastated. Chris now had a past she knew nothing about as well as a past she grew up knowing suddenly shrouded in doubt.

"I see you met Annie Mae," Agatha said, standing behind her daughter. Startled, Chris turned around to find her mother standing at the top of the steps. "I didn't mean to startle you, dear. I was worried about you after I got a call from the mayor saying you had left town in a hurry. I called Beverly, and she informed me of what happened at the house," Agatha said, walking over to where her daughter sat. "By the way your place is a mess," she added.

"Why didn't you ever tell me?" Chris asked. She could feel the tears swelling in her eyes.

Agatha sighed. "I did but you were too young to remember. And when I did want to tell you, your father forbid me to." Her mother sat down on the floor next to her. "I guess, when I asked you to go to Jacksonville, I secretly wished that you would bump into Annie Mae, so, I could stop feeling ashamed for neglecting to tell you the truth myself."

"It was Dad wasn't it? I remember coming home from Jacksonville and Daddy telling me, I was not related to 'no niggers'. He forbid anyone in the house from even speaking about Jacksonville," Chris exclaimed.

"That was the first time, I took you and your father with me to Jacksonville. I felt like I could no longer hide my past from your father. I felt it was time he knew. At that time, I had gotten tired of hiding it from him."

"That was the reason Daddy never went with you to Jacksonville again...Isn't it?"

"Yes, it is darling."

"It is also the reason, why he pounded it into my head that I was not related to nobody black and how I was never ever to speak of Jacksonville?"

"Yeah...Your father refused to have his little girl associating with anybody black. The funny thing about it was here he was lying in bed with a woman who was the descendant of a black woman."

"That is why Dad had an affair isn't it?" questioned Chris.

"I guess you can say that partially had something to do with it. Like I tell you, life is much more complicated than you think," her mother sighed. "You got to understand Chris, your father was born and raised in a different time and era. There was not all this supposed, political correctness that is going around now.

He grew up in a time when things were very much black and white. There were no shades of gray."

"But if he hated the fact some of our relatives were black that much, why did you stay with him?"

"Because I loved him Chris, and it was quite clear to me he loved me too. He could of left me if he wanted to, but he didn't…He stayed. Your father was nothing more than a man torn between the way he grew up learning the way things were supposed to be and his love for us. Despite the fact he was married to a woman who was related to individuals who happened to be black, your father chose to stay. He chose love above all else. See, in the end Chris, it did not matter what color people were in my family; our love was what mattered the most.

"I can understand, how finding out your wife was related to someone black could've been a surprise to him. In all honesty, it was just as much a shock to me when I was finally told the truth. I was raised white. I went to an all white private high school. All of my close friends were white. I am, by all standards white. When your grandmother revealed our past to me, I did not believe her. To me, she was playing some cruel and inhumane joke. I was in my mid-twenties at the time for God's sake, when she decided it was time to tell me. But, I managed to live with it and over time embrace it for what it was…my past, my history. Regardless, if I wanted to or not it is who I am.

"Of course, I could have continued on with my life like nothing had changed, keeping my family background a secret for the rest of my life. But I decided I did not want to live that way. I was not going to live in misery, trying to hide a secret or fear that someone might find out. I chose to not live like your great grandmother Celia, because not only was it a disservice to me but our family as well. Besides, when I thought about it, I had nothing to be ashamed of because this is who I am. It took me sometime to reach that point of acceptance, but eventually I got there…Just as you will."

There was a brief moment of silence between the two of them, while Chris stared at the photo of her great grandmother. Chris could sense the world changing, shifting, around her. Her mother did not intend for things to change. The world simply felt different, like she had taken off the shades that blinded her. It was inevitable after making such a discovery.

"Did you know Hope's mother, Josephine, passed away last year?" Chris sniffled, breaking the silence.

"Yes, I attended the service. Josephine was a dear friend of mine. She was my best friend. I loved her dearly."

"Why, I never heard you speak of her until now?"

"Because, I chose to respect your father's wishes."

"Even in death?" questioned Chris, tears streaming down her cheeks.

"By the time of your father's death, it had became hard for me to say anything, I feared how you might react." Chris could understand her decision in not doing so. She still wished, her mother had told her the truth. It would have allowed her to avoid the shock she experienced in meeting Annie Mae and Hope in Jacksonville.

"Her daughter, Hope, wants me to call her, so we could possibly get together," said Chris, wiping her eyes.

"Why don't you?"

"I don't know," said Chris, shrugging her shoulders.

"I think it would be good for you. You two were like kindred spirits the first time you met."

"Yeah, I heard."

"She is a beautiful person inside and out, Chrysanthemum. You should really make an effort to get to know her. Give her a chance."

Agatha got up from the floor and walked over to the stairs. "I'm going to go downstairs and make some coffee, do you want a cup?"

"Sure," responded Chris. Before her mother could get away, Chris had one last nagging question to ask her, "Do you know what the 'gift' is?"

Just the mentioning of the word "gift" stopped Agatha in her tracks. However, she chose to answer Chris' question with a question of her own. "No, what is it?"

"I don't know. I thought you might know. Hope, mentioned it to me in a letter she gave to Annie Mae to pass along to me."

"I'm sorry, but I don't have a clue as to what she's talking about. That sounds like a good reason why you should call her up to me," said Agatha, heading down the steps.

"Do you mind if I keep this?" yelled Chris, holding up the picture of Celia.

"It's yours to keep," her mother replied, with a smile.

As her mother went downstairs to brew them a fresh pot of coffee, Chris could not help but marvel at how over the course of a day, one's life could change so drastically.

CHAPTER 19

▼

With Beverly and her mother's help, Chris was able to clean up the mess Frank had left behind with little hassle. It took them the entire day, but they managed to get it done quite efficiently. Without their help it probably would have taken her, a week to get the house back in order. The police came by and took down the necessary information as well as brush for fingerprints. It was not like they had to; Chris could have easily pointed them to the culprit. Regardless of Chris' insistence that it was Frank, the police officers still had to follow procedure. By the end of the day everybody was too exhausted from cleaning to do much of anything else, so they made plans to get together for dinner the following evening. The remainder of that evening, Chris simply sat in front of the television after scheduling an appointment with the doctor for the following morning to find out just exactly what was ailing her.

Around ten o'clock there came a knock at the door. Chris contemplated not answering it, since she had already turned in for the night. It became painfully obvious by the persistent knocking whomever it was at the door was not going to simply go away. So, Chris reluctantly got up off the couch and stumbled to the front door. She unwittingly opened the door without first checking to see who was paying her a visit...a big mistake. Frank immediately barged in as soon as the door had been cracked wide enough for him to slip in.

"Where in the hell were you at the night before last?" he shouted, stumbling inside. "Huh, where were you?" he yelled again. He reeked of alcohol.

"That is none of your damn business Frank. Now, will you please get out of here? I am not in the mood for your shit tonight. I'm tired, I'm not feeling well and I don't want to be bothered with you."

"I'm not going anywhere till you tell me, where the hell you were!...What? Do you have another man in here?" he roared.

"Frank, that really is none of your business. I can't believe you would even have the audacity to ask me such a question? You really got some nerve."

"Where is he at? Huh?...Upstairs?...He's upstairs isn't he? The bastard's upstairs!" yelled Frank, charging up the steps. It did not matter, what Chris said; he was determined to find out for himself. His preoccupation with another man taking his place and the alcohol had dramatically impaired his judgment.

Chris gave up trying to reason with him, she knew it was a waste of time. So, she decided to let him parade around the house until he got exhausted. He was drunk and didn't intend on listening to reason. Chris sat down on the couch, and lit up a cigarette. She took a long drag, while she listened to Frank stomp around upstairs searching for her imaginary lover. The last time she had smoked a cigarette was the first time she caught Frank cheating on her. Chris only smoked when she felt stressed. It often managed to relax her nerves. With the revelations of the past week, Chris felt she was overdue for a good smoke. However, this time around the cigarette did more in regards of making her nauseous, than releasing pent up frustration.

"What the hell are you doing? You smoke now!" bellowed Frank stumbling down the steps.

Chris put the cigarette out, before getting up and walking over to the door. "Believe me Frank, there is a lot of things about me you don't know. Now, if you're done ransacking the house for the second time. I think it is time for you to leave. If you refuse I'm sure the police, who now have your fingerprints on file, will be more than happy to ask you a few questions about what happened to the house over the weekend. Since I called them while you were upstairs." Chris gave him a sinister grin before conveniently opening the door for him to leave.

"Like hell you called the police?" His uncertainty as to whether to believe her or not caused him to phrase his statement more like a question.

"Suit yourself. Just don't say I did not warn you," she warned. She calmly stepped away from the door and sat back down on the couch.

Chris could tell he was debating on whether to call her bluff or not, before deciding it was best to not take any chances. "I can't believe what has become of you!"

"You know Frank, I could really care less if I disappoint you, because you are no one I want to impress."

"Fucking smart ass," he groaned, stumbling out the front door and down the steps.

"Save the pleasantries for your mistress," shouted Chris.

"Fucking bitch!" he retorted.

"No, fuck you Frank! Fuck you!" screamed Chris, slamming the door shut.

CHAPTER 20

▼

Chris could have done without Frank coming over late in the night like that. It seemed to only aggravate her condition. Still, regardless of everything else the doctor did not tell Chris anything new the following morning pertaining to her mysterious illness. After running a battery of test, he informed her she had nothing more than the stomach flu. A conclusion she had pretty much surmised before arriving. The doctor gave her the customary flu prescription of rest, fluids and an over the counter medication before sending her on her way. However, before sending her out the door, he assured her he would contact her if anything unusual showed up in her test. He simply confirmed Chris' opinion surrounding physicians; they were a waste of money. Every doctor she ever visited always recommended the same thing, rest, fluids and an over the counter medication. Of course, followed by their regular line of "it should blow over in a couple of days." It was because of such poor advice; Chris rarely went to a physician unless the situation was dire.

Later that evening, Chris attempted to cook dinner for Beverly and her mother as promised. Although, she hated to admit it, she missed cooking for Frank. To know he used to come home looking forward to her meals gave her a sense of pride. Of course, that feeling was based on the wrong thing, Chris' dependence on him to justify her existence. Still, regardless of that fact she missed it. She could not help but look forward to cooking for someone, even if it was just her mother and Beverly.

Chris had made several attempts at starting dinner, but found it hard to muster up enough strength to get in the kitchen. She could not figure out why she felt so sluggish. She had not done anything out of the ordinary or strenuous during the day, other than go to the doctor's office. In fact, she had taken her doctor's advice and rested most of the day. Still, her lack of energy concerned her. After giving it some thought, she blamed her lethargic behavior on the medication she had taken to fight her cold. So, when Chris' mother called and canceled, Chris was relived. It was drawing near the time she had told them to arrive, and she had not begun preparing the meal. Since it was now only going to be her and Beverly, Chris decided to skip the hassle of whipping something together and instead ordering take-out.

Although she did not feel well, Chris looked forward to sitting down talking with her friend. She was rather eager to tell Beverly about her trip to Jacksonville. At first, she was reluctant about sharing with Beverly what she had learned. Yet, after giving it some serious thought, she saw no harm in telling her. She was after all her best friend. Besides, Chris wanted Beverly's advice as to what she should do about possibly taking Hope up on her offer and contacting her. If Hope had not mentioned the "gift" to Chris in the letter she left with Annie Mae, Chris doubted she would have been considering her overture to get together at all. Chris had enjoyed Hope's company while in Jacksonville. It was just that she was uncertain on whether visiting Hope was a good idea. Still, Chris had found it hard to simply forget about her mentioning of the mysterious "gift".

Beverly arrived at Chris' house right after the delivery service had dropped off their dinner. It was perfect timing. While Chris prepared their plates, Beverly set the table. "Um, um…There is nothing better than cashew chicken, and a good Chardonnay," insisted Beverly, smelling the cooked cashews.

"Thank God for take-out," said Chris, laughing.

"Yeah, tell me about it. So, tell me what gives Chris? Why didn't you call the cops on Frank last night?"

"Please Beverly, I got enough problems as it is, Frank has quickly became the least of my worries." Beverly paused for a moment, surprised to hear her say such a thing. As far as Beverly knew Frank was Chris' only problem.

"And when did this happen?" questioned Beverly, gazing over at her. It was when Chris noticeably avoided returning her stare, when Beverly exclaimed, "Okay, spill it. What gives?"

Chris hesitated before saying to her, "I don't think you're quite ready for this one yet."

"Try me," insisted Beverly, while Chris placed their plates on the table.

Chris took a deep breath before saying, "What if, I told you I found out that I was the descendent of a slave?"

There was dead silence, before Beverly looked over at her and burst into laughter. "You're joking right?" Chris calmly shook her head as she sat down at the table.

"Your serious aren't you?" Beverly gasped, taking a seat.

"Yes I am," said Chris, getting up from the table. She went upstairs only to return with a faded black and white photo in her hand.

"Who is this?" asked Beverly as Chris handed her the picture.

"That is my late great grandmother Celia."

"You must be kidding me?" Beverly said, examining the picture. "My God, the two of you could almost pass for twins."

"I know, isn't it creepy."

"Where did you find this?"

"At my mother's. She had it buried away in a box, with a bunch of other old photographs."

"So, why are you showing me this," inquired Beverly.

"Because she's black...at least half black."

"She appears white to me."

"Despite appearances she's half black," Chris assured her. "Her mother, my great-great grandmother, Nettie, was at one time in her life a slave."

"Why did your mom wait so long to tell you something like this?"

"She didn't. I found out the hard way. I met a few of my relatives from the other limbs of my family tree, while I was in Jacksonville. My mother claims she wanted to tell me, but couldn't find the heart to do so. She claims my father wouldn't let her, which is true."

"Wow, I really don't know what to say," said Beverly, absently twirling her hair. A habit she displayed when she was stunned or confused.

"You don't know what to say, how do you think I feel. I mean, not only is my marriage in shambles right now, but also I'm not even sure who I am. It is like this bad dream, I can't seem to wake up from."

"That is not true. You're still the same person. It is not like, just because you found out your great grandmother was black, that you have been living a lie all your life. As I see it, your life has been made richer by finding this out," Beverly consoled.

"I hope so, because I am truly confused. I mean, why did she even try to pass as white. Maybe if she had stayed black, I would not be going through this identity crisis right now," proclaimed Chris.

"Chris you are who you are. You can't change that. Everything that has happened in the past and what is going to happen in the future will not change that fact. You're who you are—period. Most importantly, you are still my friend." To hear Beverly say that made Chris feel better.

"Thanks Beverly, I really needed to hear that."

"Don't mention it. I was lying through my teeth, but who gives a shit." Beverly smiled.

"Very funny," said Chris, returning her smile with one of her own. "I also have another problem."

"What's that?"

"One of my long lost cousins lives here in Atlanta, and she wants to reconnect."

"So? What is wrong with that?"

"What if we wend up not liking each other? Of course, we got along fine while I was in Jacksonville, but we only got to interact for a short period of time."

"So what?"

"Well, what if I'm not what she thought I was going to be. You know, what if I act too…" Chris hesitated.

"Too what?" asked Beverly, unsure of what she was getting at.

"You know," said Chris, dancing around the subject.

"What…too white!" exclaimed Beverly.

"Yeah!"

Beverly laughed. "Believe me Chris, I think she knows you are white. Just because you found out your great-great grandmother was black and your great grandmother was half black, does not mean you all of a sudden have to act like you're black. You just need to be yourself. I'm quite sure, if you just be yourself everything will work out fine."

"Maybe, I'll call her like I promised," Chris replied.

"I don't see a reason why not," insisted Beverly. "So, do you have any new found male cousins?" Chris immediately knew where she was going with that comment. She could not help but shake her head in disgust. It didn't take long for Beverly's attention to turn to men.

"Because, I've always been kind of curious when it came to dating a black guy. You know a Mandingo," Beverly added.

"A what? What in the world is that?" questioned Chris.

"I don't know. I over heard some black women call this gorgeous black guy that before. I took it as meaning he was good looking. Who knows?…The fact of the matter is I've never dated a black guy before, and hey if I find someone whom I can relate to for God's sake and whom I can trust…I'm all for it no matter what their skin color. Lord knows I've given plenty of other bums a chance."

Chris rolled her eyes. "I just don't know what to do with you Beverly."

"Don't worry about it, I don't even know what to do with myself...Hey how about I help you relax. Why don't the two of us go out to the country club tomorrow and play a few rounds of golf?"

"I really don't know about that Beverly. I'm really not feeling so hot."

"Come on. What else do you have to do other than sit in this house and sulk? Besides, it will do you some good to get out. Exercise helps get rid of a cold much quicker than sitting around the house feeling sorry for yourself."

Chris knew she was not going to stop pestering her until she said "yes." "If you insist," conceded Chris.

CHAPTER 21

▼

The humidity was way too much for Chris to handle. The heat coupled with the humidity totally dehydrated her, which for her was not good, since it only made her feel worse. It also did not help that her golf game stunk. After five holes, she decided it was best to simply watch from the cart rather than endure not only the heat, but also a lousy round of golf. To endure both was torture. Although the cart provided a little relief from the sun, it did very little in regards to cooling her off. She would have much rather stayed at home and moped about a house with air conditioning, instead of being outdoors in weather that felt like a sauna. Riding in the cart, however, did give Chris plenty of time to think. She thought about Frank. She thought about Annie Mae and Hope, but surprisingly she found herself thinking about Dr. Deshpande of all people. What he had said to her during her last visit had suddenly struck a chord with her. Chris found it quite ironic, that the story Dr. Deshpande had relayed to her in regards to the reason why she suffered from chronic back pain, sounded very much like the story Annie Mae had told her about her great uncle Cletus. Although, Chris tried to discount the similarities in their stories as coincidental, she could not ignore how much they were alike. Dr. Deshpande had told her the ghost that was sup-posedly haunting her was black. He also told her, the ghost had been lynched and was nothing more than a kid at the time of his murder. According to Annie Mae, Chris' great uncle Cletus was also lynched as a child. Chris was never one to believe in the paranormal, yet, she could not resist the apparent connection that existed between the two stories.

Chris was glad they had agreed upon playing only nine holes. She seriously doubted she could have withstood watching Beverly play an entire eighteen. So, when Beverly had completed the ninth hole, Chris was relieved that they were heading over to the clubhouse where there would be some respite from the sweltering heat. Yet, despite achieving shelter from the heat, Chris could not escape Dr. Deshpande words.

"Chris! Chris! Are you listening to me?" shouted Beverly, snapping her fingers.

"I'm sorry Beverly, what were you saying?" Chris had blanked out.

"Where the hell are you at? I didn't ask you to come out here, so you could zone out on me. If I wanted to talk to a zombie, I would have brought along a guy."

"I'm sorry, I just got a lot on my mind. I much rather go home."

"No way, you'll do nothing of the sort. No friend of mine is going to go home and sulk. Now snap out of it. To hell with Frank, let him go. Believe me when I tell you, life goes on."

"If I remember correctly, you were the one who had a nervous breakdown when Harry left you," remarked Chris.

"Yeah, maybe, but I'm a veteran now," snapped Beverly, polishing off another Bloody Mary. She paused for a moment to notice the butt of a waiter passing by before exclaiming, "So what do you think?"

"What do I think about what? That guy's butt?" asked Chris; unsure of what Beverly was referring to.

"No, of my attempt at administering tough love. You can't say it did not work for you." Beverly smiled.

"Was that what you call yourself doing? I must apologize I did not recognize it," replied Chris, not finding much humor in her flippant behavior.

"Screw you. I'm trying my best to cheer you up."

"Sorry," Chris replied, realizing she was being overly harsh. "Can I ask you a question?"

"What's on your mind?"

"I have been thinking about something Dr. Deshpande said to me, that reminded me of something someone had told me in Jacksonville."

"And what is that?"

"I rather not get into the details right now. It's just that the stories sound similar and I'm starting to wonder if there is some truth to it."

"Well, why don't you call your cousin as I suggested and find out? That is the only way you're going to get your answer."

"Yeah, you're right."

"Look, the waiters around here are moving too slow. I'm going to the bar and get myself another Bloody Mary. Do you want anything?" Chris shook her head no. She didn't say so, but she felt Beverly had already had one too many Bloody Marys.

"I'm fine with my water," she replied.

"Suit yourself," said Beverly, hurrying off to the bar.

While Beverly was at the bar refilling her drink, Chris' mind once again drifted to Dr. Deshpande. She found it odd that the doctor and Annie Mae's stories were so much alike, when they had no connection to one another what so ever. If that was not eerie enough, the episode Chris had in the clearing that afternoon outside of her great-great grandfather's mansion in Jacksonville was frightfully similar to not only her dreams, but also the story Annie Mae had spun for her of how her great uncle Cletus had passed away.

"How is it going Chris?" Margaret Trumball, a woman Chris bitterly despised, had managed to sneak up on her while she daydreamed.

"Fine and you?" said Chris. She gave Margaret the phoniest smile she could muster.

"I'm glad to hear that. I know it must be difficult for you right now, with Frank and you splitting up after so many years. Not to mention the shocking news about your family. I can't imagine the horror of finding out such a horrible family secret," stated Margaret, acting shocked.

"Excuse me? What shocking news about my family are you referring to?" Chris did not have a clue as to what Margaret was talking about. Chris knew she could not have been referring to the discovery she made in Jacksonville, because she had told no one except Beverly.

"Not like the trauma of losing Frank wasn't enough." Margaret ignored her. "You turn around and find out you're related to blacks. The horror of it all!" she continued, acting repulsed. "I'm quite sure the country club will not revoke your membership, since that technically means you lied on your membership application. Besides, you've been a long standing member of the club."

Chris knew that was nothing more than a veiled threat. Margaret sat on the membership committee. Margaret was an attorney, so she knew revoking Chris' membership would result in a lawsuit and Chris would sue just to get under her skin. Still, Chris could have cared less about being a member of the country club. She was quite astonished to hear Margaret knew about her family secret.

"Who told you such a thing?" asked Chris, curious to know how news of her family had spread so quickly.

"Oh, there goes Ann," said Margaret, ducking the question. "I had promised her I would have lunch with her this afternoon. I hope everything works out for you. Ta, ta." Margaret gave Chris a plastic grin before hurrying off. Chris sat there in shock.

"What was that all about?" asked Beverly, watching Margaret walk off.

"Margaret just informed me, she knows about my family. How the hell is that possible, if I just found out a few days ago myself?" Chris knew, outside of her mother, Beverly was the only person who knew. So, when Beverly said nothing the moment Chris posed the question, Chris knew it was an admission of guilt.

"Please Beverly tell me you didn't?" pleaded Chris. Still, Beverly said nothing. "How could you?" Chris screamed. "You are supposed to be my friend!"

"Well, last night after I left your place, I saw Margaret and her husband, Richard, over at Houston's. I'm not absolutely for certain, but we got to talking about one thing or another and it might have slipped out."

"Oh great! It might have slipped out? That's just fucking great! If I wanted the whole world to know what was going on in my personal life, I would have gotten on a bullhorn and just stood on this god damn table and announced it to the world!"

"Will you please calm down?" proclaimed Beverly. She noticed the unwanted glares they were getting. "I'm sorry okay. Besides, I only told Margaret and Richard," Beverly replied, bringing her voice down to a whisper.

"Oh that brings me great joy to know that you only told the biggest big mouth in Atlanta!"

"Look, I'm sorry okay. I was a little tipsy. I had wine at your place and then a few more drinks at Houston's."

"You're always tipsy! You're a fucking alcoholic! I can't believe you! I confide in you and you betray me! Like I don't already have enough things on my mind! Now I got to deal with everybody staring and whispering behind my back!"

"Chris will you please calm down! You are making a scene!" said Beverly, urging Chris to keep her voice down.

"I don't give a damn! Fuck them! They're already looking at me! I thought you were my friend!" shouted Chris, picking up her purse and storming out.

It took Chris some time to settle down. She could not believe Beverly would have betrayed her in such a manner. Beverly had made several futile attempts at calling but Chris refused to take her calls. Instead, she sat at home alone, trying to figure out how everything could have changed so fast. By the time she had gone through half a box of tissue, she was both emotionally and physically spent. She wanted to do nothing more than take a nap.

*   *   *   *

Chris, once again woke up in a panic. She had the dream again. However, there was now a burning desire within her to determine if the child Dr. Deshpande spoke of was indeed her great uncle, Cletus. She also wanted to unveil the mystery behind the "gift" once and for all. To discovery if Dr. Deshpande were speaking of Chris' great uncle after all, Chris would need to talk to the doctor herself. However, after her last visit, Chris was a little cautious about going to see Dr. Deshpande. He had really scared her. Also, she was now even more frightened by the possibility of how his story could be true. If Dr. Deshpande could see the past, Chris was curious to know could he see the future. And if he was a seer, that only scared Chris even more.

Still, Chris wanted only one mystery unveiled at a time, and at the moment she was plagued by the secrecy surrounding the "gift" more than anything else. She knew there was only one person who could unlock that riddle for her, and Chris felt more comfortable confronting Hope for the time being instead of Dr. Deshpande. So, she desperately searched for Hope's letter. It took her a while to find it, but that didn't matter just as long as Hope's phone number was on it.

CHAPTER 22

▼

Chris was surprised to hear that Hope lived in Druid Hills. Chris would later admit to Hope, that she had simply assumed Hope lived in southwest Atlanta where the majority of the city's black population resided. Hope did not strike Chris as someone who could afford to live in Druid Hills. Chris was quite familiar with the area and from what Beverly had told her; homes in that area were not cheap. Chris could only assume Hope's good fortune had to be the by-product of a very successful husband.

Druid Hills was designed by the late architect, Frederick Law Olmsted, right after he had completed Central Park in New York City, the capitol grounds in Washington D.C. and several other projects along the eastern seaboard. After Druid Hills, Mr. Olmsted designed such Atlanta neighborhoods as Ansley Park and Chris' neighborhood, West Paces Ferry. He never got to see the completion of Druid Hills or the other Atlanta neighborhoods for he died during the construction. During Chris and Frank's initial search for a home, Chris had tried to convince Frank she would much rather prefer to live amongst the beautiful parks and wooded lots of Druid Hills than the gaudy flaunting of wealth that permeated Buckhead. The fact the neighborhood was centered around Ponce de Leon Avenue, gave the neighborhood sort of small town feeling while at the same time remaining apart of the city. Yet, Frank much rather preferred the prestige and status living in Buckhead symbolized, than the beautiful parks and wooded lots of Druid Hills.

As Chris had expected, Hope's home was a stately estate nestled amongst majestic trees sitting quite a way off of the main road. When she got to the door Hope was already waiting for her. She greeted Chris with a rousing "hi" and a warm embrace. Chris attempted to reciprocate her warmth and joy in seeing her, but felt awkward in doing so.

"I saw your headlights coming up the driveway," Hope explained. "Come on in gurl and have a seat." Hope led her inside. Although, Chris had seen Hope in Jacksonville, she really had not noticed how beautiful she was. She was a radiant color of butterscotch with a hint of red undertones. Her hair, which was coifed in a short but stylish hairstyle, seemed to compliment her shapely figure.

"Mama, who's that?" someone cried out from upstairs.

"It is your cousin Chris. The woman I told you about. You and your brother come on down here and say 'hello,'" shouted Hope.

"I want you to meet my boys," stated Hope with a smile. Chris tried to return her expression with a smile of her own. She could not help but feel a little uneasy about suddenly meeting more people whom she did not know, yet, who called her family. Despite her nervousness, two boys bounced down stairs to stand at Hope's side.

"This is my son Nathan, he is ten," she said, placing her hand on the tallest boy's shoulder. "And the littlest one here is Anthony and he is eight." She patted the youngest child on the head.

"Hi, it is very nice to meet you," stated Chris, shaking their hands.

"Hi," both boys said in unison.

"My, you guys are such handsome young men," commented Chris.

"Thank you," they both said, once again together.

Everything seemed to be going fine until Hope's youngest son blurted out, "Are you really my cousin?"

Chris hesitated a moment before answering, "It appears so."

"Then why are you white?" came the little boy's response. Chris was caught off guard by his childhood innocence, but she understood the source of his confusion. She, herself, was still very much confused by the events that had transpired over the past few weeks.

"Anthony!" exclaimed Hope, sounding intent on scolding the boy.

Chris looked at her and gave her a wayward smile before telling her, "Don't worry about it. I can understand his confusion. I guess this is all kind of new for all of us."

Chris gave Anthony a wink of her eye, before whispering in his ear, "Shhh, don't tell nobody. I know it may seem weird that I could be your relative, believe me I'm kind of new to this too, but it's true. Besides, just because we're a different color does not mean we cannot be friends...Does it?" Chris added. Anthony shook his head.

"Good," exclaimed Chris. "I did not want that to get in the way, because I was starting to like you." Chris smiled. She looked over at Hope, who seemed to be pleased with Chris' response judging by the smile on her face.

"What your cousin, Chris is saying is right," added Hope. "Now, you guys go on upstairs and finish cleaning your rooms. And when you are done with that, I want the two of you to get ready for bed."

"Ah ma, can't we watch TV," complained Nathan.

"First you have to finish cleaning your room, and then I have to think about it."

"All right," said Nathan, moping back upstairs with his brother in tow.

"The sooner you finish cleaning your room, the sooner you can watch TV," yelled Hope as they scurried to their rooms to begin the cleaning process.

"You have two very beautiful children," said Chris, watching them hurry off.

"Thank you. Come on, let's sit down so we can chitchat." Hope smiled, leading Chris into the living room.

"I never got the chance to ask you if you have children of your own?" inquired Hope as Chris took a seat on the couch.

"Unfortunately, I am unable to bear children," said Chris, solemnly.

"I'm sorry to hear that," replied Hope, appearing truly saddened by the news.

"It's all right. I've learned to live with it. For some unknown reason my ovaries do not produce eggs."

Hope could sense this was a topic of great sorrow for Chris, so she decided to change the subject. "You got to excuse me for being so rude," said Hope, hopping to her feet. "Would you like something to eat or drink? We have already ate dinner, but we have some leftovers if you're still hungry?"

"No, I ate before coming over." After eating the meal at Annie Mae's in Jacksonville, Chris was not going to take her chances eating another meal that did not agree with her stomach.

"Well, how about something to drink. I got grape juice, orange juice, soda pop, milk and coffee. That is unless you want a glass of wine?"

"I'll just take a glass of water, if that isn't too much."

"Gurl please! I'll be right back with that water," shouted Hope, heading into the kitchen.

Chris could hear the clank of glasses as well as the opening and closing of cabinet and refrigerator doors. "Uncle Buford was quite impressed with how you handled Gran at the diner back in Jacksonville."

"I'm sorry?" replied Chris, unable to hear her over the clatter of dishes in the kitchen.

"Uncle Buford told me what happened at the diner in Jacksonville," repeated Hope, walking back into the living room with Chris' glass of water and a glass of wine for herself. It suddenly dawned on Chris what she was referring to.

"Oh, I had totally forgotten about that. I did not do anything out of the ordinary."

"Well, whether you think you did or not it doesn't matter. You don't know how long, my uncle and I have been trying to get Gran to leave out of the front door of that place, instead of the back," professed Hope.

"It just took a little push that is all…Thank you," said Chris, taking her glass of water from Hope. "You have a beautiful house."

"Thank you."

As Chris sipped her water an uneasy silence came between them. "So, how did your parents come up with such a pretty name as Hope?" Chris asked. The silence that had descended between them made her nervous.

Hope smiled. "My dad use to tell me, that him and mama viewed me as their hope for a better world. Thus, they named me Hope." With that question answered there was once again, another awkward moment of silence between them.

"So, what exactly does your husband do for a living?" asked Chris, trying desperately to create small talk.

Once again, Hope smiled. "I'm divorced," Hope told her. "But if you're curious to know, my ex-husband DeWayne, is an investment banker. His constant traveling became hard on our marriage. Besides, I discovered he had a preference for guys rather than girls. If you know what I mean?"

"Oh, I'm sorry to hear that," said Chris, somewhat surprised. "I just thought you was married by the comment you made in Jacksonville about your boys having spent enough time with their father."

"No need to be sorry," Hope assured her. "It was his weekend to have the boys. We have managed to maintain a cordial relationship. However, believe me when I tell you, finding out your husband is cheating on you with another man, instead of another woman, does something to a woman's self esteem. I'm seeing this guy named James, off and on, but it is nothing serious."

"Well, at least your ex-husband left you this beautiful home," proclaimed Chris.

"Honestly," replied Hope, correcting her. "This home is all mine. We had to sell the house we shared together in Buckhead."

"Don't I feel like an ass," said Chris, suddenly embarrassed. "I'm sorry for insinuating that you needed a man in order to live in such a beautiful neighborhood."

"Don't worry about it, no offense taken," remarked Hope, waving her hand as if shooing off a pest. "It's understandable. It's an honest mistake. I am a pediatrician with my own practice."

"Wow! You're a doctor. I never would have guessed. Where do you practice at?" exclaimed Chris, in amazement.

"My office is near Greenbriar Mall, right off Campbellton Road," replied Hope.

"Southwest Atlanta?" stated Chris.

"Yeah."

"I do some charity work with an organization in College Park called Save Or Kids," Chris informed her.

"For real! How did you get involved with that?" questioned Hope, sounding interested.

"My family donated money to the organization to get it off the ground. I believe children from all walks of life should have the same opportunities as children whose parents are financially stable," commented Chris.

"That is kind of the same reason I went into medicine. When I graduated from Emory's school of medicine, I decided I wanted to help those who might not have much money, but still deserved quality medical care," explained Hope.

"That's great, maybe I can introduce you to the organization's director, her name is Jessica Rhimes. There are many kids she works with whose parents do not have adequate healthcare but need quality medical service."

"I would love to. If I can donate my time or expertise, I would gladly do it." Hope smiled. "It's funny how after all of this time, we still have some things in common. I wonder what other things we may share," Hope added. "I really need to remember to water this thing more often," Hope said, directing her attention to a dying houseplant on her coffee table.

In Chris' opinion the plant was beyond saving. Yet, Hope examined each individual leaf as if all it needed was a little tender loving care. Hope's comment pertaining to the two of them sharing in something did make Chris remember, the reason as to why she had called Hope in the first place.

"In regards to us sharing something…You mentioned in your letter, you left with Annie Mae something about the 'gift'?"

"Yes, I did," answered Hope.

"What is the 'gift'?" questioned Chris.

"You know, I thought you were never going to call me," responded Hope, completely ignoring the question.

"Why would you say that? I said I would."

"Yeah, ya did. Yet, it took you almost a week."

Chris paused for a moment, contemplating on whether to tell Hope the truth or make up some excuse as to why it took her so long to contact her. Chris settled upon telling her the truth. She did not want a possible friendship to get started off on the wrong foot. "To be honest with you, Hope, I was somewhat apprehensive about calling you."

"I can understand. All the stuff Gran told you would make even me, kind of leery." Hope paused for a moment. "So, you want to know what the 'gift' is I take it? I knew if I mentioned the 'gift', I would get your attention…I think you already know what the 'gift' is, Chris. The only problem is that you do not recognize it for what it is."

"I don't understand?" replied Chris.

Hope glanced down at her hands, before returning her attention back to Chris. "Gran did not tell you everything about our great uncle Cletus, your great grandmother Celia's brother. Gran simply told you he was lynched because he was a troublemaker. Now it is true, Cletus was lynched, but Gran did not tell you everything when it came to the reason why he was murdered.

"What Gran did not tell you was that Cletus was different…He was very different. See, our great uncle was slow, mentally. Despite that fact, he was blessed with a God given talent…what I like to call the 'gift'. No one knows how he got it or where it came from. It is generally believed by many of us in the family, that he was born with it. Growing up, I heard tales of how Cletus healed people by simply laying his hands on them. How he brought plants and animals back to life. I heard a story of how one year during a drought, he placed his hands in the air and made rain in order to save the crops."

"Do you truly expect me to believe that?" interrupted Chris.

"No. I know it sounds crazy but it's true. Believe me, every word I am telling you is the truth. I did not believe it either, until I witnessed its power." said Hope.

"And what was that?" said Chris, sounding skeptical.

"I'll get to that story," stated Hope. "First, I want to finish telling you about Cletus…Now, many black folk in and around Jacksonville, began to believe Cletus had a direct line to God's ear. From what I've been told Cletus performed way too many miracles to keep track of. The fact Cletus was black made many of the town's black folk in and around Jacksonville believe he was the Second Coming of Jesus Christ himself. This gave many of the town's blacks a sense of pride and hope to believe that the son of God was a living breathing black boy and not some blond hair, blue eye, white man as they had been made to believe.

"As you can guess this did not sit well with the town's white folks. The way Gran put it, 'white folk did not and refused to appreciate a miracle living in their midst.' It is because of people's fear of the unknown as to why Gran refuses to speak of the 'gift' to this day. Nonetheless, black folk began preaching about how God was a living and breathing Negro child amongst them, and that black people were truly God's chosen people. It was this type of talk amongst them that brought trouble."

"You got to be kidding me," interrupted Chris once again.

"Here me out now," protested Hope. "At least let me finish the story."

"If you must," replied Chris.

"As one can understand the town's whites did not like all this talk about Jesus being a living breathing black child for it was disturbing the natural balance between blacks and whites in Jacksonville. As far as they were concerned, blacks had forgotten their place. So, they went to your great-great grandfather Clayton Jackson, and asked him to get Cletus under control. Cletus was after all not only his son, but also his property. And being he had some claim to Cletus, your great-great grandfather, Clayton, did try to protect Cletus as best as he could without appearing to favor the boy over his fellow white kin. He kept the Klan at bay for quite some time, but after a while even he couldn't prevent the inevitable.

"The end came after a day of being teased, Cletus told all the kids in town he could fly. The story goes that he stood up on top of great-great grandma Nettie's cabin and conjured up a wind that bent trees back and made the skies howl. Many people believe that if Nettie had not stopped Cletus that day, he would have taken to the sky. You can ask many of the old black folks in and around Jacksonville and they will tell you the same story. It has been passed down from generation to generation almost word for word."

"That can't be true," proclaimed Chris.

"Why not? Is it really that hard to believe? Just a few days ago you did not believe you were the descendant of a black woman."

"Maybe so, but to believe someone had God given healing powers and possibly the gift of flight is a little hard to believe. I would be a fool to sit here and believe such a cockamamie story. It is nothing more than a folktale that has been embellished upon over the years and taken to be fact," professed Chris.

"Sort of like the Bible is a collection of folktales, embellished upon over the centuries and considered to be true," replied Hope.

"The two are in no way related," insisted Chris.

"Why not? They both are simply nothing more than folktales embellished upon over the years. Isn't that what you said," argued Hope. Chris grew silent.

"Regardless, of whether you believe it or not," continued Hope. "It was because of great uncle Cletus' desire to fly that led to his demise. By that time the town's whites had had enough. That is when the Klan came to put an end to Cletus' antics for good. So, they hung him. Like Gran said, Nettie went into a deep depression following Cletus' death, and she did vow that God would exact his revenge on those who murdered her son. Seeming to bring her prophesy to fruition, the following year a plague did sweep through town killing most of the town's children like Gran said. The only thing she did not tell you about the epidemic was that its victims were all white. It has been said that not one black child contracted the disease. Among the children claimed by the epidemic were Timmy and Jane, the son and daughter of Clayton and Emma Jackson. They had tried to have more children after that but with no success. So, grief stricken by the lose of Timmy and Jane, and longing for the sound of children in the home, they adopted Celia as their own."

"So, you're telling me that our great uncle Cletus was killed because he had this 'gift,'" muttered Chris. She was suddenly surprised to see the once dead plant on the coffee table alive and well. Chris glanced over at Hope, speechless as she pointed towards the plant.

Hope smiled. "Is it really that hard to believe?"

"You, you, have the-the 'gift'," Chris stuttered.

"Yes," replied Hope, finding Chris' sudden shock amusing.

"For how long?"

"Since, I was fourteen."

"How did you know you had it?" questioned Chris.

"Like I said, that is another story. But to answer your question, I sort of found out by accident."

"What happened?" asked Chris, staring at the plant.

"We had a dog, his name was Duke. Growing up we use to live on a busy street, it was only a matter of time before Duke wandered out into the street and got hit. I remember the day he got hit, vividly. Duke had ran out into the street and gotten clipped by a truck. I remember the truck driver didn't even bother to stop, kept right on going. Duke managed to crawl over to the curb right in front of the house. My brother, my sister and I were outside playing at the time, so we ran right over to where he laid. The moment I laid eyes on him, I knew it was not good. The truck had mangled his back legs. I knew if he lived, he was never going to walk to again.

"My dad rushed outside and told my brother, Robert, to go inside and get a towel to wrap him in. I remember breaking down in tears because I pretty much knew by the look on my father's face Duke was not going to make it. I watched as Duke slipped away, right there before my eyes, I wanted to do something to take away his pain. I recall a warm sensation coming over me, and without thinking as to why, I fell to my knees right there next to Duke and laid my hands on him. I remember the warm, hot, energy channeling through my body and concentrating itself in my hands. I don't know how long I was there next to Duke, but I do remember the shock on everyone's face the moment Duke jumped up and started running about the yard like nothing had happened. I did not have a clue as to what it was I had done to Duke, or if I had done anything at all. All I knew was that Duke was better, and that was all that mattered to me.

"That evening mama pulled me aside and talked to me about what happened that afternoon with Duke. She wanted to know, if I had done what I did on purpose. I told her, I did not know that I had done anything to Duke at all. Mama listened to what I had to say then we never spoke about it again. It was not until our next trip to Jacksonville did the subject of Duke come up again. Apparently, mama had told Gran about the incident, because after we got settled in Gran took me for a walk. We walked up to the Jackson mansion. Gran took me around back to Celia's garden and we begin tending to the flowers. She always took me up there when I came into Jacksonville. She gave me little tasks to do in the garden while we talked. It was then when she told me about our great uncle Cletus. It was also when she told me about the 'gift'. She explained to me how precious the 'gift' was and how its power was not to be misused. Before we left the garden that day she explained to me how that was her aunt Celia's garden, my great auntie Celia, your great grandmother, and how one day it would be my turn to take care of it. She also made it clear to me that I was not to use the 'gift' in anyway that interfered with the Lord's work. God has a plan for everybody."

Chris sat there silent, recalling the plant on her coffee table springing to life from her touch. "So, do you use the 'gift' on the job?" asked Chris.

"I may use it from time to time to speed up the healing process of maybe a broken arm or leg, but nothing more than that. Other than that day with Duke, I have never again attempted to rewrite fate."

"Did your mother have the gift?"

"Yes, and so does Gran. You may not have realized it while you were there, but Gran is considered to be Jacksonville's own herbalist. Before driving thirty miles to the nearest doctor most people in Jacksonville, both black and white, come see Gran first.

"See, the 'gift' does not seem to follow some preordained pattern in our family. It simply is passed on from generation to generation. For example, I got it, Gran got it, my mother had it, as well as my brother, Robert, has discovered he is blessed with it. However, my sister, Sadie, does not. I believe my youngest son, Anthony, has the 'gift,' but my son Nathan has not showed signs of possibly possessing it. If you were to ask me, I would tell you, it is us who chooses the 'gift' and not the 'gift' that chooses us."

"What do you mean by that?" asked Chris confused.

"I believe all of us, who are descendents of great-great grandma Nettie, possess the 'gift'. For some unknown reason we find a desire or need to call upon it when we need it the most, we may do this consciously or subconsciously, who knows. But I do know that once you have summoned it, there is no putting it back. I can tell, that you have opened up that bottle," asserted Hope, with a smile.

"What makes you think that?" asked Chris with a hint of curiosity.

"I see its beauty all around you. I saw it in you while in Jacksonville. I especially knew you had it when you told us that you had seen a young boy hanging in that old oak tree in the clearing. That was Cletus' ghost. He was hung in that oak tree standing watch over Celia's garden. That is why Celia started that garden there, in remembrance of her brother. Nonetheless, only someone blessed with the 'gift' can sense and feel such things as spirits. The only problem I can see standing in your way of realizing the 'gift's' full potential is your own lack of belief."

"Well, what do you expect? You tell me about some 'gift' in your letter, then you get me here to tell me this mysterious 'gift' is some sacred power passed down from generation to generation in our family. Not only that, but because of this power, people in our family have God like powers. That is a little farfetched—don't you think," proclaimed Chris.

Hope simply smiled. "It is not the belief in the 'gift' I am talking about. I am talking about the lack of belief in yourself."

"What do you mean?" Chris asked.

"What I mean, is that I've learned the 'gift' can only touch a person if that individual has an unwavering belief in themselves." Chris sat there silent, digesting what Hope had said.

As Chris sat there quiet, Hope looked her in the eyes and asked, "So, what is holding you back?"

CHAPTER 23

▼

Despite the cold tablets Chris had been taking for the past few days, she still felt ill. The mornings were the roughest part of the day. If she managed to get through the morning, the rest of the day was a breeze. The only problem was trying to weather through it. This particular morning was no different; there was the pounding headache right along with the upset stomach. She took two aspirin to ward off the headache while hoping the nausea would subside with a glass of milk. Chris partially blamed staying over at Hope's house until midnight as one of the reasons for the severity of that morning's bout of the flu. They had spent so much time talking about the "gift," Cletus, even Chris' marital problems, that she had neglected to get the proper rest. Hope was a good listener and even gave Chris some advice as to how she overcame her divorce, which Chris found helpful.

As Chris made her way down the stairs to the kitchen, a plethora of thoughts crossed her mind. As she walked through the living room she spied her plant on the coffee table and immediately thought about Hope's houseplant. She went into the kitchen and poured herself a glass of milk, hoping it would coat her stomach and ease her nausea. As usual she stood at the sink, glancing out the kitchen window at the bird feeder while she drank. As she looked out on the feeder, she suddenly remembered the incident with the birds. Chris could not help but wonder if the incident was some type of anomaly, or if it indeed had something to do with the "gift." She did recall hearing voices, although she was not sure if that was not her imagination. Even though she was not feeling well, Chris knew there was only one way to make sure it was not pure fantasy.

Chris opened the French doors that led out to the pool. She wrapped her robe around her and tied it tight. Usually, the start of a brand new day is punctuated by the sounds of birds ushering it in. Yet, that morning as Chris walked outside not one bird could be heard for miles. She did not hear a single one. There were no birds nor crickets or any insect for that matter making noise. Everything was still, very abnormal.

Chris halted there in front of the bird feeder to find not one bird. Usually every morning there had always been birds feeding at that feeder. It struck her as odd that there were none that particular morning. Chris peered into the trees that lined her yard and the shrubs in her garden to see not one bird. It suddenly dawned on her, that she had not seen a single bird since the day she had banished them. Although, she knew that could not be possible, she could not recollect seeing a bird since then. It was hard for her to believe she had commanded the birds to leave. However, the fact she had not seen one solitary bird since that day struck her as odd. She figured if the "gift" was real, then there was only one way she could get the birds to come back.

Chris was scared. If what she intended to do worked it would once again prove Hope right. If Hope was indeed right about the 'gift', Chris did not know how she would handle it. Still, there she stood bare foot in the lush green grass contemplating an act she would have considered just a day ago insane. She figured since she had come that far, she had no other choice but to go all the way.

So, Chris closed her eyes and briefly remembered what Hope had told her about believing in herself, before whispering, "Come."

In what sounded like the beating of a thousand heartbeats, Chris heard the flutter of wings. When Chris opened her eyes there were a myriad of birds surrounding her. They had gathered at her feet, perched themselves upon her head and shoulders. Where ever she looked there were birds, dozens upon dozens of birds. Their chirping filled her ears. It was almost deafening. Just like when they sat upon her windowsill, they began to sing a song that filled the early morning sky. And just like before, Chris heard every word.

Chris may have stood there for five minutes listening to their beautiful melody. Then, to convince herself that this was truly happening, Chris softly said, "Go." As soon as the word passed over her lips and out of her mouth there was once again a mass exodus signified by the beating of a thousand wings. There were so many birds in flight they temporarily blotted out the sun. As the last bird disappeared from sight, Chris could not help, but smile with delight. She was amazed to see a backyard just a second ago full of birds of all different types…empty. The sky that had just held a bounty of birds of all different varieties a minute ago was now vacant. Where, there had once been sound, there was now silence. They were gone.

Chris could not believe it. She was utterly amazed. Once again, Hope was right. She was so shocked and overcome with disbelief; she placed her hand over her mouth in an attempt to suppress a nervous laugh that had bubbled to the surface. If there was not numerous bird feathers scattered about the yard and on her bathrobe, she would have believed that what had transpired was nothing more than a dream. Yet, it was real and she knew it was real. The gravity of what had just took place brought tears to her eyes. Chris figured, she was either completely insane or she truly did possess some unimaginable power.

Still, Chris wanted to make sure that she was not hallucinating. She had heard tales of people who had wanted something to happen so bad, they induced themselves into believe that it actually had occurred; when in reality it had not. Chris wanted to make sure that was not the case. So she looked up into the sky, and called out to them once again.

*   *   *   *

After calling the birds back a second time, Chris decided that was enough for one day. She had proven it to herself that the first time the birds responded to her call was no fluke. Besides, she had grown hot. Her body was on fire. When she had broken out into a sweat, she had contributed it to the weather outside. However, she quickly realized it was her that was creating such heat. She related the feeling; to the sensation she received when she accidentally shocked herself while changing a light bulb. To Chris, it felt similar to electricity coursing throughout her veins. It was a tingling sensation running throughout her body and her limbs. She did not know if it was the feeling Hope had attempted to describe to her when she told her of her first experience with the "gift" or if it was her nerves, or outright fear. As she closed the patio door behind her, she stood still for a moment in disbelief of what had just transpired also to let the feeling of electricity coursing through her body wear off.

Once the eerie feeling had died, Chris was struck with fear in what she had just done. Suddenly so many questions began to career through her mind. How did she control this immense power? How many people in the world were there like her? What did she do next? She knew that she had to learn how to control this "gift" quickly. If she did not, she knew she could be in trouble. Chris was well aware of how people reacted when they witnessed something or someone they could not explain; they turned them into lab rats. Chris had no intentions of living the rest of her life in some laboratory with people poking and prodding her. She quickly resolved she needed to call Hope.

As Chris stood there in deep thought, she tried to pick the bird feathers from her bathrobe and hair. Realizing it would be much easier and less laborious of a task if she were to brush them out of her hair instead of picking them, Chris headed to the bathroom where she had a brush handy. If Hope's demonstration with the houseplant had not convinced Chris about their great uncle Cletus' Godly gift, then her exhibition with the birds definitely did.

Chris picked a few feathers, she immediately noticed in the mirror out of her hair, before grabbing the brush out of the cabinet drawer. Now, Chris had heard stories of how certain tribes in South America, refused to let photographers photograph them because they feared the photograph captured their soul. She had also heard of how some Native Americans, during the colonization of America feared seeing their reflection in a mirror, because they believed the mirror revealed the portal to one's soul. Yet, when Chris had heard these tales, she thought of them as nothing more than one's ignorance towards the advancement of technology. Yet, when she looked back into the mirror to brush the remaining feathers out of her hair, she could not help but see the truth in what she had once considered to be primitive beliefs.

At first, Chris was startled by the reflection that greeted her in the mirror. She instinctively yelped in fear. Once again, her instincts told her to run. However, this time she suppressed that urge long enough, to notice the gaunt face of the little boy staring back at her. It was the same little boy she had seen in her bathroom before. Although, the vision lasted only a split second, Chris was able to recognize his woolly hair that was such a deep color of red it was almost crimson. Despite the texture and color of his hair, the young boy had the complexion of coffee when too much cream was added. In such an instance, the coffee takes on a tan, almost off-white, coloration, a fair complexion. Yet, the strength of his nose, the pronouncement of his lips and the innocence in his eyes, told Chris this was none other than her uncle Cletus. Chris did not know why, but for that brief moment, that split second, she felt a rush of happiness wash over her.

As his image faded, Chris stared into the mirror in vain, hoping he would return. She probably would have stared into the mirror all day if it were not for the sudden churning of her stomach. Although, she had only a glass of milk that morning it became clear to her it was not going to stay down. It was a good thing she was already in the bathroom, because Chris doubted she would have been able to make it to the toilet from any other room in the house.

CHAPTER 24

▼

"Now do you believe me," professed Hope.

Although, Chris felt terrible after puking her guts out for five minutes, she could not contain her need to call Hope and tell her what happened. Her stomach lurched slightly against her abdominal wall trying to dispel whatever remnants were left, but she was empty. Her bout with the dry heaves was testimony to the fact she had nothing left. Once Chris was done hugging the toilet, she quickly got up and rinsed her mouth out before madly searching for the phone book. Since it was early in the day Chris was certain Hope would not be home. It took her no time to find the number to Hope's private practice.

"I do now," replied Chris.

"Look, I got a patient. Why don't you come over to the house tonight for dinner, and we can talk about it there? I want to hear about everything that happened, plus help you understand how I go about controlling it."

"As long as you don't serve that stuff I ate at Annie Mae's. I was sick to my stomach the rest of that night," warned Chris.

Hope laughed. "I'll see what I can do. Do you like seafood?" asked Hope.

"Yeah."

"Well, since today is Friday, I'll go down to the Bankhead fish mart and see what I can do. I see, I'm going to have to hip ya to soul food," said Hope, laughing.

"I've had soul food before," protested Chris.

"I'm not talking about that stuff you get in a restaurant prepared by a chef. Gurl, I'm talking about the real deal," exclaimed Hope.

"If you say so," conceded Chris.

"Good, I'll call you when I get home tonight."

"Okay."

"Bye."

"Bye."

Chris hung the phone up and lay down on the couch as her stomach churned. She found it uncommon for her to be sick for so long. She was starting to get worried that it might be much more than just the flu. She contemplated calling the doctor and scheduling another appointment, but was not sure if it was truly necessary. She went back and forth with this idea for sometime before the doctor ended up calling her. This caught Chris by surprise because he requested her to come in and see him...immediately. Although Chris knew something was not right, she did not like the tone of the doctor's voice nor was she prepared for what he had to tell her.

*   *   *   *

Chris waited in the examination room, wearing the customary patient's smock. The doctor had simply told her over the phone, 'He found something unusual in her test and he wanted to bring her in for additional testing'. Chris knew that could mean anything. As she paced back and forth in the room, she could not help but fear the worst. She feared it might be cancer or even worst. Her biggest fear was that Frank, in one of his many indiscretions outside of their marriage had contracted HIV and unwittingly passed it along to her. The doctor's extended absence after running additional test did not help soothe her fears.

"Well, Mrs. Adams," said the doctor entering the room.

"What is it?" interjected Chris, not giving him time to speak.

The doctor gave her a warm smile. "Well, I can assure you, you are not going to die." To Chris that meant nothing, it still did not entail she was not ill.

"What does that mean?" she demanded to know.

"To be quite honest with you Mrs. Adams," his tone became more serious. "What is troubling you has me a bit perplexed as well."

"What is it?" begged Chris, fidgeting back and forth.

"It is nothing bad, in fact it is quite amazing."

"Amazing?"

"Yes, indeed," he answered.

"Then what is it?" demanded Chris.

A huge smile crossed over the doctor's face before he said, "Are you ready for this?"

"Can we dispense with the games please?" insisted Chris, becoming irritated.

"Well, it appears that you have not been suffering from the flu at all. Instead, it appears to me, you suffer from what we call morning sickness," the doctor said, getting straight to the point.

"Excuse me?" stated Chris in shock. Chris knew exactly what morning sickness was associated with. However, such a thing was not possible with her because she was supposed to be sterile.

"You're pregnant Mrs. Adams. From the looks of it you are about six to eight weeks along." The doctor smiled.

"But how can this be?" asked Chris in utter confusion. "This is not supposed to happen."

"I asked myself the same question when I had seen your test results. Nonetheless, after retesting you again, I have come up with the same answers."

"You've got to be kidding me?" said Chris, suddenly feeling lightheaded.

"I have seen terminal ill cancer patient's, cancer go into remission, with no apparent rhyme or reason. I have seen people, who had been in a coma for two to three years, all of a sudden wake up like nothing had happened. Yet, after all these years, I have never seen someone who physiologically can not bear children, become pregnant," proclaimed the doctor.

CHAPTER 25

▼

Beverly was the first person Chris called upon leaving the doctor's office. Chris had tried contacting her mother, but was unable to reach her. She thought about calling Hope, but she knew she would probably be too busy to take her call. Chris was feeling overwhelmed upon leaving the doctor's office and desperately needed to talk to somebody to calm her nerves. Since Beverly was the only one accessible, fate had chosen her.

Up to that point, Chris had not spoken to Beverly since their blow up at the country club. Beverly could sense by the panic in Chris' voice as they talked, something was terribly awry. Beverly was on her way out the door at the time Chris called, to show a home in Ansley Park. However, she decided it was imperative that she be there when Chris arrived, judging by the panic in her voice. Of course that meant she had to come up with an excuse that could possibly delay her closing on the home for another month, but that did not matter. Chris needed her, and quite honestly Beverly missed her. Beverly hated to admit it to herself, but Chris was the only friend she had. It saddened her to know she had inflicted such an unduly amount of pain on her friend by telling Margaret her secret.

Beverly monitored the driveway while impatiently awaiting Chris' arrival. The anticipation in waiting to find out what was so important that she had to tell her immediately had Beverly in a tizzy. She could not stop tapping her feet or wringing her hands as she waited. When Chris finally pulled up into the driveway, Beverly could tell by the look on her face as she got out of the car, she was upset.

"Chris what is wrong?" asked Beverly as she rushed outside to greet her. "I hope I haven't taken you away from anything important," replied Chris in a daze.

"No, not at all," Beverly lied, following her inside. She felt there was no need to tell her she had to postpone a showing on account of her.

"So, tell me what the hell is going on?" repeated Beverly, shutting the door behind them.

"To tell you the truth Beverly, I wish I knew. The last two days have been hard to believe."

"Are you sure you're all right?" asked Beverly, noticing how despondent she acted.

"No, I am not all right. Nothing is all right," snapped Chris, beginning to feverishly pace about the room.

"Chris, you got to talk to me. Tell me what is going on? Did Frank do something to you?"

"Oh did he ever!" Chris was having trouble finding the words to explain to Beverly what the doctor had revealed to her. It was still, hard to believe, let alone explain.

"Well then, what did he do?"

"I just came from the doctor's office," proclaimed Chris.

"And?" replied Beverly, fearful of Chris' response.

"You're not going to believe this. You remember I told you, I was not feeling well…That I had the flu."

"Yeah."

"Well, the doctor ran a few more tests on me this morning. As it turns out, the headaches and nausea, was not the flu but morning sickness."

"You got to be kidding me?" said Beverly in disbelief.

Chris paused for a moment to let the ramifications of her announcement soak in. "I'm pregnant." Although she heard herself say it, Chris felt as if the words had came out of someone else's mouth.

Beverly simply stared at her in shock before leaping up and embracing her. She was happy for Chris. She knew, how bad Chris wanted to have a child. "Wait a minute! Are you trying to tell me you're pregnant with Frank's child?" screamed Beverly.

"Who else's would it be?"

"I don't know? I guess I was just doing some wishful thinking."

"Now, is not the time," snapped Chris. She knew Beverly's next sentence would be directed towards Frank's insidious behavior.

"Okay, okay…but I thought you were…"

"Sterile?" said Chris, finishing the sentence for her. "So did I. So, did my doctor. I don't know how this can happen, but it has."

"I think we all got a good idea of how it happened," quipped Beverly.

"You know what I mean," snapped Chris.

"Oh my God Chris, I can't believe it. I am so happy for you." Beverly embraced her once again. "So, how far along are we?" she asked, wiping the tears from her eyes.

"Six to eight weeks," announced Chris.

"How long has it been since you last did it?"

"Almost six weeks," answered Chris. Chris quickly remembered the night Frank had virtually raped her.

"And you're sure it was Frank?" teased Beverly.

"Are you implying it would be with anyone else?" said Chris sarcastically.

"Like I said, I guess I'm just hoping," stated Beverly in her defense.

"Yeah, me too," sighed Chris, wiping the tears from her eyes.

"I don't understand. Other than the child being Frank's, I don't see what the problem is? I would think you would be a lot happier than you are acting. I mean this is something you have always wanted, right," commented Beverly, noticing Chris' subdued behavior.

"I know, I know," stated Chris, flinging her hands in the air in a bout of frustration. "I do want to have a baby, but under different circumstances than the one I am being faced with right now. I mean look at me. I am going through a divorce, and I just learned that my family tree has a few hidden branches to it I knew nothing about. I still have not totally grasped the concept yet of how I am suppose to nurture another human being through life, when I can't get my own act together."

"Don't worry about that. Take it from someone whose life has been in shambles most of her adult life. I went through a nasty divorce, had a nervous breakdown, saw a psychiatrist, and still had to come home at night and be a mom. I know I'm not the world's perfect mother, but I feel I've done an okay job. The stuff I don't know, I figure, hell, I can just figure it out along the way. Although, I did catch Bobby with a joint the other day and Jill is much too young to be getting it more than her mother. I still feel I am doing an okay job.

"Life isn't easy. Sometimes we have to make due with the hand we are dealt. Beside, I will be here for you every step of the way...Now sit down, you shouldn't be on your feet."

"I appreciate that," said Chris starting to cry. She was touched by Beverly's show of support. Chris sat down next to Beverly, and for a while they simply sat there, weeping together.

It was not until Beverly told her, "I have some good news of my own."

"What is that?" Chris sobbed, once again drying her eyes.

Beverly smiled. "I enrolled in Alcoholics Anonymous."

"You what?"

"Yep."

Chris suddenly felt a spell of guilt come over her. "Beverly, I hope you did not take what I said at the country club literally. I was just upset."

"Don't worry about it, Chris. You were only telling the truth," admitted Beverly. "I knew I had a problem. There was one too many nights, I found myself drinking alone. It was good I heard it from someone, in particular you." Beverly paused for a moment before suggesting, "Why don't we go into the kitchen and celebrate to both of our good news."

"Sounds good to me," said Chris, smiling. Beverly led Chris into the kitchen, where they sat down at the kitchen table.

"You want a cup of coffee?" inquired Beverly.

"No, I can't. It's got caffeine in it. The doctor says I've got to watch what I eat and drink from now on," Chris insisted.

"That is right. You would think after having two kids of my own, I would know that. How about some water?"

"No, I'm fine."

"So tell me, what did the doctor exactly say?"

"When? After he shitted in his pants or before?" Chris laughed.

"I'll take after he shitted his pants," said Beverly, smiling.

"Well as you can guess he was just as much in shock as I was. He could not find the words to explain it."

"Have you told anybody else?"

"No, you are the first to know," exclaimed Chris.

"Well, I am honored. Do you plan on telling anybody else, like your mother? I'm quite sure she would be delighted to hear she is going to be a grandmother. I also know you don't want to, but Frank needs to know as well. Even if you don't want to have anything to do with him, he does have a right to know. You have to give him the choice to be an active participant in the child's life."

"I know," said Chris, sounding disgruntled.

"I know you don't like it, but you're sooner or later going to have to deal with Frank."

"I know," stated Chris, really not wanting to talk about it.

"I'm just telling you Chris, because he is the child's father and he has a right to be apart of the child's life. I don't make up the rules, nor do I care much for them. Nonetheless, they are there and we all have to do what is best for our children. Believe me, I wish my two children didn't have to see their two-timing father, but I can't stop them for that would be selfish of me...Believe me, I spent plenty of money on a shrink to come to that conclusion. So, I think I'll save you some time and money by sharing that with you now."

"I know that, but how do I know he will treat our baby differently than he has treated me?" professed Chris. "I mean he has treated me and our marriage like dirt. I don't want him to be apart of my child's life if that is how he intends to treat our baby."

"Listen to me Chris, sooner or later you're going to have to come out of this cocoon you've spun around yourself. I'm sorry sweetheart, but Snow White and Cinderella were fairy tales. There is no running away from life. You're going to have to deal with him.

"Now, enough with the serious conversation. I've said my piece. Let's celebrate. How about a nice big fattening chocolate sundae?" asked Beverly, smiling.

"That sounds down right sinful," Chris replied. Although she did not want to admit it, she knew Beverly was right.

CHAPTER 26

▼

Beverly was the only person in the world Chris accepted hearing that from. Chris had to accept the fact that now since she was pregnant, Frank was going to forever be a part of her life. There was no escaping it. She even had to come to terms with her past, which was no longer some figment of a by gone era of the antebellum south like *Gone With The Wind*. The reality of it was that her history was one marred by tragedy and based on one woman's perseverance against insurmountable odds to have a better life, even if it meant sacrificing everything...including her identity. Although, it was a past Chris had grown up not knowing, it was nonetheless a past that she now would have to claim.

As Chris sat there back home in her kitchen, thinking about the events that has shaped her life over the past few weeks, she could not help but feel everything had been orchestrated. There was the incident with the birds, her mother asking her to go to Jacksonville in her place, the vision in the clearing while in Jacksonville, the chance meeting of Annie Mae and Hope as well as her pregnancy. Chris was not a big believer in fate, but everything seemed to have been arranged. With the many strange and un-natural occurrences she had witnessed in the prior weeks, it would not have surprised her, if such a thing as destiny did exist.

As Chris placed the events that had transformed her life into perspective, she realized that everything happened soon after she had met Dr. Samir Deshpande. Chris had intended seeing Dr. Deshpande after having visited with Hope. However, her fear of what he might say next kept her away. He had already told her about her past, now Chris was more than ever curious about her future. Yet, her fear of hearing what he might say had made her reluctant to pay the doctor a visit. Still, the fact that Dr. Deshpande had informed Chris of her great uncle Cletus, long before Annie Mae had told her the story, made her inquisitive to find out what else might lie ahead for her. He had spoken of how her back pain was tied to the spirit's eternal agony. He also mentioned a deed left undone, which is causing the spirit to remain restless. If the ghost, Dr. Deshpande was speaking of was indeed Cletus, there was no telling what task he may have left unfinished. The more Chris thought about what Dr. Deshpande had said, the more it troubled her. Now that she had finally achieved the one wish her heart desired, she wondered if all these premonitions would rob her of enjoying her child. After giving it some thought, Chris realized she had to go see him.

*   *   *   *

The last person Samir Deshpande had expected to see standing at his door at nine o'clock at night was Chris. It took her some time to track him down, but with a little help from Beverly and the telephone directory, she was able to find him.

"Mrs. Adams?" said the doctor, surprised to see Chris standing at his doorstep. A woman crowded him at the door, to see whom it was visiting at that hour of the night.

"Hi, doc," said Chris giving him a weary smile. "I hope I am not intruding." Chris noticed Sasha, his receptionist, standing behind him. Chris surely hoped his receptionist was not his wife. Judging by their apparent disparity in age, she would have believed Sasha to be his daughter, instead of his spouse.

"No, no please do come in," he said letting her inside. Judging by the look of desperation on her face, the doctor, could not rightfully turn her away.

"You do remember my daughter, Sasha?" he asked.

"Oh, yes I do," said Chris, trying not to sound relieved.

"Sasha is helping me out around the house while her mother is in Bombay tending to her mother," Dr. Deshpande professed.

"I am sorry to hear that," Chris replied, waiting there patiently.

"No need. My wife's mother is one hundred and five. She has spent a wonderfully long time on this earth. We can not live forever." He turned to Sasha and whispered something into her ear. She smiled and nodded her head at Chris, before promptly leaving the room.

"How about we go into the study, where it is a little more private. Besides, my son has fallen asleep and I do not want to wake him," he suggested.

"Look Dr. Deshpande, if I came at a bad time, I can just come by your office tomorrow," proclaimed Chris, realizing she was intruding.

"Don't worry about it, obviously something is troubling you. Or you would not have come to my home seeking my help. So, please come," he said, leading her into his den.

Chris followed him as instructed. In comparison to his office, which was adorned with beautiful East Indian art, his den was a bit more modest. Instead of rare art, there were photos of his family. She noticed a woman in the photographs who appeared more along the lines of what Chris thought his wife should look like. The numerous scented candles that adorned his office were replaced with hundreds upon hundreds of books that sat in bookcases that reached the ceiling. For being one of the cheapest chiropractors in Atlanta, Dr. Deshpande lived a fairly comfortable life.

"Have you read all of these books?" asked Chris marveling at his collection of books.

"Some of them," he said taking a seat. "Most of them I have simply bought for my collection. I am an avid collector of vintage books." He watched as Chris' eyes scanned the bookshelves.

"So, tell me Ms. Adams, what brings you to my home? I know it was not so you could marvel at my book collection?" He smirked.

"Ms. Jackson-Moore," replied Chris.

"Excuse me?" he asked, confused by her response.

"I am no longer Ms. Adams. My husband and I have parted ways. Moore is my maiden name. And you're right, I did not come here to read your books," Chris informed him.

"Well, then what seems to be the problem?"

"The last time I was in your office, you told me that a spirit from a past life was the cause of my chronic back pain."

"Yes, I recall," answered the doctor.

"You had said, it was the spirit of a little boy, a little black boy to be exact, whose life ended abruptly," stated Chris.

"Yes, I believe I told you the child was lynched. Thus, being the reason for your neck and back pain. Speaking of your back how is it feeling?" he asked. With all the excitement that had been going on the past week, Chris did not realize until the doctor had asked, that she had not had any problems since returning home from Jacksonville.

"To be honest with you fine," she said, unexpectedly shocked.

"That is good."

"Here's the funny thing though Dr. Deshpande, I stopped having problems with my back as soon as I came back home from a trip, to a small town in southern Georgia called Jacksonville. My family is from there. In fact the town is named after my great-great grandfather."

"Is that so," replied Dr. Deshpande.

"Yes. Nonetheless, while I was there I discovered that my great grandmother had a brother by the name of Cletus, who was lynched as a child. From what I understand my great uncle, Cletus, was a gifted individual. He had the ability to do things normal people simply cannot do. And the weirdest thing of all is that he was black." The doctor's eyebrows rose slightly when Chris revealed this bit of information to him. "I know that may be confusing judging by my appearance, but it is indeed true. Believe me, it is a very complicated story. One I will save for another day."

"This is interesting. Let me guess, you have found out that you have a talent similar to that of your ancestor's?" questioned Dr. Deshpande.

"How do you know?" said Chris in amazement.

"Because, it is written all over your face."

"That is just it Dr. Deshpande, I can do things now that I never believed to be humanly possible. Not to mention on top of that, I have become pregnant after a slew of doctors had told me, I would never be able to bear children."

"And you are wondering if the discovery of your great uncle had something to do with all of this," Dr. Deshpande interrupted.

"Not only that, but since you can so clearly see the past, what now lies ahead of me," Chris murmured, fearing his answer.

Dr. Deshpande paused for a moment. He gazed at Chris before smiling. "Amongst the many great literary works I have here, there is a poem by a poet by the name of Robert Frost. Are you familiar with his work?"

"Yes, I am."

"Have you read a poem written by him called, '*The Road Less Taken*.'"

"I recall reading it in college, but that was so long ago."

"Well, it does not matter. What does matter is that Frost wrote that poem about a man in the woods who comes to a fork in a trail and is forced to make a choice on which path to take. The poem is a metaphoric look at someone having to make a decision in their life."

"The tale is somewhat coming back to me, however, I do not see what that has to do with me?" questioned Chris.

"What I'm trying to say to you Ms. Moore is that you, just like the traveler in Frost's poem are on a path, or trail. And whether you know it or not you have already reached the fork in the road and chosen your path. This is evident in the events and occurrences you tell me that have already taken place. I hate to tell you, I cannot see what lies down the road you have chosen for the outcomes are infinite. Thus, making it difficult for me to see.

"You must simply wait and see where the path leads you. However, I am certain, just like the gentleman in Frost's poem, your life has now become all the more richer for your choice." Chris was puzzled. She did not understand why he always spoke in riddles.

"I don't understand?" said Chris bewildered.

"What I'm trying to say is, I cannot tell you your future because I do not know it." Upon hearing that, Chris realized she did not need to waste anymore of his time. She only wished, he could have skipped the reference of her life to the character in Frost's poem, and simply told her, 'he did not know' in the beginning.

"Well, I want to thank you for seeing me and helping me figure things out. Please, tell Sasha, I'm sorry for imposing," said Chris, getting up to leave.

"Don't worry about it. I am glad, I could be of some help," Dr. Deshpande said, escorting her to the door. But before Chris could leave, he stopped her and said to her, "You simply have to believe in yourself, Ms. Moore, and all your questions will be answered."

CHAPTER 27

▼

Chris had thought a lot about what Dr. Deshpande had said as she left. It was not the first time she had heard that statement. Hope had said the same thing. Throughout the muddled mess of thoughts that swam through her head, it dawned on her that she had not called her mother and told her the good news. She also realized, she had missed Hope's phone call inviting her over for dinner as well. It was late, so Chris decided it was best to call Hope in the morning. Chris did not want to take the chance of waking her boys. Besides, she had already imposed upon one family that evening and did not intend of imposing on another. However, she did decide it was wise to give her mother a call before turning in for the night. If her mother found out she was not the first one to hear of her daughter's pregnancy, Chris knew she would be highly upset.

"Hello?" said Agatha, sounding surprised to be getting such a late night call.

"Hi, Mom," said Chris.

"Hi snookums. How are things going?" Chris could tell her mother had been asleep.

"I'm sorry to be calling so late, but I have good news to tell you," teased Chris.

"Oh do you?"

"Yes, I do."

"That is good to hear. Am I privy to know the reason why?" inquired her mother.

"Of course you are." Chris could not help but smile. "You're going to be a grandmother." There was a slight hitch in her mother's voice like she intended to respond but did not know what to say.

If Chris had not asked, "Mom, are you still there?" there was no telling how long her mother's silence may have endured.

"I'm here, I just don't know if you're serious or playing some cruel joke on your mother. And if you are, you should not play such games like that with me," she insisted.

"It's not a joke, Mom. It is the honest to God truth," gushed Chris.

"You're kidding me!" yelled her mother.

"No, I am not."

"But how?" she asked.

"Your guess is as good as mine."

"Oh my goodness, I can't believe it! I'm going to be a grandmother!" shouted Agatha. "I am so happy for you Chrysanthemum! I know how bad you wanted this. See, sometimes if you make a wish, your wish will come true. Just how far along are we?" her mother inquired.

"Six to eight weeks."

"So, does this mean you and Frank are going to be working things out between the two of you?"

"No Mom, it doesn't mean me and Frank are going to be working things out." Once again the topic of Frank, had ruined another joyous occasion.

"Now, Chris, you know a child needs a father," she advised.

"There are plenty of strong women out there raising children on their own," snapped Chris.

"Yes, that is true, but I can guarantee you their having a tough time at it."

"You know Mom, I'll worry about that when the time comes. Right now, I have just over eight months to worry about a parental agreement," complained Chris.

"All right, I'll mind my own business. You have at least told him right."

Chris remained silent.

"You have told him?" repeated her mother.

"No," sighed Chris.

"Once again, I will mind my own business from this point on but I do think you should tell him. It's only right."

"I will, I will," replied Chris. Chris hoped since she had convinced her she would tell Frank he was going to be a daddy, she would at least change the subject.

"Who would have ever thought, I would be a grandmother!" beamed her mother.

As Chris had hoped, the conversation strayed away from Frank and on to more practical things of concern for a woman expecting a child, such as baby clothes, cribs, carriages and the many other accessories necessary for the arrival of a child. Still, Chris could not shake what her mother and Beverly had suggested in regards to her contacting Frank.

The only question Chris continuously asked herself after hanging up the phone with her mother was…should she?

Despite, feeling she had handled his infidelity quite admirably, there was still plenty of hurt that remained. However, her mother and Beverly had a point. She could not deprive her child from knowing his or her father, purely on the basis of her own selfish reasons. It was unjust to the baby. Chris glanced over at the clock. The red neon digits read eleven thirty. She contemplated calling him, but told herself it was too late.

Yet, Chris knew if she did not do it that night, at that moment, she would lose the nerve to do it at all. She knew she had to do it, while she still had the courage. She was well aware that it would be awkward, trying to hold a civil conversation with Frank after everything that had transpired between them. Nonetheless, she knew she would feel better in the morning because it was the right thing to do. So she looked for the piece of paper with Rita Thorin's telephone number on it. Once she found it she picked up the phone, and dialed Rita's number. Chris was certain; she would find him there.

CHAPTER 28

▼

Dawn sprinkled itself sparingly across the morning sky. After a long night, Chris surprisingly found herself lying awake in bed. It was more like someone or something had jolted her awake. She wondered if Frank had been jostling about. She quickly concluded it couldn't have been him for he lay clear on the other side of the bed. How or why she lay there in bed wide-awake staring at the ceiling, after a long night of talking with Frank was a mystery to her. Now as she lay there deep in thought, she wondered why she even gave in to Frank's pathetic pleas to come over.

No longer was he seeing Rita. In fact he was not allowed. After the circus act Chris had put on at her condominium, Rita told Chris she had kicked him out. Rita also informed her, Frank's inability to tell her the truth was justification enough to throw him out. He had told Rita he ended their marriage the weekend at the cabin on Lake Lanier. Chris knew that was probably more than likely his intentions behind taking her up to the cabin and being so attentive to her the entire weekend. Yet, somewhere along the line he had gotten cold feet. Rita told her that the trip to Grand Cayman was supposed to be their way of celebrating. Plus, Frank's incapacity to grasp the fact Rita had called it quits, forced her to file a restraining order against him. So, ever since the incident at Rita's condo, Frank had been living with Russell. Of course, Chris now wished she had sent him back to Russell's last night.

Maybe, it was because she longed to feel the warmth of another human being lying next to her or maybe she simply felt sorry for him. Whatever the reason she let him stay, his presence definitely left her in a predicament when it came time to tell him to leave. Although deep down inside, she wished they could work things out, Chris knew there would be no reconciliation between the two of them. In her heart and mind, it was over. The wounds he had inflicted ran too deep, not to mention the expanse that now separated them was too vast to be traversed. Even while they lay in the same bed it felt equivalent to them lying on the opposite sides of an ocean. Chris cared for him, but she no longer loved him.

She got out of bed, making sure not to wake Frank. Once out of bed, she watched as his body rise and fell with each breath. Chris recalled, how there used to be a time when she simply wanted to breath the same air he breathed. At the time, she wanted to believe that with each breath, he was inhaling a piece of her. No longer.

She noticed, the picture of her great grandmother on the dresser. It looked regal sitting there. She had dressed it in a beautiful frame that complimented the dark brown tones that weaved their way throughout the photo. Chris walked over to the photograph and held it in her hands. She could not resist smiling. A sudden sense of peace eased over her. She put the picture back down on the dresser and waltzed slowly over to the balcony doors to look out onto a new day.

She opened the balcony doors and stepped out into a world, fresh with the earthy smell left behind after a good down pour. Interwoven in the smell of the earth, Chris could smell a hint of lilacs and jasmine. It was reminiscent of the sweet smell of the flowers in Celia's garden in Jacksonville. Just the smell of flowers seemed to stir something within her. At that moment she felt like she was the only person staring out on to that picturesque canvass called the sky. The vibrant splashes of orange and red draped upon a beautiful backdrop of an ever-deepening blue. The day almost seemed to stand still. A calm induced by the tranquility of the morning seemed to come over her. Chris' thought went to visions of hot summer days sitting out on the porch in Jacksonville, sipping sweet tea. Thoughts of Jacksonville made Chris remember she needed to return Hope's phone call sometime that morning before she forgot.

As she gently rubbed her belly, she could not help but wonder if it was Jacksonville calling to her in its hot steamy voice of summer that morning. The so many sun-kissed fields choked with weeds, beckoning her back. She stood there listening to the countryside's call and watching the day spread across the sky like runny watercolor paints, mixing and blending with all the other hues until eventually every color became a shade of blue. At that moment a sole, solitary, thought entered her mind. As she mulled it over in her head, Chris peered down at the pool beneath the balcony and wondered. She knew it was a crazy idea, but she couldn't help but be curious. She could not resist using the "gift" to talk to the birds, so it was inevitable that the thought of flying would eventually come to mind. She remembered Hope and Dr. Deshpande telling her, all she had to do was believe. Still, communicating with birds and attempting to fly were two different things. The risks associated with one were not the same for the other. Of course, the pool would break her fall, but what about the fate of her unborn child. She had waited too long and came too far to risk losing her child. And yet, despite the danger, her curiosity urged her to try. Her conscience told her if she just believed then it was possible.

Chris felt almost compelled to grab the balcony railing. Not fully understanding what insane urge was driving her to attempt such a lunatic act. Still, Chris mounted the balcony railing. With her knuckles a ghostly white from holding on so tight and her feet firmly planted on the wrought iron rail, Chris closed her eyes and tried to think of flying. She found it hard to concentrate on flying, when she was flirting with death and if not death then definite injury if she failed.

Just when Chris was ready to give up and admit that it was a foolish idea, she began to feel her body grow warm. She recognized the feeling of electricity circulating through her body from when she beckoned to the birds. At the same time, she sensed a light breeze stir and gather strength. And she heard a voice deep within her tell her to simply believe in herself. Before she knew it, visions of soaring amongst the clouds began to come to her freely like a lucid dream. The more vivid the vision became the warmer she became. In turn the warmer her body temperature, the stronger the wind grew. The sky seemed to ebb and flow almost like it was breathing…like it was alive. By the time Chris let go, to balance herself on the railing with her arms spread wide, the wind howled and the trees had begun to sway. She could not help but smile in disbelief as her hair danced and her nightgown flapped uncontrollably in the wind. When her body felt like it was on fire, visions of flying felt real and her feet felt as light as feathers. She wanted so badly to soar into the sky and touch the sun, such as Icarus.

Now, Frank had been awaken by the roar of the wind. He had never in his life heard of a windstorm in Atlanta, or anywhere else in the south for that matter. Yet, what he was witnessing could easily be classified as a freak act of nature. When he realized Chris was not in bed with him, he glanced over to the open balcony doors. He could not believe his eyes. Chris was standing upright in the face of the wind, but also more incredible than that she was balancing herself on the balcony railing with little effort. A feat in such weather, he knew had to be impossible. He attempted calling out to her, but realized she could not hear him over the din. So, he figured it was best that he grabbed her before she lost her footing and possibly blown back into the flapping balcony doors, which would more than likely be fatal. Frank desperately screamed out to get Chris' attention.

He struggled to get close to the balcony to grab her but the wind impeded his ability to move quickly.

Now, Chris did not hear Frank calling out to her. Even if there had not been the roar of the wind in her ears, it is doubtful she would have heard him. Chris, now, only existed in a world of deep blue skies filled with beautiful sunburst and clouds as soft as pillows. That is why, when Frank had gotten close enough to reach out to feel the wisps of her nightgown dance along his fingertips, he was too late. For Chris simply leaned forward and let the wind catch her, leaving Frank to behold a miracle.

"Know from whence you came. If you know from whence you came, there is really no limit to where you can go."

—*James Baldwin*

Acknowledgments

This has been a long journey. It's hard to believe I was a sophomore at Clark Atlanta University over a decade ago when I came up with the idea for this novel. This has been a labor of love, and I am glad as well as sadden that this long gestation period has finally came to an end.

I want to say thanks to: my mom, Patricia Hampton, for always telling me to following my heart; my father, Preston Hampton, for instilling in me the virtues and values necessary in being a man; my maternal grandmother, Geraldine Quarles, for being the rock everybody leans on; my late paternal grandmother, Elzena "Grannie" Hampton, for bestowing upon me my oral history long before I knew the value in the stories she constantly told me; my late uncle Hugh "Uncle Poin" Hampton, who instilled in me an unwavering pride in who I am; my aunt Alice "Aileen" Hampton, for always being there for me when times got hard.

I want to give thanks to: my brother, Makeem Hampton, for not only being my brother but my best friend; my sister, Danielle Dibba, who despite life's ups and downs has managed to stay apart of my life; my cousin, Ralph Redmond III, remember kicking around ideas in my apartment in Atlanta; Cheryl Curry for letting me type the first draft of this novel on her computer in the Career Placement Center at Clark, not to mention feeding me during those lean months while in college. Of course, I cannot forget Ms. Georgia Jones; Ms Ernestine Pickens, my English professor at Clark, who dared me to dream; Mr. Charlie Carter, my Economics professor at Clark, who looked out for me and pushed me to excel.

To my in-laws who treated me like family from day one. I want to say thanks: Lynda Jackman, for loving me as if I were your own; Wallace "Jack" Jackman, who made me feel right at home when he called me "Cricket" the first time he met me; Dauhn Jackman, for simply being Dauhn, and Thomas "Tommy" Jackman, for being like a brother to me.

To my numerous friends who begged to read the novel, but whom I constantly told it was not ready yet. I know many of you began to believe this was nothing more than a figment of my imagination. Thanks to: Stevie J, Randy "Ran", EJ "Coach J", John and Tracey, Ken and Amber, Byron and Twanya, Stephen and Shawn, David "KJ" and Bridget and all those I may have not mentioned but definitely did not forget.

I have to thank my extended family, the numerous aunts, uncles, and cousins who guided me along throughout the years: the Hamptons, the Matthews, the Hubbards, and the Redmonds. I am sorry I cannot name you all by name. Just know I love you.

Lastly, I have to thank my wife, Tonya, my daughter India, and my son Phalen, without you guy's support and understanding this would not have been possible.

0-595-27450-1